THE GAME

THE GAME

FRANCES LIARDET

MACMILLAN
LONDON

First published 1994 by Macmillan London Limited

a division of Pan Macmillan Publishers Limited
Cavaye Place London SW10 9PG
and Basingstoke

Associated companies throughout the world

ISBN 0-333-60128-9

135798642

A CIP catalogue record for this book is available from
the British Library

Typeset by Cambridge Composing (UK) Limited, Cambridge
Printed by Mackays of Chatham PLC, Chatham, Kent

SARAH

ONE

'I didn't see him, Graham, honestly, he came out of nowhere,' I pleaded as the blue truck blared past, headlights flashing, an inch from my bumper.

'He came out of that little slip-road,' said Graham.

'They think they own the road, bloody navy lorries.' I restarted the engine with a howl, my hands shaking.

'No harm done.'

'That's about the fifth one I've seen.' Scrabbling for the indicator I turned on the wipers. Horns started behind me. 'OK!'

'They must have a lot to do at the moment. Forge on now, angel, easy does it.'

I forged over the roundabout and joined the southbound evening traffic. Out of the corner of my eye I saw Graham getting his pipe out. The sucking noise irritated me beyond belief so I slowed down a bit and he put it away. We travelled down a dual carriageway through a built-up area typical of the coast, the sort of ruination of flats, wasteground, Stu's News, Hair Universe – Hair Universe, I ask you – which looks like the back end of nowhere and sprawls so far you have to unfold the whole road-map if you don't know your way around, which luckily Graham did. The rush hour was over and people were moving about at a leisurely pace, vans parking and unparking, women pushing push-chairs out over the kerb to halt the traffic. Never seen a man do that, I thought. The road curved, and the sun dipped under the visor. Suddenly I expected the sea.

'Where the hell are we?' I said, and changed down with a crash.

'Steady —'

'What's going on? Where are you taking me?'

'Sarah, shall we pull in for a bit?'

We've been doing this since January. Generally we drive around for a couple of hours, stopping furtively in lay-bys and leafy side-streets. Anyone who saw us on that round-about – him so much older and glummer than me, me snapping at him – would think I was telling him to leave his wife if it weren't for the sign on the roof, PASS WITH GRAHAM STILGO. I could still be telling him that, of course. The sign is perfect cover. In fact, I think Graham's quite glad he's got that sign, judging by the suggestive way he leans over to murmur 'Gas, gas, angel,' or 'Watch that bike,' into my ear.

He gave a noisy sigh. 'Portsmouth,' he said, now that we were stationary. 'This is the outskirts. You said you wanted to find your old house.'

My jaw dropped. 'When did I say that!'

'You kept on about it. I thought you'd remembered. Why did you think we were flogging all the way down here?'

'I didn't notice until it was too late!' Really, for a basically nice man he must have a record number of annoying habits. The 'angel' stuff is one, the pipe-sucking at high speeds another. His watch must be set to bleep the quarter-hour, it goes off so often, and he can never turn it off. And then there's the brilliantine; I mean, it's 1982 and he can't even be forty and he wears brilliantine. And, *and*, he takes me literally, all the time, as if everything I say is cast-iron intention and gospel truth. 'Do you mean, before I went on holiday, when I said that I'd like to go back to my roots? That's all I said. "I wouldn't mind seeing Pompey again,

4

that's where my roots are." I didn't mean . . . Graham, you are extraordinary!'

'Not my fault if your head's in the clouds,' he said. His bland, watery eyes met mine. No sign of a crinkle today. 'You're much worse than last time – in fact you were a proper hazard back there. We've got—' he looked at the watch – 'over an hour still. Plenty of time to look. But if you don't want to, then I'd just as soon owe you the hour and go home and have my tea.'

He was right, I was driving appallingly. On top of that I'd been rude. I leaned forward and put my head on the steering-wheel, mainly to hide the blush. 'We'd never get back in time if we started looking,' I mumbled. 'There was more than one, in fact there were four or five, and I can't remember which was which.'

'Oh, well.'

'I was little. I expect they've been knocked down for all these new multilane freeways and interchanges and so on. Really, it was a stupid idea, I'm sorry.'

'Not to worry. Just start concentrating, there's a love.'

'Crazy idea. Out of the question.'

'Look, suit yourself.'

We did a few hill starts. I stalled again and blamed him for never giving me the same car twice, what did he expect, and then we drove off in thoroughly bad tempers.

All around it was just like I imagined it would be. It was me that didn't fit. It should have been pleasant tooling around the coastland again after so long with the radio on in neighbouring cars at the traffic-lights, Graham's watch trilling away, the spring evening sunlight in my eyes, out of my eyes, in my eyes again as we headed west, south, west through the small streets and round the roundabouts. We were approaching the shore now at last – the light brighter, the buildings lower and uglier – coming to a plastic pub with plastic chairs on the grass outside, then a clatter of halyards on masts as we went past a sailing club and then we were by the sea, for a minute, until the road took us away again.

'Hell,' I said, and, 'Somewhere . . . !' and Graham said, 'I thought you weren't looking!' and I said, 'I'm not!' and it was exactly like I thought it would be except for this winding unplaceable tension dogging me all the time, tailing me so close that I didn't realize that Graham had been saying left, left and I had been obeying him until we were in the city itself and heading for the docks.

'Le Havre or Cherbourg – which would you prefer, darling?' I asked him. One last attempt to make a joke of it. He began to explain how the driving school and his wife and boys would object to our leaving the country, but his voice was drowned by the roar of a train as we went under a railway bridge. In the sudden noise and darkness I felt cold and awake. When we came out from beneath the bridge I had forgotten what Graham had been saying.

I knew exactly where we were now. Tall red-brick buildings, illustrious pubs. The harbour wall, the local ferries, the street turning sharp right at the end. The spars and struts of the historic sailing-ships and the entrance to the naval base.

'Oh no. No. It can't be,' I said, quite loud, very clear, and stamped my foot down on the accelerator.

Graham sat up straight. 'Whoah! Steady, angel!' he gasped, but I hardly heard him. I roared down to the end of the street and it looked for a minute as if we were about to plunge through the gates of the base, but I swerved with the street round the corner and into the fast lane. Soon I was driving as fast as I could. We squeezed ahead of a queue of navy lorries (the place was crawling with them), coasted over junctions in the gap between red our way and green the other, cut people up on roundabouts. I was looking for signs that said OUT OF CITY; I took all the signs that said OUT OF CITY until we were in lane for the motorway. By this time there was no turning back and Graham was too scared even to get out his pipe. 'You're not allowed, you're not allowed this way,' he pleaded, but we sped past the slower traffic and up on to the bridge and I heard myself saying, as if in reply, 'I lived everywhere round here, everywhere, how do you expect me to find it,' as the harbour hove into view below us, the warehouses and dockyard cranes and the assembling fleet, winking and flashing in the sun.

Graham took me all the way home instead of dropping me outside the Fruit and Veg as he usually does. 'Promise me,' he said, 'promise me you won't do that again,' and I promised him.

My mother and sister were just getting out of the car when we arrived. Mum waved to Graham but went straight on in without saying hello.

Flora had bought the dog a toy puppy to play with to make her more maternal. We stood in the back garden for a while watching her dismember it as she does with all her toys. As we went inside Mum said I looked pale. Before I knew it I was telling her about my driving lesson. We held our conversation against a background of 'Men of Harlech', the first four bars of which Flora was playing maniacally on the recorder, as if someone had stuck repeats in at that point and she kept forgetting it was the second time round.

'I couldn't help it,' I said lamely.

She was washing jacket potatoes at the sink, plunging them into the water one by one. 'Sounds very silly to me.'

'Well, yes, it was.'

I watched her prick the potatoes all over with a fork and then, when she had finished, sit down at the kitchen table and take her socks off. She was wearing pearlized varnish on her toenails. She slid her feet into the house sandals she kept under the table. 'You need to be experienced to drive on the motorway,' she said, as she went into the sitting room to get herself a drink.

'How do you get experienced if they don't let you on them!' I pursued her. 'I thought it was a breeze, myself.'

'I'm surprised you didn't give Mr Stilgo a heart attack.' She was pouring herself a small whisky, holding it up to add water as if it were medicine. I hadn't told her why I'd done it.

I sighed. 'All right, it was stupid, I know. I thought I'd

tell you, that's all.' I waited for her to ask why, but she didn't. She sat there smoking one of her filthy menthol cigarettes, staring into the middle distance. I don't know how she smokes menthol. She looked incredibly young.

'You're eighteen now,' she said suddenly.

'I know,' I said. 'I didn't do it on purpose, actually. I did it because I was scared.' I paused. I couldn't keep it from her any longer. 'Mum, the reason I took off. Down by the docks. I think I saw' – *God* – 'I saw someone who looked like Genevieve.'

She appeared not to have heard me. She sat staring at her hands. I didn't know whether to say it again, and I wasn't sure if I could, but just then she got to her feet and came towards me. I thought she was going to brush past and leave the room but she stopped and put out her hand. Gently she rubbed between my eyebrows with her thumb, like she used to when I was a kid. 'You'll get a —'

'A frown-line, I know.' We both laughed a bit but I could see her eyelashes were damp. My heart thumped, God, I hate it when she cries.

'Sweetheart,' she said, 'things are quite hairy enough without you . . . without you risking your neck in these capers.'

'Yes,' I said quickly. 'I'm sorry.'

She sniffed. 'I'm going upstairs for a bit,' she said. 'I don't think I can stand any more of those "Men of Harlech". Put the spuds in the oven, will you, darling?'

And then at the door she turned and said: 'Don't tell your father about it, Sarah. He'll go spare.'

I know she just meant the driving episode in general. I don't think she even registered the bit about Genevieve.

When I was a child I used to lie in bed at night and press my fingers against my eyelids, press quite hard so that the black would slowly suffuse with sunbursts of colour. Then the sunbursts would fade and I'd be left with these splotches and streaks of green, blue, silvery-grey which spread and sprawled and somehow hovered just out of reach in my mind's eye. I did it when I wanted to remember some special event, to conjure it up so that it was really sharp and clear . . . I think I was quite odd when I was small, one of those odd, frowny kids. I wonder if I can still do it, call up the past like that.

My brother called her a hippy once, when he was old enough to know the word. Genevieve, I mean. Mum happened to mention her in passing and Jonathan said: 'Is that the hippy one who used to be an actress?' That was years after he met her, and he only met her the one time, the first time, in London with my uncle Nicholas and aunt Juliette. He only knew her as the sister of his French aunt. He never knew her as a person . . .

Mum's in a panic because Dad will be back for the weekend. So will Jonathan, from school. She'll go mad with Baco-Fresh spray – especially in their bedroom, where she has 'an occasional cigarette'. (She makes Flora stand in there and sniff, and when I say in exasperation that you can't smell a thing she says I wouldn't be able to tell.) Flora and I will dump books unsorted back on to the shelves, throw armloads of our clothes into the wardrobe and tie the door-handles together. Every loose utensil in the kitchen will be swept into the nearest drawer, and none of us will be able to find anything for weeks. Once when guests were arriving – this was back when it was the fashion to wear wigs – my mother tossed a wig of hers away out of sight up the stairs. Some time later it fell down through the banisters on to the sofa, and nobody even noticed it was there until a neighbour asked Jonathan if our cat was all right. But at least with Dad and Jonathan there we won't have the Fruit and Veg conversation, where she suggests that with all those A-levels I do something more constructive than sell greengroceries, and I say I've done constructive things since I was a tiny girl, and I've got my university place for October, and she replies yes, but I still think . . . She does it quite nicely, she's not cruel, but it's a bore . . .

There's a photo of the two of them, her and Genevieve,

at Uncle Nicholas's wedding in France. Both families are standing out in front of Juliette's mother's house, beneath the trees. People always remark, when they see this photo, on how handsome Nicholas looks, and how Juliette could be a model, with her dark hair under the white veil.

The group is huge, but even so you can see that my mother's in the wrong place. She should be near her newly wed brother, but she's out on the other side with Juliette's family. She hasn't met my father yet, he isn't there; she's standing on the French side with Genevieve. And Genevieve herself should be right next to her newly wed sister, but she isn't; she and my mother are right on the edge of the group, one in pink and the other in lemon-yellow, in those short coats and matching pointy shoes people wore then. It's a bit shadowy, in fact you can hardly see my mother's face at all, but you get the impression that they're both convulsed with laughter, the way only old friends can be, and if you look closely you can see that they're each wearing one pink and one yellow shoe. My mother used to tell me how they had run off together after the wedding into the woods and climbed up a tree, and had to come down in a hurry for the photo session. She used to tell us this story every time we looked through the album but then she stopped. She hasn't told it for a long time now, although she knows I still look at the picture now and then.

They both look so naughty and young. This evening, just for a minute, my mother looked as young as she did in that picture.

But she's not young any more, none of us are. We've all grown older – all of us, that is, except Genevieve. I saw her down at the dock. She looked just as she did when I first met her, right down to the red lips and the diamonds in her ears. I saw her standing there among the sailors as plain as day.

Right down to the red lips and the diamonds in her ears.

Lips a deeper red than the velvet curtains which enchanted me.

Press, press against my eyelids. Call it up, sharp and clear. Come on, Genevieve, where are you?

TWO

The window comes first. The first sharp image of the first time. The tallest I had ever seen, rising from a low sill almost to the ceiling. Eight square panes, as clear as if there were no glass at all, showing the empty flooded street, a few bare trees with the last dead leaves still clinging, the high brown Thames, the city beyond. The sky was grey. It was early.

And the velvet curtains fell deep red to the floor; deep red with a faint grey nap to it, from the dust, or the winter light, or cigarette smoke, or age. They thickened the air in the room, intensified the silence.

Genevieve lay debauched on the sofa behind me, horribly transformed from the previous night, but I didn't know she was there. In my mind she was still the glowing figure of the party. It had been such a long Sunday – church first, in Portsmouth; yes, the chapel as bare as a dry dock, where the chaplain, shiny black shoes poking out from under his surplice, said *Jesus* to rhyme with *please us*. Jonathan was sent to the Sunday School where he drew a picture of God in a naval uniform (Ha ha ha, what a killing little boy you have, Mrs Finney), but I fidgeted in the pew as my parents took Communion, ill at ease in my green coat with the velvet collar. Jonathan had an identical coat, but smaller. And after the service a visit to our grandparents: portraited generals, flanked by their medals and swords, staring impassively down at the roast beef. On the mantelpiece a knuckleduster we could not fit our fingers into, a bugle we grew choleric trying to blow. The firelight glowed on the oak panelling and gleamed on the swords as father and son sat on either side of the hearth in identical postures (legs outstretched, feet crossed, fingers templed) and father talked to son – my father – about the War.

Then my mother speaking in an undertone, and I could hear the excitement in her voice: 'We're going to London tonight, to Uncle Nicholas's party,' sliding a teaspoon on to each saucer. 'We ought to leave soon if we're to be there by seven,' dosing each cup with milk; and then we were in a London street flooded by the river, wading in our wellingtons to the tall brightly lit house, muddily climbing the stairs. 'Remember what I said, children, they come from a very grand French family, your two aunts, so you must behave well like French children . . .' We entered a vast high-ceilinged room. Chandeliers to make you gasp, and candles – a whole Christmas tree decorated with candles. A bedroom full of coats – a pile it seemed entirely of furs and brocades and velvets on the bed where Jonathan and I later slept. A great variety of sumptuous foods, drinks in glasses of all shapes. Aunt Juliette dark and cooing in French, Aunt Genevieve – yes, I called them both aunt, they had been introduced as aunt – in a black velvet dress with a gold glittering shawl hanging down at the back. Juliette was certainly grand and beautiful but Genevieve was kind and exciting, and hoisted Jonathan into her arms and carried him around and threatened to throw him away down the lavatory which was huge and green like a marble sea tunnel, and we nearly died laughing; and after everyone had gone she gave us bread with hundreds and thousands on it and promised us a trip to the Natural History Museum and to a café, and it was a fantastic party, Aunt Genevieve had made it something – out of this world, she was *fantastic*!

And it was over. The house was silent. I had no idea

what time it was or how long I had been awake. Everyone
was asleep: Uncle Nicholas and French Aunt Juliette, who
had arrived from France the previous day; Aunt Genevieve,
French sister to Juliette; Jonathan, my brother; my parents.
The person who would turn out to be Flora possibly kicking
in my mother's womb, but not enough to wake her, not yet.
I was sure that I would be alone for hours.

I turned at last from the leafless scene, the plunging
curtains instilling hush. It seemed that the tall window was
the only splendid thing left from the previous night; the
decorations were tawdry in the dim light, the thickly carpeted
floor and the polished tables covered with debris – dishes,
ashtrays, scraps of wrapping-paper, pine-needles. Smeared
tumblers by the score, wine-goblets with gritty purple dregs
in the bottom – all empty. I wondered whether everyone had
drunk up or whether someone had gone round finishing off
the 'heel-taps', as my father called them.

I picked up Genevieve's glittering shawl from the floor.
Draping it over my shoulders I paced slowly around the
silent room, threading my way amongst the glasses and
plates. I pretended that I lived there and that I was an actress
like Aunt Genevieve, that I had a lot of parties like the one
last night, thronged with handsome men nonchalantly eating
cheese straws. So engrossed was I in this fantasy that,
although she was bleary and disgusting on the couch, when
she said that I looked like a film star it seemed obvious,
somehow, as if I should say in reply: 'Of course. What else
should I look like?'

I watched her cough, stretch her limbs and lever herself
on to her feet. It took ages. It was painful to watch. Finally a
thin, wretched woman stood before me, tentatively patting
her body and the rumpled covers as if she'd been mugged
during the night. She was wearing a thin shift of a nightdress, a hospital-type garment stained and wrongly but-
toned. I could see the skin of her stomach through it. Her
cheeks were smudged with lipstick, her black-rimmed eyes
open wide. She looked shorter and also quite sick.

'Aunt Genevieve?' How did I find my voice?

She blinked and focused on me. I expected her to smile but she didn't. 'God, Sarah,' she said. 'You look like a film star!' And I replied, thinking: Of course, in my mind, but saying only, 'Oh really, do I? Do you think?' mechanically, because I was so shaken.

We stood there, looking uncertainly at one another.

'Where is your brother?' she asked after a moment.

'He's asleep.'

'Shall we have breakfast?'

'If you like.' She didn't move, however; merely continued to stand by the couch, wriggling her toes and swaying slightly. 'What about your mother and father?' she asked next.

'I think they're asleep too. I think everyone is, except us.'

'No, I mean, what do they take? What do they eat for breakfast?' Her voice took on a hoarse, querulous tone.

'Well, they have the usual things.' This was dreadful. 'Coffee, toast and marmalade is what they usually have – except when my father's away my mother just has tea and sometimes a Limmits.'

'Limits?' She squeezed her sooty eyes shut, as if I were trying her patience.

'It's a biscuit.'

'Oh, I see.' She shivered.

I held out the shawl ungraciously. 'You must be cold, just out of bed.' I felt foolish and ruffled. It was as if the party had not happened and I was just a boring stranger who had woken her too early.

We went into the kitchen. It was small and there was a dirt in there far older than the party; plates piled with unfamiliar food and a bad, ancient smell. I tried not to look at the take-away cartons, sticky bottles of sauce, eggshells, sprinkles of coffee and pasta, but my eyes were drawn irresistibly to a lone tomato slowly losing its shape on the floor.

'Nicholas managed to keep Juliette out of here yesterday,' Genevieve said, kicking one cupboard door shut and opening another. 'They only arrived yesterday from France and already she has given a party. This is typical of her.'

'So how did Aunt Juliette do the party food,' I asked, still sullen, 'if she wasn't allowed in?'

'She catered it from outside.' She giggled. 'Nicholas is a wonderful man,' she went on. 'He understands Juliette very well, and he understands me.'

This was too much. 'He's my uncle!' I said. Nicholas must not be associated with this dirty person. To think we'd been told to call her aunt!

'So? He is my brother-in-law,' Genevieve tittered again. 'And he has been my brother-in-law for longer than he has been your uncle, little Sarah. Oh yes!'

She had put a bedroom mirror on top of the fridge. I could see my red snubbed cheeks in the little piece which wasn't covered by postcards and small notices saying things like: Etienne, 563 2330 . . . Salut, Genevieve . . . Paris St-Lazare . . . Bridge Street Farm . . . Madeleine Players. There were things on the door too, posters of Genevieve in black and white, mouth half open and bosoms laced into a bodice, staring upwards at some writing above her head. *Audiart, Ezra, Arnaut*, they said. Some had the address of a theatre in Provence, others that of a theatre in London. I couldn't see her name anywhere.

Genevieve was clattering away near the sink, talking to herself in French. I assumed she was searching for breakfast things and opened a drawer to help her, but found only a black cake of mascara, a rolling pot of deep red make-up and a bra – which she suddenly leaned across me to grab and hurl towards the dustbin, forcing me to shrink against the door. 'It was torn!' she said, when she saw my surprise. 'I don't find the bread, by the way— Oh!' she exclaimed horror-struck, palms flat on her cheeks. 'We ate it all last night, do you remember, with the little . . .'

'Hundreds and thousands.'

'Hundreds and thousands, yes, and now there is none left.' She sat down heavily on a stool. 'I feel unwell,' she said next, closing her eyes. Sweat had broken out on her forehead and she swayed where she sat.

'We can go and get some more. Or if the shops are too far away, we could have cereal instead.' I racked my brains. Perhaps I shouldn't have said that my parents ate toast.

Genevieve moaned. 'Ohh, you don't understand. Juliette will be so . . .' She swallowed, and opened her eyes. Then she stood up, turned smoothly on her heel and retched into the sink.

I was stunned. I said 'Christ' for the first time in my life, but didn't feel any steadier. I wondered if I should wake my mother or Aunt Juliette, but Genevieve, as if she had read my mind, said, 'No! Stay – be quiet, don't make any noise,' before retching again.

'It's you who's making all the noise,' I retorted. Agog and repelled at the same time, I lingered for a moment before returning to the drawing room. I began to collect together the glasses and plates. I considered going back to bed, but I didn't want to wake Jonathan or anyone else while Genevieve was so indisposed.

After a few minutes I heard her running the taps in the bathroom, splashing and humming. Then a long silence, broken only by the lapping of water, tinkles, sighs, rattles. The clock said five to eight.

'Sarah, I'm sorry,' she said later. 'I'm sorry I vomited.'

The way she said 'vomited' made me giggle. 'Maybe it was because you had too much to drink,' I ventured.

But she only laughed. 'After everyone had gone to bed I drank all the glasses people had left. I polished it off,' she added, in Nicholas's voice. 'I suppose your parents have parties like this?'

'Oh yes, they do, quite often – not as grand, though.'

'But I bet they don't vomit afterwards.'

'Daddy threw up in the flower-bed once. But that was when we lived in Hayling Island.'

'That would explain it,' said Genevieve.

We sat on the drawing-room floor, eating avocado dip and fish paste with celery and carrots. The taste of the fish in my mouth in the morning was unfamiliar, rich, shocking, coating my teeth in a manner suggestive of sin. She raked her finger round her back teeth – 'Do this,' she said – so that I could see the inside of her mouth.

'Yuk.'

'Fussy girl.' Tenderly this time, more like the tall shining aunt. But I had the feeling she would never be exactly like that again – not in the daytime at least. She was pale; it was a dead matt pallor curiously unlike skin – make-up, of course, I realized later. Expensive make-up which gave a thrilling, unclean look to her face. She was dressed in black, a jersey and narrow trousers, both wool, and she had bare feet. Her eyes were light blue, a kind of opaque enamelly turquoise, a colour I had seen before on the backs of my grandmother's coffee spoons. You could say she looked more like my own mother than fresh plump dark Aunt Juliette.

No, you couldn't. Not even though she and my mother are both fair, you couldn't.

'I can't believe Aunt Juliette is your sister,' I said slowly, when she caught me staring.

'Sisters don't always look alike.'

'You speak English much better than she does, as well.'

'We have led utterly different lives!'

I snorted, brave again now. 'How different? You both went to university in London. That's how Mummy met you, and how Uncle Nicholas married Aunt Juliette. Your lives can't have been *utterly* different.'

'Ohh!' She pouted and growled, leaning backwards, beady eyes wide. 'Interrogator! You ask my sister if you like, why I speak English better than her. She will tell you it is because I run around Europe all the time like a call-girl. I say it is because Nicholas speaks French to her all their married life, so their dull children missed the chance to be b— to speak two languages, but you can take your pick.'

This time there was nowhere to hide my treacherous cheeks.

'You may well be ashamed. So rude to dispute like that. At this time in the morning as well.'

I said nothing.

'Her children are dull, believe me. They are absolute . . .' Genevieve searched – 'dolts!' and rocked with mirth, clasping her feet in her hands. That was so rude that I had to laugh as well. I took hold of my feet like her and we both rolled on to our backs. 'Dolts!' she cried again, which made me laugh even more. Finally we lay exhausted side by side. I turned my head to look at her. 'You were nasty earlier.'

She grinned. 'Sometimes I am.'

'Mummy said that you like acting. Have you been in any films?'

Her mouth narrowed in a thin smile and her eyes went gimlety. 'At least two or three,' she said. 'And many plays. So many!' She reached out and gave me one deliberate poke in the side.

I had one quick thought: *She's lying*, which did not distress me, and one slow, delicious realization: that this whole conversation was a game. I could say what I liked.

I smiled. 'French plays or English ones?' I asked. 'After all, you could act in either, couldn't you, being *bilingual* yourself?' and Genevieve cackled, heaved herself on to all fours and crawled to the sideboard. 'I think we should eat cookies now,' she said. 'I must have my cookies in the morning.'

She had deep red lipstick, deeper than the curtains, the same red as the pot of colour in the kitchen drawer. As we ate the cookies – which were a kind of Italian biscuit, more like a cake – she rocked back and forth cross-legged, breathing noisily through her nose, giving me the gimlety look from time to time, waving celery as she spoke. She had terrible manners. Her big diamond earrings pulled her earlobes down; the earlobes themselves were the colour of ivory, without the remotest pinkness.

I tried to grill her some more, but she wouldn't oblige me. Why should she? She was only amusing a child of eight. She told me she wasn't an actress, she was only working for a theatre company, but apart from that she gave the most monosyllabic answers.

So I regaled her with stories of my school, how there was a boy in my class called Philip who had carried on sharpening and sharpening his new pencil until there was nothing left but a huge pile of shavings, and when our teacher asked him why he did it he said he couldn't help it, it was an illness with him. I liked the school, but got fed up with being in the same class as Philip.

I had to keep her there. I talked on and on. I found myself telling her about the house where I had buried my silver christening spoon in the garden and never found it again, and where I had tied my tooth to the door and slammed it. And about the house where Jonathan got stuck under the bed all the time, he didn't know how to crawl forwards yet, you see, only backwards; and the house you could see the hovercraft go out from, and the one where there was a boat-trailer in the garden and we played the desert island game every day and got no further than the shipwreck — which we did again and again because our imaginations were so fired, surging and surfing over the roaring breakers, because in comparison desert island life is boring, boring . . .

Her earlobes were so pale. The pulling of the heavy earrings made me want to touch and cup my own ears. I didn't like looking at Genevieve's ears but I couldn't stop.

THREE

We had barely finished the fish paste and already I was enthralled by her. An hour later I would be saving her from Nicholas, Juliette, the entire family. I would lie and keep her secret safe. She was so different from the others, she didn't seem like a relation at all, I had to stop them finding out. Anyway, we were companions by then.

When did she tell me about her lover Henri Palastrier? I seem to connect his name with this first time . . . It was towards the end of that day, just before we went back to Portsmouth. Just his name, nothing more. It wasn't until I was twelve, and we were in her house in France, that she told me all about him and by then he was out of her life.

But, oh, he was so romantic. He had given her diamonds and taken her to a big hotel for their first New Year together. Yes, this is why I think of it now: she said that the London flat had reminded her of this distant romantic New Year. I remember that as I listened to her describe it all – the chandeliers, her fur coat, the marble foyer – all I could picture was the drawing room of the flat. And although I was twelve and we were sitting in her stifling bedroom in France I remember shivering as she spoke and feeling eight again, just for an instant.

To be honest I can't recall much more of what she said about Palastrier. Apart from that London-flat shiver I was bored and puzzled, I was four years older, I was hard on the heels of more vital information. I brushed aside this talk of past winters and men who were no longer important. But there was something so ecstatic, so fixated in the way she sat and spoke about the flat, the hotel, Palastrier himself – she actually started crying – that I wished now I'd paid attention. She could well have talked about us also, together in London. I would have remembered and understood everything, too, if I'd listened – because of course by that time I understood her absolutely – and now I realize how nice it would have been to share our memories of our first meeting. I was clever but I was eight; I know that things about her escaped me. I didn't recognize all those signs of transience – the way she perched there nestling in the cushions, wriggling her toes, never sitting down properly. The way she filched vodka and cassis and stowed it in her suitcases. The suitcases themselves, spewing clothes all over the hallway (and her clothes were all for festival, she hadn't one single plain hard-wearing thing). Her kitchen about to be cleaned tomorrow and tomorrow, stacked with half-eaten delicatessen foods, nothing cooked. It was obvious to any adult, but to me she didn't behave like a visitor. No wonder I was mistaken and thought that she lived there . . .

Why did she go on and on about Henri Palastrier all that time later when we were in France and he was gone? Why did she cry?

I can't stand the thought that I missed anything. From any of the times we were together.

Jonathan awoke, refused fish paste, demanded a real breakfast.

'We must go shopping,' said Genevieve, 'I had not prepared for so many,' – in a hostess fluster which made me laugh, as if she had sat up late at night garnishing treats and pressing napkins in preparation for her sister's arrival. 'The flood is still high, children, put on your rubber boots.'

Lucky for her I couldn't keep away from bathroom cabinets. Otherwise she'd have been sunk. But it sat, mirrored and secretive, above the loaded shelf and the prospect of alien drugs and lotions was too much for me. So I clambered up on to the stool, opened the doors – and saw something which had no place there. It was so unexpected that I exclaimed, lurched, and grabbed the shelf, causing it to tilt and crash and take a great many jars and bottles down with it, smashing over the green marble fitments and scattering red-and-black capsules across the tiles.

I stood surrounded by broken glass, blood pounding in my ears, miraculously uncut. I couldn't swallow.

I climbed up and looked again. Then I reached out my hand. Careful not to drop it – it was heavier than it looked – I lifted it out. Once I had it in my hand I couldn't put it back. Quickly, shakily, I hid it away where I knew it would be safe.

The morning lowered, darkening almost as soon as it began. The air was like iron in our mouths, the sky impacted as if with snow. Genevieve took my hand in one fur mitten and Jonathan's in the other and led us out into the flooded street. 'It doesn't matter now,' she said, 'they were my medicines, and we can clear it up later, right now the bread is more important – don't hoot like that, Jonathan, Sarah will not be "in for it" later . . .' I let myself be taken, still drymouthed, thinking: She must have been drunk to leave it there, dying to tell her what I had seen and done but prevented by the presence of Jonathan; dying also to clear up the glass, but it seemed that Genevieve had to get out of the house fast, and once out we couldn't turn back.

The street was deserted. The water still lapped the kerb. Jonathan screamed in delight as Genevieve stepped out to test the depth – it looked like another river where she waded, thick and green and glacial; and she was so incongruous, bent over with laughter, holding up the skirts of her coat. I wanted to follow but Genevieve said, 'No, not till I know it's safe,' and then she carried Jonathan piggy-back to the other side. 'I can walk myself, thank you,' I said, 'my boots are high enough,' and Genevieve replied that it was lucky, since she doubted she could lift a great lump of a girl like me. Jonathan thought it was the perfect chance to escape; Uncle Nicholas would never be able to follow us through the flood since Genevieve was wearing his boots. We could make a run for it; just round the next corner and we could get a taxi. And then where? To the station! And then where? To the boat! And then where? To France . . . !

Who started that? Jonathan or Genevieve?

'You know I could really go,' she said as we turned; 'I could just slip away and leave you and go to France if I wanted. I've got my passport in my bag.' She stood on the corner pretending to hesitate – I know she was acting – laughing when we said that the water was too deep for us to go back on our own. 'I suppose,' she said, spinning it out, watching our faces, 'I suppose I could dump you in the hall and make a run for it' – 'Oh no *please*, Geneveeeve, stay with us, what about the Museum, what about the glass, Genevieve, we've got to clear it up before the others' – 'Oh yes, the glass,' she cried with great peals of laughter. 'Come on then, little housewife, home to the dust-spade and the brush . . . !'

She hadn't remembered what she had left in the cabinet. She was still holding my hand and laughing as we strolled into the drawing room and Juliette screamed at her: '*You ruined it, you bitch, you spoiled my party and turned my flat into a pigsty.*'

I couldn't understand what they were saying, but I can guess at it now. The drawing room was tidy now. The debris had been replaced with Juliette's anger. Everything – the bulbs on the chandelier and the wall-lights, the green glass balls massed on the Christmas tree, the stuffed cream-silk cushions – seemed rounder than before, as if brimming with her temper. '*And now one of my guests has injured himself because of your slovenliness, just imagine, it could have been one of the children.*' I saw my father sitting embarrassed on the couch where Genevieve had slept, one foot shoeless and dumpy with bandages, protesting that it was only a tiny cut and there was no glass in it at all now. Nicholas stood by the fire, helpless between the two screaming women. *'The children were with me! How could they have been hurt! And how have I ruined your party? I thought Nicholas and I entertained everyone very well, while you sulked as usual.'* It felt like the dog-fight in the summer when Jonathan and I had stood on the table at the pub and clung to each other while the Alsations tore each other to bits under our feet. *'Oh, I should thank you both, should I, for saving the day! I should thank you, Nicholas, since it is due to you I find her squatting here?'* Then she remembered; her grip tightened, my fingers were squeezed, I looked up at her frozen face and tugged her hand, I tried to tell her that Juliette hadn't seen anything, but she took no notice of me. She shouted on more desperately. *'Don't bother, Nicholas, your wife will never understand generosity, I have known her for twenty-eight years.'* 'Daddy,' I said louder, 'tell them I broke the shelf,' but he didn't hear me. *'And you do understand it? Ha! By God, you tap everyone's generosity, you suck it dry, even that ageing parvenu whose home you treat like a pension.'* My father was now rising to his feet. I began to panic. *'So! You have found me out, have you? And what do you intend? Are you content with shaming me in front of these people or will you telephone my ageing parvenu as well? Do it then! Tell Palastrier! I no longer care!'* She tore her hand from mine and advanced on Juliette, oh God, she was going to give herself away. My father was limping towards the door like a good guest, leaving the family to quarrel, leaving me alone in this room with the round mirrors and marble tables where I was powerless to prevent disaster. *'Yes, I have discovered you in all your filth. I have entered a stinking apartment which I was under the impression was my home, where my sister has not the decency to pass a rag over her grime, where my husband's family has been exposed to the shock of finding, upon going into the bathroom —'*

'I broke the glass,' I said at last, in a loud, clear English voice, and there was silence.

Their heads turned towards me. They had not expected anyone to join in.

'We were going to clear it up immediately,' I continued, 'but we decided that the breakfast was more important. And it took us a long time to get to the shops, because of the flood.'

Genevieve, at a loss, glanced wide-eyed from her sister to me.

'I just slipped, that's all. I slipped on the floor.'

Nicholas smiled. 'Oh, Sarah,' he began, 'nobody minds,' and the quarrel began to break up, with Nicholas moving away from the two women as he spoke, making calming gestures, and Juliette looking at the floor, pursing her mouth, curling a lock of hair behind her ear and sniffing.

My father, however, paused in the doorway. He was so relieved the row was over that he sounded quite indulgent.

'I suppose you were peeking in the bathroom cabinet,' he said. 'When will you learn?'

There was silence. My mother could be heard in the next room, talking quietly to Jonathan.

Genevieve cackled. 'Oh God. Sarah,' she said, whey-faced. 'Sarah.'

'No,' I said. 'No. There wasn't anything in there. I mean I didn't really look. I hardly even opened it, in fact. Anyway I didn't see anything.' Genevieve was chewing at her finger, eyes darting from me to Juliette and back again. I couldn't help her, not here with all these people.

'She's incurable,' my father said. 'Not usually so clumsy, though. Come here, you little clot, and apologize for your bad manners.' As I went over to him he leaned down and asked, in a stage whisper: 'Find anything interesting?'

A short high scream came from Genevieve's mouth. 'Shut up! Shut up!' she cried. 'Must you put your big soldier's boot in it? Oh! Ask her then, if she found anything! I don't care! I don't care! Do what you like with me!'

Then she strode out of the room. A few seconds later she could be heard savagely tugging a broom from the cupboard in the hall and sobbing drily.

It was so melodramatic I nearly laughed. Juliette said: 'Ah, la-la.' Nicholas put his head in his hands. My mother appeared in the doorway, exclaiming, 'Darling! What on earth did you say!'

My father's lips twitched. 'I'm a sailor, not a soldier,' he said. 'And I couldn't get a boot on, at the moment.' He spoke as mildly as if Genevieve had been a hysterical child.

'You must excuse her—' Nicholas and Juliette began in unison, and then they stopped; and that made the two couples laugh abruptly and break into a flurry of apologies, from everyone and on behalf of everyone. I left the room to the sound of exclamations, soothing murmurs, the knuckle-crack of a new gin bottle being opened.

I found Genevieve in the bathroom, weeping and sweeping.

'Careful, sweetie,' she said. 'There's a lot of glass every-where. You don't have to help me. Go and play with your brother.' Then she bestrode the pile of splinters and pills and leaned on the broom, sniffing copiously and wiping her streaming cheeks with the back of her hand.

The cabinet was completely empty now. She had swept the tubes and lotions frantically into the basin.

I picked up the dustpan and brush. 'He's looking at the river with the binoculars,' I told her. There was such a lot of glass, big shards from the bottles and small sugar-dice pieces from the shelf. 'What are these pills? They look big enough for a horse!'

'They make you go to sleep,' Genevieve said, still weeping. 'Let's put them in the bin. Oh, Sarah, I have been a fool, an imbecile!'

'Don't cry. It's all right.' Juliette and my mother were in earshot, passing up and down the corridor outside the bathroom, but my voice was gentle, almost cool. It was astonishing; I had never been so excited in my life, and yet I was able to remain completely calm. I swept the diamonds together and crashed them into the bucket. It was satisfying the way the brush got even the smallest feathery glinting bits.

'I'm sorry,' I said, when there was no one near by. 'I should have told you what I did, but I never got the chance, and then you started making such a scene with Juliette . . .

And you were pretty rude to my dad as well!' I added, in awe. 'Why? It had nothing to do with him.'

Genevieve was staring at me. 'What did you do!' she hissed. 'Please, darling, sweet Jesus, did you really find – did you find something?' She put her hands on my shoulders and shook me very gently. 'Did you give it to Nicholas or Juliette? Please God you didn't, Sarah, tell me what you did with it!'

'With what?'

She shook me harder. 'Don't play with me, you little —'

I squirmed away, laughing, and picked up the brush. 'Look! This piece really is a diamond!' I exclaimed. I held it in my cupped hand and brushed the splinters off it. 'It's one of your earrings.' I held it out to Genevieve. 'They're so big, they must be really heavy.'

'Sarah, before anyone comes, please – I'll give you the diamonds if you like, just tell me what you did with it!'

'I haven't got pierced ears.'

'You could get them done.'

'No fear. Anyway I bet they're fake.'

As I held the jewel up to the light my father was suddenly behind us, standing in the doorway, the passageway so dim that we could hardly see his face.

'Apparently we're going to the zoo instead of the museum,' he said heavily. 'Is that a piece of glass in your hand, Sarah? Careful you don't come a cropper, like me.'

'It's only an earring,' said Genevieve. 'She cannot harm herself with it, not unless she swallows it like a baby, that is.'

Still bent over our task, we looked up at him. We couldn't see his expression. He stood there for a moment, and then when neither of us spoke he moved away.

The London lights shone blurred and gleaming through the steady rain as we travelled homeward through the evening traffic. I sat in the corner and stared up and out at the drizzled red and gold, the traffic lights and flashing signs, the movement and the roar. The earring was lodged tightly in my grip like a walnut I was trying to crack. A small piece of glass had pierced the skin of my fingertip and made a tiny prick, a tender pink wound which bloomed when I pressed it. It was a gift from Genevieve, for keeping the secret.

It was after my father had gone away that I had relented. 'Don't worry,' I had whispered. 'I did see your gun. It was me who took it out. Nobody saw me. It's in my suitcase, for safe-keeping.'

'You clever, clever little girl!' she had exclaimed, embracing me in joy and relief. 'Quick! We must remove it before your daddy comes to supervise your packing!'

Genevieve is like a prince or a knight, I thought in the car, the way she led us across the water. She should have a sword.

She has blue eyes and pale skin, but I can tell it's the kind of skin that will go brown in the sun. She's not the least bit rosy.

'Genevieve, I love it at your house,' I had told her when we were out of earshot of the others, in the café after the zoo. 'Please let me stay with you, it's the holidays now, I could stay until Christmas.'

But Genevieve, lopsided with the one earring, had undeceived me. 'It's not mine, Sarah, I am only staying. It belongs to Nicholas and Juliette.'

'Oh! But where do you live? I thought you lived *there*!' My disappointment was impossible to conceal.

'In France. I must return there now.'

Downcast, I fiddled with a spoon. 'So I won't see you again.'

'Of course you will!' Genevieve smiled gaily. 'You can come and stay! You can come and visit me and Naomi. Naomi is my daughter.'

'You've got a daughter!'

'Why shouldn't I have a daughter? She is nine. The same age as you.'

'I won't be nine until February . . . You didn't tell me you were married.'

Genevieve smiled. 'We live with a very nice man. His name is Henri Palastrier. I am not married to him.'

I was momentarily dumbfounded. I opened my mouth but Genevieve gave me the gimlet eyes, so I closed it again. Finally I said: 'You seem too young to have a daughter my age. Younger than my mother.'

'Ah, well, marriage, it can age you.'

'That's so rude!' I said in delight . . .

I thought: She should have a sword and not a gun. A sword is better. She said it didn't work but I don't believe her. Grandfather has a gun much older than that and his works. Why would it be a secret if it didn't work?

I thought: Look at that lorry going past, with stickers and signs from every place in the world. I want to be in that lorry now and go wherever it is going. I want to be on a journey for ever.

I could hear my father saying 'needs her head examined', and my mother reply 'changed a lot' and I knew they were talking about Genevieve. I thought: We could just travel for ever. Me and her.

Was it a dream or did she really say it, come and stay? I pictured Genevieve with the one earring – which I could not have dreamed – as she said: 'You can come on the train, we can have a lovely time, you and me and Naomi. Just think, you can come on the train . . .'

But how strange it was, when it actually happened! How much everything had changed, by the time we met again!

And how shocking it was when Genevieve stood before me, hands on hips, and said: 'My word! You are a different little girl now, aren't you!'

FOUR

Last night I got the suitcase down from the loft, the suitcase I put the gun in. It's too battered to use now. Flora tried to run away with it last year but the handle came off before she reached the bus-stop. Jonathan and I found her in the road, trying to drag it behind her; cruelly, we wept with laughter at our desperate little sister. I tried to fix the handle back on with a kitchen knife, I didn't want to go and get a screwdriver in case someone saw me. I sat there twiddling for hours but I couldn't manage it.

It was my mother's originally – it still has her maiden initials embossed on it, KW for Katharine Whelan – but it was coveted by both her daughters in turn. Even now you can see why. It's the perfect small girl's suitcase, a pale blue outside and a silken oyster-like interior with flimsy straps of the same material for holding everything in place, ruched pockets in the sides for the jewel box, the sponge bag, the shoe brush. It was made for folded blouses, shoes choked with tissue-paper, lavender bags. Lavender bags, for Heaven's sake! Imagine a firearm nestling in one of those ruched pockets! Imagine that . . . *object* in this case which my mother lent to me so trustingly for that winter weekend in London, the case she gave to me three summers later for my first trip to France – and by then I wanted to replace the KW with SF for Sarah Finney, but there was too much history in it for that. It was my mother's last maiden suitcase, the one she had taken with her, too superstitious to take off the W beforehand, on her 'going away' . . .

Imagine putting it in there, that heavy black thing! Because it was black, and it was heavy – I remember how it looked and felt before I got used to it. I shoved it in under my party dress and banged the lid down but it still made a lump, it was revolting. If my mother had seen it in there she would have gone 'Ah!' with disgust, just as if she had found a dog-turd on the carpet. 'Ah! Dirty!' And I knew that it was dirty. I knew I was in it up to my elbows from the minute I touched it, from the minute I lurched off the bathroom stool and brought the shelf down. I should have told. I should have told my daddy but I did not. I hid the gun away in the borrowed virginal case and handed it over in return for a fake jewel, with a round-eyed, serious stare; I was sworn to secrecy and I didn't smell a thing. What did I think I was doing!

For that matter, what did she think she was doing?

I didn't ask. Although I didn't believe her when she said it didn't work, I didn't ask. I was too busy exchanging filth for trash – look how I enjoyed teasing her back, making her wait! – to give it a thought until it was too late. Only when I went to France for the first time would I even begin to get a glimpse of the answer. Until then I simply waited. I told no one about it because I had too much hope in the promise – *You can come on the train!* – to tell; and I knew, furthermore, that if I did tell I would never see her again. To think what would have happened if I had told! They would have taken Naomi for a start; they came damn close to doing that anyway. No, no – inconceivable never to see her again.

And almost inconceivable to count the number of times I did see her again, to arrive at three, the three summers in France when I was eleven, twelve, thirteen, and then she was gone. How many weeks did I know her? How many days was I with her? Every one of them I can recall, sharp and clear, except the last day. I can't remember that.

Nicholas said that she must have dropped me at a station somewhere on the way to Toulon, because I turned up the next day at Siorac and walked to their house. I stayed the night in this station, wherever it was, because I must have missed the last train. Everybody agrees with this, and I myself remember walking away from Siorac Station in the morning, so it must be right, but I can't remember the night at all, I've never been able to remember it. When I came home Mum said I probably slept on a bench and woke up all stiff, it doesn't matter now, never mind, darling, cradling my head, it's all over . . .

The radio goes booming through the house now we've got the hi-fi. We used to have a transistor in the kitchen and a coffin-like record-player on legs with a turntable that was intermittently live, you had to put on rubber gloves to change the record . . . Right now I can hear some American politician saying 'prioritize', it kills me the way they talk. Or it might be a military man – isn't it one of the American generals who uses this weird jargon? I'll have to ask one of my friends, I'm not bothering to follow the reports. There's no point when you're on the inside and you know what's really going on. Some people are so arrogant, they think they can pick everything up from the media. I met an Argentinian like that when I was in Spain – it was only a week ago. The buildings were great but the boys said *Hola rubia*, hello blondie, all the time. I tried to sneer at them but you can't sneer to order, you just look daft. Anyway, I met this Argentinian photographer in Madrid and when he discovered I was English he said *Hola amiga* instead. I didn't get it, so he said it again with an uncomfortable steely smile. 'Oh, honestly,' I said, 'there won't be a war, not over a couple of islands, they'll solve it diplomatically.' He replied: 'No, I fear we will fight. This is what the papers say.' So I told him he was a fool if he relied on the papers, and a double fool if he thought he could teach me anything about it. Who was he to go around saying he *feared* this and he *feared* that? Someone like him, a photographer, he doesn't know the meaning of the word!

I mean round here they call some of the villages HMS for a joke, the whole place is thick with us, you'd think that would count for something, when it comes to being in the know! I told him that. Since I came back I've given up reading the newspapers.

Oh, thank God. Mum's turned the beast off.

We lived in a house on the heath, right next to the sea. The heath turned into sand-dunes around the house. I remember white walls and white washing flapping on the line, and that's all. We can't have stayed there very long.

I wasn't lying to Graham, really, I'd never find any of those houses again; even with the addresses it would be difficult because it's true, there has been so much demolition and expansion that half of them have probably gone. You never know where the hell you are down there. And apart from this heath house they were all so similar, square-windowed pebbledash, one of a row, one row in several. Shops at the end of the street, the sea in one direction and the city in the other. Good places for children to play – hardly any through traffic, and they weren't rowdy communities, where people broke bottles in the street. I remember standing barefoot in the road, chewing gum, the tarmac warm under my feet.

Inside they were all the same as well, flat-pack coffee-tables, carpeting designed to last. Big trouble if you broke anything – not that I did, I was usually careful, but Jonathan made up for it – because there was an inventory. You couldn't just strip the wallpaper if you felt like it, or bang hooks in for extra cups. I remember sitting in one of those kitchens eating cereal out of a mug, the bowls not yet unpacked, and hearing my mother upstairs measuring for curtains with a group of wives who were telling her how thin the walls were. Jonathan and I tied our ties and went to school – each school was different but only slightly, so we soon got used to the changes in the rules, where to queue for assembly and hang your shoe-bag and so on. I had a blue tunic and cardigan, then a blue skirt and jumper. But it came to an end, this era of indistinguishable houses, shortly after I met Genevieve. We moved to Dartmouth, and when we moved back to Hampshire again it was to a small town, inland. On a clear day if I went up the hill I could still see the refinery on the coast – but not the estuary, cluttered with rusty boats, where we used to go for walks. I went to a convent school for a year, and then, the summer I was eleven, I went to France.

By this time I didn't care enough to tell anyone about Genevieve and her gun. I had saved her and she had forgotten about me. I had lost the diamond earring in Dartmouth; now I lost my hope in her promise and my trust in her as a person. If Sister Mary Ignatius, by some super-natural power, had got wind of it and sat me down and said: 'What did you see in that cabinet, Sarah? What did you do with it?' I would have shrugged. What difference did it make now? It was of no concern to me now; how could it matter to a nun? In any case it was something out of the jurisdiction of nuns, who were bothered by more paltry things, like scraping your chair oafishly when you stood up to greet them or producing needlework of bullfinches and blue tits where the back was not as neat as the front. Nuns stood behind you and dealt out books and food. You could look up their wide sleeves and see how the tubes of wool covering their forearms stopped at the elbow as if they were socks without feet. In the beginning I had called them 'miss' by mistake. I had stuck up my arm and said 'Please, miss!' and they had told me it was 'not beautiful' to address them like that. What could such people have to say about automatic pistols?

The school-houses at the convent were called after saints. At the end of term the house with the most gold stars – or the least red, if there was a dead heat – received a prize. I spent my three terms in St Dominic, an unsuccessful house. We wore dashing berets in the winter. I remember my grandfather showing me how, pushing it right down over the side of my head; I thought it looked rather silly. Then that school was over, and the following term, after the summer, I would go to boarding-school.

I wasn't sure if Aunt Juliette – or *Tante* Juliette, as I was to call her now – had always sent Christmas cards to my parents. I hadn't taken much interest in the woman or her cards. When Nicholas came to England to visit my mother and grandmother, Aunt – Tante – Juliette generally stayed at home. But I had looked for three Christmases for a card from Genevieve and each time I was disappointed; and instead, as if on purpose to wound me, came large crested ones, printed with the name of Nicholas's wine company and signed with a flourish by Juliette. I managed to excuse Genevieve for that, on the grounds that she was not a true aunt, but merely an uncle's wife's sister; I had excused her, already, for not being an actress, after all. But when it became clear, after a long time, that not only was Genevieve non-actress, non-aunt and gun-woman but also houseless, that she did not even have a house for me to come and stay in – *Ah! Ça c'est le comble!* as the more spirited nuns would cry.

'She can't have meant it, darling. She left that man a few months after she went back to France, according to Juliette. Juliette gets postcards from all over the country, she's such a bird of passage, extraordinary, really . . .' That man! My mother's phrase. I always imagined Henri Palastrier as a big bear of a man. I still do. I've never seen him.

'She left him almost as soon as she went back to France. Extraordinary . . .' My mother speaking, telling me that, standing on a step-ladder one Twelfth Night to take the decorations down. Standing with her back to me in the dim winter daylight, her arms raised above her head and a long kite-tail of cards, paper-clipped to a red ribbon, looping to the floor on one side of her. Was I nine soon to be ten, or ten soon to be eleven? Had one year or two years elapsed since our first meeting? I have the impression that my father was at sea, in which case it was the latter Twelfth Night, for the year before that we were still in Dartmouth and he was at home in January. Yes, I was ten, yearning to be eleven when my mother told me, in the dining-room with the pine-needles all over the floor. My father gone, leaving his usual palpable presence behind, a sort of dim cloud which I never saw, which was always around the corner, out of sight in the other room, but I knew it was there . . .

But Genevieve was fake and trash and didn't even have a house, and so couldn't have meant it when she said, 'Come on the train,' and I blamed myself just as much for being young and stupid enough to believe her. It seemed like a joke by now, that whole night and day, something dis-remembered, knocked down, lying back beyond the borders created by the two moves, the two more schools, the Christmases, the eleven plus; the fact, coming up on me, that next term I was going to boarding-school and I would stay there. It seemed obvious, finally, although I did not dislike her any the less now, that when I went to France it would be with Juliette that I would stay, and that Katrine and Lucien, Juliette's children, would be my friends. I jeered at myself. To think that I'd been so taken in as to wonder about Naomi, what she was like and what she did, and whether she would ever come to Portsmouth! Naomi I suspected was another lie. She probably didn't even exist. It sounded like a name you would make up on the spur of the moment, to convince a small girl.

The suitcase was cleansed. It contained nothing more malevolent than striped T-shirts, balled ankle-socks, and a carefully folded dress on top bound crosswise by the two silken straps. It lay on the rack above my head as I sat in the hot train, slit-eyed against the sun and heat, catechized and scripture-read, deceived and disabused, trailing red and gold stars, eleven.

The train window was dirty, but it couldn't dim the sunlight. The woman sat opposite me and smoked.

Not a strand of her hair showed beneath her head-scarf. Her lips were almost as pale as her face and her eyes were outlined with black. She made an 'O' with her mouth as she breathed out her cigarette smoke, and after each puff brushed imaginary ash off her wool trouser-suit, swish, swish, swish. I couldn't imagine how she wore such thick clothes in this weather. She looked as if she was suffering from a slow-growing internal disease.

'Thiviers,' she said.

'Thiviers,' I repeated as the train came to a halt. Juliette's handwriting had given me trouble. The 'r' in 'Thiviers', in Juliette's letter, looked like an 'n'. The woman had obliged me by listing all the stations on the line and then repeating them as they passed. I was to get out at Siorac and not Sionac as I'd previously thought.

I pressed myself back in the seat to keep out of the sun and shaded my eyes with my hand. Beyond the window the drought ticked away in the silent village streets and the stone huts, abandoned for decades, in the small oakwoods. The south-west would survive the summer; it would eke out the green, it wouldn't parch like Provence, but I didn't know this. For me this careful, stretched warmth was the hottest thing imaginable.

'Niversac,' said the woman.

'*Ah oui*, Niversac,' I agreed, glancing down at Juliette's letter in my hand.

It was a small local train. The French railway is good, everybody knows that, but this was nineteen seventy-five. Modernization had not spread all the way into the Perigord. The seats were upright, the carriage jolted, there were cigarette-butts all over the floor. As the train turned the sun moved over the top and the window on the other side became a square of yellow light. I dozed in the brief shadow – to be woken an instant later by: '*Nous sommes arrivées, Mademoiselle!*' Blinking, I rose hastily to my feet and got out along with my fellow passenger, who hadn't once smiled. Perhaps the disease affected her teeth.

Now she walked away, black-clad, along the platform into a shimmer of heat. I watched her pick her way over the line to a path on the other side and disappear into the trees.

As she hadn't said goodbye, I began to follow her before realizing that the station lay in the other direction.

It was cool inside the building. I waited for Tante Juliette, wishing I hadn't refused the bread and sausage offered me by the brown-fisted men just south of Limoges. The official who escorted me across Limoges Station had put me in the carriage with those men. I thought I could probably have found my way alone at Limoges, but I had been glad of Nicholas in Paris to meet me off the boat-train and take me to Gare d'Austerlitz. Nicholas worked in Paris nearly all the time. He wouldn't be coming down until the fifteenth of August. He said that Paris was hell on earth, and I had agreed.

The men with the sausage had chucked me under the chin in an unpleasant way, which was why I had refused the food.

I thought about going into the WC to brush my hair, but I was afraid that Tante Juliette would come when I was in there.

I realized that I had left my pullover on the train, and thought: At least you won't need that here.

I waited for Tante Juliette.

It was the fact that he was rough and kind, the station master, and that he thought that I was crying when I wasn't, which made me start crying in earnest. I hadn't checked the sign on the platform. The woman had misunderstood my list. His loud, urgent tone needed no translation. 'Can you not see? You have alighted at the wrong place. You should go to Siorac! Siorac!' Before I managed to convey that it was sweat and not tears, he was wiping real tears from my cheeks with his huge calloused thumb – 'Don't cry, little girl. It is not your fault you are so stupid' – before turning away and bellowing: *'Marguerite! 'Ya une p'tite Anglaise ici qui est perdue, qui pleure!'* And it was while Marguerite was hurrying over that a car drew up outside the station and Genevieve got out, calling my name.

'I thought this was Siorac!' was the first thing I said, and then, as my convent manners deserted me: 'What on earth are you doing here!' Without waiting for a reply I flung my suitcase into the back of her car, planting my feet firmly apart on the ground so that I wouldn't totter under the weight. Then I climbed into the front seat, pulling the buckle of the seat-belt away from her helping hand and avoiding her eyes.

'Don't worry. This is Siorac. You've squashed the plant with your case,' she added in a matter-of-fact tone, as if we had parted yesterday.

'I've got money, I can buy you another plant. Is it always as hot as this?'

'Think yourself lucky we're in the Perigord. It's forty degrees down on the Côte d'Azur.' Genevieve twisted in her seat to reverse the car. 'I'm sorry I'm a little late. Juliette was going to fetch you, but she had to take Katrine to a tennis lesson. Lucky I was here, really.' She said this in such an infuriating, off-hand way that I burst out; 'Oh, you're too kind!' and that so bitterly that she braked and turned to meet my unblinking gaze.

God, the woman had become ugly. She was gaunt, she could really be called gaunt now, and she was very brown, I knew she would be brown like that. It made her eyes an even paler, shocking blue, the whites dull. She was sweating. She wore no make-up. Her hair was longer and sun-streaked, her orange dress grimy and damp under the arms.

She put out a hand to brush a lock of hair from my clammy forehead. '*Qu'est-ce que tu as?*' she said, and, meeting only my brazen stare, repeated, 'I'm sorry I'm late!'

'"I'm sorry, I'm sorry",' I mimicked. 'I'm sorry I'm late, I'm sorry I vomited, you're always sorry!'

She cackled. 'Fancy you remembering that.'

I turned to face the front again. 'Shall we go now? I'm tired. I've had a long journey. Paris was hell on earth, if you want to know.'

'Yes, so Nicholas said,' she replied, smiling to herself. 'He telephoned this morning.'

We drove through glorious countryside but I didn't notice, transported as I was by a fury which made my voice thick and unsteady and my body sticky in the heat. I could hardly focus my eyes. We passed under walnut trees and through vineyards, the houses lying white in the sunlight and golden in the shade, and I replied woodenly to the questions Genevieve put to me.

'How is your school? Have you still got that boy in your class, the one who sharpened his pencil?'

'We don't live in Portsmouth any more. I've been to two schools since then. The last one was a convent.'

'A convent with nuns?'

'Of course with nuns.'

'Did you have to go to Confession?'

'I'm Protestant, we don't do that. Only the Catholic girls went to Confession.' I tried to imply that Genevieve should have realized that, in fact probably had, and that I wasn't fooled by her attempts at conciliation.

We came over the brow of the hill and the valley lay beneath us, the river-plain a patchwork of small dry fields cut across by narrow roads. The hills rose abruptly, looking higher than they really were because they were so steep, green with trees and broken by the occasional outcrop of grey rock. Further down the valley, where the plain narrowed and the hills approached the river, the outcrops became a cliff overhanging the river road. 'See that house?' said Genevieve, lifting her chin. 'That's Juliette's.'

I didn't turn my head or make any comment. Eventually I said: 'I'm awful at tennis.'

'Oh, well, I don't suppose you'll have to play.'

'Where's Naomi?'

'Naomi is not here.'

'I suppose you're just staying as well.'

'I leave this afternoon.'

'Huh. Same old story.'

The road reeled us in down the hill, towards the house. I pressed the soles of my feet against the floor of the car. 'Will I see you again?' I asked.

'Maybe. I think they are planning to go to the sea for part of your stay. You will all go to Arcachon next week. I will perhaps be here when you get back.'

'It's a bloody big house,' I said, speaking fast out of fear.

'It's a bloody big family. There is our mother, who you will call Madame, and my brother François. His two teenage sons are always fighting with Katrine and Lucien – who are Juliette's and Nicholas's children, as I expect you have been told. Katrine has fifty dolls—'

'Oh God.'

'—and Lucien is a little pig. I think you will have a lovely time.' Genevieve stopped the car under the trees in front of the house and grinned at me.

I wanted to slap her. 'Well! Thanks *very* much for the lift,' I said hotly, 'and I suppose I might see you again if I'm not *dead* when you come back!'

And it was then that she said it, as we got out of the car. As I pulled my luggage from the back seat I looked up to see her standing with her hands on her hips in the shade.

'My word!' she said. 'You are a *different* little girl now, *aren't* you!'

I dumped my suitcase on the ground. 'Of course I'm different!' I cried. 'In case you haven't noticed, I'm not little! I'm eleven now! What do you expect me to be like! I don't even know why I'm talking to you, since I didn't come to see you anyway!'

Genevieve reached into the car for my travelling bag and flung it on the ground beside my suitcase. Then she got back into the car and tore away down the tree-lined road without another word.

FIVE

Solid, liquid, ether or dough, I don't know what it's made of, I squeeze my eyes shut and find it there, shot with silver, streaked with blue, points of light darting and shivering in shoals inside it. And there I am, I can see myself, eleven again, angry again, with her and with myself – furious to discover that all this time later I'm still hurting from her shabby desertion, that in spite of that I still want to be with her! My own oldness, her great ugliness are no defence at all and I cannot hide my rage. *Genevieve, how nice to see you again. Tante Juliette could not come? How kind of you to take me to her house!* Do I say that? I cannot say that. I open my mouth and out pops something really quite different in nature. I hate it. It's a matter for shame. I hear myself say: 'Will I see you again?' as if I were eight again, a Portsmouth child excited by a party!

Damn you, I think, you've even asked where Naomi is!

But I couldn't stop it then any more than I can now, whooh, here we come, up over the hill to see the valley beneath us, the light so bright that my eyes, though my face is in shadow, are screwed up. I am staring sullenly ahead, sullen and sightless with a string of plastic beads around my neck and a cotton T-shirt filling with the breeze. Genevieve, orange dress, tanned skin, one hand on the wheel as she changes gear, flicks her gaze for an instant towards my pale and rigid face, my untanned arm crooked on the edge of the open window. I am thinking *Cow* of Genevieve, who in turn is thinking *Bad-tempered child* as she says: 'That's the house,' and I say, 'I'm awful at tennis' – but even our thoughts are superficial because beneath that, as the valley spreads monumental and grand before us, runs the real swim of things where I am feeling: *It's just like it was*, and where Genevieve is feeling . . .

Ah. I still don't know how she feels at this moment. Not even after all this time and insight can I do more than guess at how she is feeling now that her foreign ally is here, her little helpmeet is back, no longer round-eyed but slit-eyed, scowling this time, making a row. Perhaps she's preoccupied with other things, there's a lot of mess and danger around; perhaps she's forgotten what I did for her. Does she even remember inviting me all that time ago? Even now I cannot be sure. I know my eleven-year-old self doubts it; I am furious; I have just realized that I never forgot Genevieve for a *minute* and she doesn't give a damn!

But we're here, the two of us! I can see it all so clearly; the sweat shining on our faces as we come over the hill, the poplar trees lining the river far below, straight, small, separate, green. Soon Genevieve will be tearing down the road, and maybe she will come back in a week or maybe not for a year. I may wish I had the earring still to fling it in the dust in the wake of the departing car, I may wish to sink imploring in same dust to my knees; but whatever the actions then, whatever the results, down in the swim of things I don't care if she remembers or not. I have the power to make her remember, the power to make her come back – I can feel it surge in me as I come over the top of the hill and see the valley for the first time. I know it will always be like this, it will always be fierce like this. It doesn't matter what I say. I have a hold on her.

Who has a hold on whom? Can you even tell, when it is this strong? Does it matter so much, since we're in it together?

The tennis ball hit me in the eye, I wasn't ready, I didn't see it coming. I half-hoped the eye would turn black, but it didn't. I pricked my finger, quite badly, on a pin in one of Katrine's Spanish dolls. I longed to dive from a rock in the river where the boys dived all day, but they said I would probably injure my head. Tante Juliette said that my swimming-costume was too old to wear and bought me another one, but I kept the old green frayed costume and swore that I would throw away the new yellow bikini when I got home. I said to myself that it was grotesque. I wore it under duress.

There was an air of guilt about my arrival. I had appeared on the front step alone, able only to report that Genevieve would return, perhaps, next week. Genevieve had omitted to give me the plant destined for Tante Juliette's conservatory and this was a matter of some gravity. At the end of a long and elaborate dinner – served by a maid called Toinette and throughout which Madame had complained of her *diabète* – I had drunk from the fingerbowl, causing Katrine to scream with laughter. I wouldn't have minded had not the uncle, François, alone among the adults, joined in. At the end of every ensuing dinner, François mimed drinking from the bowl and laughed, unaccompanied, for about a minute. 'He is a widower,' said Juliette one evening, as if to explain it.

I was an unsatisfactory guest. I substituted a glassy stare for conversation, I was late for breakfast, I crept away to read in the attic or the garden. I apologized for nothing, fearing that if I started saying 'sorry' I would never stop. I wished at least that Nicholas was there.

On the sixth day, the eve of the trip to Arcachon, François drove me with my cousin Lucien to the troglodyte village in the river cliffs. It was something interesting for Sarah, special to the region, educational, historical. Lucien and Sarah were the right age for such things. In any case, Lucien and Sarah should spend more time conversing together.

We made an ill-assorted three as we strolled along the path by the rock-face, past the caves in which life-size models of Cro-Magnon man constructed stone implements and fought off predators with flaming brands. I found the tableau featuring a sabre-toothed tiger the most affecting. The teddy-bear glint of its eyes, the window-dummy postures of terror and defiance made me give a high peal of mirth which François mistook for a scream, and he asked me solicitously whether I was frightened and would I like to hold his hand.

We went for a picnic lunch in the woods not far from the troglodyte village. We marched single file along the forest path, Lucien swiping surreptitiously at the backs of my legs with a switch he cut from a tree – I presumed for that sole purpose, since he did nothing else with it. The sun beat down as we collected logs and stumps to sit on, for the ground was treacherous, all dips and hollows and leaf-mould. We ate bread and cheese and pots of yoghurt.

Mouth crammed, I counted grasshoppers, glad at least not to be sitting at that table bristling with cutlery, with the maid Toinette and Madame who would only eat the white heart of the lettuce. I broke the long silence by announcing that there were many grasshoppers in the wood, whereupon François clapped his hands and exclaimed, '*Elle a parlé!*' When we finished eating he tipped his cap – which was of the kind I had seen only children wear in England – over his forehead. It became apparent after a short time that both he and Lucien were asleep.

I finished the lemonade, replacing the cap of the bottle without a sound. Around me the wood clicked and buzzed in the mounting heat. I crept away from the camp, walking faster the further I went. By the time I reached the path I was running full pelt. I came upon a small stone hut, and sat inside it for a moment before climbing further up the hillside through the trees. Eventually I reached a clearing which had a pile of stones in the middle surrounded by empty Evian bottles and cigarette packets. The trees were oaks, but they seemed oddly smaller than English ones. They all looked the same, as did all the paths and clearings now.

It was better to go down than up, at least. I crashed and stumbled, cutting across from path to path, sucking the weeping scratches on my arms. Occasionally I saw a flash of colour through the trees which looked like Lucien's shorts or François' cap, but each time it turned out to be a piece of litter. Before I knew it, I had reached the road.

There was a road-sign of tumbling rocks which I didn't remember having seen before. I stared in both directions, but there was nothing familiar about the landscape. Above me the woods were silent, steep, rocky. On the far side of the road the slow green of the river gleamed between the trees.

I stood there for a moment, and then started walking.

The policeman who found me, after speaking immediately on the radio to his headquarters, told me that the family had been in contact with the gendarmerie. I sat in the back seat, tousled and dirty, my pants, wet from a short cooling river swim, stuffed into the pocket of my shorts. I kept thinking of the sabre-toothed tiger and giggling weakly. By the time I arrived at the house things had become slow and uncertain and I could only say, 'I'm very sorry and I am hot, I am very sorry and hot.' A doctor was sent for, who pronounced sunstroke. I was put to bed by Toinette, protesting that I would pay the doctor's bill before losing consciousness.

I lay there for an eternity, coming to, remembering Arcachon, forgetting again. I was thirsty. The woman in the train came and sat opposite me and smiled continually, revealing black stumps of teeth. I turned on my side so that I couldn't see the woman but I could still hear her brushing the ash from her wool-clad thigh, swish, swish, swish. I burned and froze through silence, I realized that I had swallowed the earring and it lay cold and lumpen in my belly. I was thirsty. The woman asked me, '*Qu'est-ce que tu as? Qu'est-ce que tu as?*' in a voice made of the sound of brushed wool and I couldn't make her shut up. I came up over the hill and down the other side, sinking as if I were in an elevator until two arms embraced me and pulled me up, held me close, made me hot. I fought off the arms but it was no good, I was carried about, there was an icicle in my mouth but I spat it out and so they stuck it up my bum and the woman laughed and said *pilule, pilule, pilule*. I awoke at sunset to see the light streaming in, and there was no one in the room. And I was thirsty.

I sat up and trampled the sheets down to the end of the bed. The room was silent and bare, full of bright light.

She came in with a glass of water. I took it from her without a word.

'Do you want to pee?' she said.

I shook my head.

'You should keep drinking until you want to pee. And take these. They are salt.'

'Where is Toinette?' I asked when I had drained the glass.

'They've taken her with them. How could they do without Toinette?'

She was wearing the same orange dress, but it was dirtier now. It looked as though she had been wearing it all week. Her eyes were ringed with brown, her face sallow and shiny. She stood, alternately chewing her fingers and running them through her hair, looking out through the window at the setting sun. The house was quiet. 'You mean they've gone?' I asked.

Genevieve shot me a bitter glance. 'Of course they've gone! Why do you think I am here? I am your nurse!' She gave a bark of laughter, and looked once more out of the window. 'I am convenient to them. I arrive, and they are free to leave. They could not cancel the hotel or disappoint all the children. So I am trapped for five days until they return.'

I opened my mouth, dazed. 'It's not my fault.'

'Certainly if you had not been so stupid I would not have to be here.'

I went crimson. 'Well!' I exclaimed. 'Well! You should

have stayed with me in the first place, shouldn't you! Then I wouldn't have had to go to the troglodyte village with that nasty boy!' Then I couldn't believe that I'd said that, but once I had said it I couldn't retract. 'Shouldn't you!' I repeated, my face flaming.

Genevieve turned and stared at me for a long moment without speaking. She chewed at her finger. She seemed not to have understood.

'Where have you been!' I cried. 'And where do you want to go so badly, anyway! And if you wanted to be there, why did you come back here!'

She said nothing, only gnawed her fingernail with a lost look in her eyes.

'Don't you want to know where *I've* been?' I went on; I was shouting now, and I could not stop. '*You* don't know! *You* didn't write! You thought I was in Portsmouth all this time!' I tried a contemptuous laugh, but my breathing was too irregular. 'I've been – everywhere! I've moved and moved all over the place and you didn't give a – a damn!'

And at last Genevieve spoke; she said: 'Sarah, Sarah,' softly, 'Sarah,' and sat down on the bed. 'Don't say this. Don't say these things, not now. It's not fair.' Enraged, I saw that she was crying. Floored by the tears I said: 'Ha. Yes, cry,' but my heart wasn't in it now. 'Yes, you cry. Look at me, I'm not crying.' Genevieve sat weeping, rocking gently back and forth on the end of the bed, her face turned away from me. 'You needn't think I cried when you went.' I was speaking softly now, as Genevieve sat rocking and the light faded from the room. 'I don't go about crying whenever anyone goes away, like some kind of baby . . .'

The room was almost dark now, but neither of us moved to turn on the lights. I lay in my rumpled sheets, a big, slamming pain in my head, staring hard at the now motion- less woman.

Genevieve bit through her fingernail with a tiny cube of

a noise. She lifted her head. 'Are you hungry?' she asked me. 'There is some food for you in the kitchen.'

'Oh, no, it'll be the *pulpe*. The whole house still smells of it. I'm not eating that.'

'You should eat, you have had nothing for two days.'

'It feels like a dead baby in your mouth. I'll be sick if I have *pulpe*.'

'Really!' Genevieve spat the chewed fingernail on to the floor. 'Some people think it's a delicacy.'

'I've never heard of it.'

'It's squid,' said Genevieve, and smiled for the first time that evening. 'Squid is what it is.'

I rolled over and vomited into the bucket by the bed.

Genevieve gave a low, delighted laugh. 'Now we're quits,' she said.

SIX

She wanted her daughter. She was on fire for her daughter. Fingertips pink and sucked and wet from chewing them in hunger for her daughter.

'Naomi is not here.' Naomi never was, these days, not if 'here' meant 'with Genevieve'. Naomi had already begun her slow move into her new territory and Genevieve couldn't think of a way to stop her. The heat was sickening, the summer infected. The high walls of Juliette's house, the golden stones, were full of dark infection as if there were a plague locked up in there. She must have imagined Naomi locked up in that plague-house with Juliette, François, Nicholas, her mother, the three boys and Katrine. Then she would be gone for good. Juliette and Katrine would eat her.

I had fallen sick from the plague of this house. I felt it too. It was Genevieve's own fault. She dumped me in this house and I yelled in pain, and she left me.

Nothing can compare with that hot button-eyed scream of desertion. You can mistake it for nothing else. It struck Genevieve to the very innards. She couldn't meet my eyes. She sat turned away from me as I stared at her hotly, lying despotically in that unmade bed, punishing. The scream was so loud that she was astonished. 'Naomi does not bellow like that,' she said. 'What are you thinking of, to bellow at me like that?' She asked it innocently, but she had just given the game away.

'So you leave her too,' I said into the silence, and it was not a question.

I listened to her. I heard, again, the name of the 'very nice man', of 'that man', Henri Palastrier. Genevieve informed me that Naomi had been living with him, coming to stay regularly with her cousins at Tante Juliette's house. Now she would come to live, full time, with Juliette. That was all. It was simple.

I thought: So this is what it looks like. A woman who does not live with her child. There was something so pathetic about Genevieve's matter-of-fact words. They were so at odds with her patent guilt and grief. I thought: I knew all along, from the moment she said 'Naomi is not here.'

'I didn't mean it,' Genevieve said later. She was feeding me toast in Madame's chinoiserie drawing room where the walls were painted red. Toast fingers made with Madame's special *pain de mie*. 'I didn't mean to disappear like that, I had no idea . . . I should perhaps have written to explain.'

Written to explain. What did a letter ever explain? We wrote letters all the time, sending them off fat with daily deeds to BFPO Ships in London (No, Jonathan, it doesn't mean that Daddy's in London) and we got letters back, one for each of us in every envelope. The day after he went I used to wander like a dog through the house chasing that dim cloud he left behind, restless, unsoothed, and not one of those letters ever explained a thing. Not one of them had the power to dispel that palpable, palpable *absence*. Written to explain. Did she think she could palm me off with that?

I raised my eyebrows, licked my fingers, gave her my sourest stare. 'Oh!' I retorted, with all the contempt I could manage. 'I get enough letters already, thanks!'

I felt her eyes on me as I stretched my limbs and slid down the leather sofa to rest my head on one arm and stick

my feet out over the other. I gazed at the red walls, the
screens, the black-laquered cabinets of the chinoiserie room.
I must have looked tall to her – I must have been taller
than Naomi by far, with my long, pale legs. My feet were
bigger. I could never have got my feet into Naomi's little
slippers.

I spoke now into the air above my head. I hadn't finished
by a long chalk. 'So what about Naomi?'

'I told you. It's all sorted out,' Genevieve replied. She
was sitting with her legs slackly apart, one hand in her lap.
There were glasses all over the table, all empty. Whenever
she fetched herself another drink she took a clean glass; there
was a tribe of tumblers and ashtrays which followed her
slowly from room to room, most of them faithful, some
lingering behind until the lemon slice was rimmed with
mould. She lifted the nearest glass and sucked noisily, like a
calf from a bucket, before realizing that it was empty.
'They've . . . sorted it all out between them.' Heavens, she
wanted to get off the subject.

The leather sofa creaked as I turned on my side to look at
her. She was still slewing the glass in her hand to emphasize
the finality. 'So you didn't decide?' I asked. 'They did? Tante
Juliette and your, your man? You didn't decide?'

There was silence. Genevieve blinked. 'Why should I tell
you!' she asked suddenly, crossly. 'It's nothing to do with
you. Who are you to judge me? I shall do as I think fit. I owe
no one nothing, I mean I know oh one, ha . . .' She leaned
back and closed her eyes, and sighed. Then she spoke clearly,
as if her tongue worked better with her eyes closed. 'Naomi,'
she said, 'is an adaptable girl.' She rose to her feet and
walked to the garden door. 'There is no problem as far as I
can see. Is it not clear to you now?'

Of course not. Of course not. How could it be clear, an
answer like that, to me who bellowed in the bedroom! How
could it be sufficient! I sat bolt upright.

'I'm an adaptable girl!' I yelled at her back. 'It doesn't
make any difference!'

The doorway was dark. I didn't know where she had

gone, all I could hear were the crickets. The realization came, for the first time.

'It just makes it easier for people like you!'

She set the gas-lamp down on the wooden table. It was even hotter out on the terrace than in the house. 'Now I need to know, my darling, how well you feel,' she said to me. 'How well do you feel?' The night was pitch dark, the midges cats-cradled around the lamp.

'I'm a bit hot,' I replied.

'A bit hot. But apart from that, you feel well? Apart from your little fever?'

'I hate you like this.'

'No.' She slumped forward over the table, head in hands. 'No, I am not nice, I agree.' She held her finger above the flame of the lamp to see how long she could stand the heat.

'Naomi will be here soon,' she announced after a pause.

'When? Will I see her?'

'No. You will be gone.' She sighed. 'She will sleep in your bedroom. It will be her room.'

'And what about you? Will you be here?'

'No. I won't live here.' She had held her finger in the fire too long; hissing in pain, she put it in her mouth for a moment before holding it over the flame again, but this time I slapped her hand away. The lamp toppled over; I shouted in fear, seized the rolling lamp and put it out. 'You moron!' I shouted. 'Do you want to set the whole place on fire?'

There was silence. She sat hunched, racked by regular, screeching inhalations of breath.

I had leaped to my feet. I was trembling, still holding the extinguished lamp in my hand. 'What's the matter with you?' I cried. 'You don't want her to come here, you hate Tante Juliette, I know you do! Why are you letting them —'

'Ah, Sarah, look at me!' she moaned, rocking to her feet. She walked away down the path, towards the wall at the bottom of the garden.

I stumbled after her with the dead swinging lamp. 'I can't

look at you. I can't see you!' I called. She reached the wall and turned. 'Look at me,' she repeated.

'I am drunk,' she continued. 'You see I am. You said that I am. I am always drunk, now, since I left him, my Mr Palastrier. He is a kind man, but he cannot devote himself alone to an eleven-year-old girl. Since I will not return to him, my dear sister will take my child because I have been judged *incapable* by them both, do you see, because I am *drunk!*'

'Ha. Because you don't care any more, you mean!' I said. 'You gave up on her and left her.'

'No. It was Henri Palastrier I left.'

'Rubbish. You don't love her. You don't think of her or me or anybody.'

Silence.

'Oh, well. I expect you've got *far* more important things to do than worry about us, haven't you. Why don't you just fuck off again, I don't need you.'

Silence.

'You don't need to stay around for me, I mean it's not as if I did anything for you ever, oh no. *I* didn't help you out when we were in London, did I. *I* didn't hide your . . .'

The shadow by the wall had grown rock-still. Then a match cracked, a flame blossomed to be snuffed out, with a flick of her wrist, as the second orange fire was sucked into life. She came closer, so close that it seemed that she had risen before me in the darkness like a wraith, and her words came out with smoke, indistinguishable from smoke.

'Oh, yes,' she said. 'Oh, yes. You were a clever little girl. A brave little girl.' She gave a low laugh. 'You kept my silly little secret, didn't you.' Her eyes shone in the darkness as she dragged on her cigarette. Mirthful half-moon eyes, glimpsed and then gone. 'OK, Sarah, let's take a trip together. Just you and me. Would you like that?'

And then, harshly, 'You dare to say I don't love my daughter. You know nothing.'

And then: 'You shall come with me.'

Spoken out of the dark by a shadow. I should hardly

have known where she was were it not for the cigarette's glow, the smell of tobacco smoke, the smell of the woman's body.

I woke at dawn to hear her downstairs, scraping something into a tin dish and calling the cats, making coffee, padding from room to room locking all the doors and windows. She was preparing to depart, but I knew she wouldn't go without me.

At seven she came into my room. I blinked once and got out of bed. 'I will put out clean clothes for you,' she said. 'Go to the bathroom quickly. I want to start before it gets too hot.'

When the telephone rang Genevieve was already out by the car and I was about to close the front door. It was Tante Juliette, saying: *'Genevieve? Genevieve?'*

'She's asleep,' I said. 'Would you like me to wake her, Tante Juliette.'

'Sarah! No, leave her sleeping. How are you? Have you recovered, dear?'

'Yes, thank you, Tante Juliette,' I replied. 'I am perfectly well. We are both well. Everything is fine here.'

'We are returning tomorrow, Sarah. There is a heatwave at the seaside. Sarah, are you there?'

'May I give Genevieve a message?'

'Tell her that we are returning tomorrow afternoon. That is all I wanted to say.'

'Yes, I will do that. Goodbye.' I replaced the receiver and closed the front door. I went out to the car.

When I thought about it afterwards I found that I could only remember the following two days in pieces because I kept falling asleep all the time, overwhelmed by dehydration and a slumber beyond panic, by that deep fatigue you get when you can't change what will happen. I knew only that it had started a long time ago, that we were in it together, that it

had been like this ever since I took the diamond. I lied to
Juliette and climbed into Genevieve's car as I had longed to
when I was a little girl. I got into the car and we travelled for
miles and miles in the bright sunlight, with the roof down
and my hair in my eyes, and it was just like it should be.
What else had I wanted except to travel like this, to roar
along the road with her, to wake, to sleep, to be travelling?

'Where are we?' I asked as we reached the city, and
Genevieve said 'Toulon.'

'Are we going to Palastrier's house?'

'No,' she replied. 'We're not going to see Palastrier.
We're going to another man's house.'

'Why?'

'Because that's where Naomi is.'

'But you said she was—'

'She's having a little holiday. Be quiet now, please,
Sarah.'

We parked in a narrow shady street opposite a small
white block of flats. I could see the front doors on the side of
the building, joined by a whitewashed zigzag of steps.
Genevieve told me to wait in the car and went up to the
second floor.

Naomi wore a white cotton dress and carried a doll. The
doll's head bounced on her arm as she came down the steps,
hippety-hop, her black hair swinging across her face. She
came down the tall flight of steps alone. Genevieve stayed at
the top of the steps, by the doorway. This other man, this
man who was not Palastrier, was waiting in the doorway but
I couldn't see his face.

Genevieve was standing the way she had during the
quarrel in the drawing room in London, her shoulders high
and tense, legs braced, feet apart, no weight on her heels at
all, as if the anger were lifting her up off the ground. Only
this time her arms were stretched out in front of her and her
hands clasped around the butt of her gun. She was pointing
her gun at this man.

I couldn't believe my eyes. Naomi was crossing the road
now. I willed her not to turn round because if she did she

might see. I tried to look at Naomi as she came towards me but my eyes remained fixed on the man's hands as he stood in the shadow of the doorway at the top of the steps; raised just a little to either side of him and spread out flat, moving slightly as if to say: Careful, careful. As I watched, he and Genevieve went into the flat. It was only a second, two seconds at most, but I knew what I had seen in that moment of lucidity and I believed my eyes utterly.

Then she took us to another place, I thought in the same town, a tiny flat where the water and the electricity were cut off. We stayed there for the afternoon, I didn't know why, before beginning the long and inevitable return journey.

We arrived in the evening. The big family Peugeot was in the drive alongside a second unfamiliar car. Juliette opened the front door to us. She sent Genevieve, Naomi and me immediately up to my room and locked the door.

I held Naomi in my arms as she became hysterical, as the man pounded massively on the door and the house became alive with the noise of men's voices and the screams and cries of women. Genevieve was screaming: 'Belar! Arrête! Belar!' I cried, 'Qui est Belar!' as the door vibrated and the house seemed to rock beneath my feet. 'Who is he!' I shouted, and Naomi said: 'He is my father.'

Genevieve is gone now. The woman I saw was somebody else, someone who looked like her when she was young. She exists only in the teeming memory-tank of the past. I try to keep that in mind, but time and again I fail. I recall instead one other thing from that summer, which was that just as we came into Toulon I opened my eyes to see a ship on the sea turning in a blaze of light, a warship so heavy but weightless in the water, a wedge in the haze like a thundercloud; and seeing that, feverish still and just woken, I thought for an instant that I was at home.

SEVEN

'There,' I said to Graham. 'Perfect.'

We were neatly slotted between two other Stilgo cars in the driving school car park. Graham smiled for the first time.

'A great improvement on the other day,' he said. 'I think you'll make it. Tomorrow, isn't it?'

'What? What is tomorrow?'

'Your test.' He sounded surprised. 'What else?'

'Oh, yes. Yes it is. Will you come and hold my hand?'

'You'd have difficulty changing gear.'

He had made a joke. I crowed appreciatively. 'Do you know what?' I went on. 'You've hardly called me angel at all. Did I frighten you so much last time?'

He looked sheepish. 'Another of my young ladies told me it was sexist.'

'Oh, Graham.'

'She left me for BSM. It was rather upsetting.'

'I thought you were a bit down today.'

He looked at me sombrely. 'Do you think it is? Sexist?'

I felt a sudden, helpless rush of tenderness for him. 'I think, probably, sadly,' I said, 'that out of all your pupils, it's the ones you call angel who hate being called angel the most.'

'I'm old-fashioned.' He sighed. 'I don't mean anything by it.'

'I know.'

'It just slips out.' His watch bleeped: another thing beyond his control.

'Maybe if you had daughters —' I began, but changed my mind. This was going too far. 'Oh, I don't know. Shall I come into the office and book a pre-test lesson?'

Relieved, we took off our seat-belts. Then I had to repark the car because we couldn't open the doors. Our minds weren't on the job at all.

Poor Graham. I felt guilty. Perhaps I should have warned him. After all, I had found it distracting myself, especially in the beginning. But there were so many other things about him which irritated me equally – watch-bleep, pipe-suck, brill-hair, literal-take – that I did not focus on the 'angel'. Perhaps it was the same for the other girl. Perhaps the only difference was that in her case the 'angel' was the last straw. I don't know.

Too many confusions today. Unknown factors. I can't decide anything today.

After my driving lesson I lingered and loitered in the shops before going unimaginatively to the Cadena Cafeteria for lunch.

Clive, my fellow worker at the Fruit and Veg, was there as usual. He was sitting with several of my class-mates from sixth form college; Vivienne who had been in my French group, accompanied today by her younger sister Amanda; Scott who had given me a beautifully carved bust of our history teacher in soap; and Julian, who was tall and sardonic. Together we formed the rump of a larger group who used to meet there in order to skive, then to study, and then to revise for exams. Now those of us who were left, who had not gone to London or India, consoled ourselves with a guiltless cup of coffee and a chat; we had at least earned our leisure time now. I loved sitting there on the creaking plastic seats which were joined back to back so you see-sawed whenever anyone sat down behind you, huddled in the corner next to the steamed windows in my coat and jersey on cold days with the warmth of bodies around me. I had liked it from the beginning, the whole college business, the way we were called 'students', the lack of uniform; I was especially tickled by the way it had stopped at four o'clock in the afternoon and we all departed with our school-bags as if we were tiny children. I remember myself, fresh from boarding-school, standing with Vivienne on the corner by the bus station as Vivienne chatted with a teacher from her old school – I remember thinking: I will never wear a skirt the whole time I am here. And I never did.

And never, no never not once, did I go to church.

Clive and Vivienne – now into her tenth week as an office junior – were the only ones officially on a lunch-break. Amanda should have been in college, Scott had 'resigned' from Safeway's the previous day and Julian was on his way to the cinema where he hoovered and ushered and occasionally managed the box-office. He looked up from his newspaper as I came in.

'Where are the L-plates?' he asked. 'You should be throwing them over your shoulder like in the advert.'

'I've got no more USE for THESE! I've PASSED with GRAHAM STILGO!'

'PASS with GRAHAM STILGO!'

'ROUNDUP!' For all your CROP NEEDS!'

'What?'

'That's the next one – after pass with Graham Stilgo. At the Cannon. You should know that, Julian.'

'Scott, honestly!' Amanda's ringed hand on the back of his young male neck, shaking him gently back and forth.

'I haven't passed yet!' I protested, giggling. 'I haven't taken the test yet!'

'Clive said you had.'

'I thought it was this morning.'

'Silly Clive.'

'It's tomorrow.' I sat down next to Vivienne. 'Where do you want to go – *if* I get it first time?'

'Southampton!' Scott suggested.

Snorts. Southampton!

'Brighton, then!'

'France,' said Clive.

'Yes!' In unison. 'We could go one weekend.'

'I'm working and I haven't got any money,' I heard myself say rather sharply.

'Whooh, only a suggestion.'

'Only a shugeshtion.'

'She's cross with you, Clive. You've been making her lift the potato sacks again.'

'She longs for the sweet south, though, look at her. You can tell she reads, much of the night, and goes south in the winter.'

'Oh, shut up, Julian.'

'It's not the winter, though.'

Julian smirked at this literalism, unfolded the *Guardian* on the centre spread where the projected fleet was displayed. 'Look at this, the Armada,' he said, and shunted the newspaper across the table, making engine noises as he did so. 'We're off to the Malvi-nas, tra-la-la-la!'

'Jules, not funny.'

'Now you've spilt my tea, you pillock.'

'I wank, much of the night, and –'

'*Scott!*' Amanda banged her teaspoon on her saucer. 'Who's going on the demo? Sarah? Are you coming?'

I opened my mouth, unprepared, still thinking how outrageous Scott was. 'Now you can soap your fanny with Dr Coombs,' he had said earnestly when he gave me the model he had carved, as if it were the most normal thing in the world . . .

'Oh,' I said at last. 'I hadn't thought. Do you think it'll make much difference to . . . to whatever they decide?' Vivienne and Amanda had stickers on their bags saying *Take the Toys from the Boys*. I had seen the badges as well, on coats and caps, bearing the words *No War in the South Atlantic*. 'I mean,' I struggled on, 'I haven't decided not to, or anything . . .'

'Never too late to do something completely pointless, that's what I always say,' said Scott.

There was a pause. I was supposed to say something back.

'Leave it, Scott. Don't push her. Maybe she will and maybe she won't.' Julian's level gaze met mine. 'And generally she don't. Isn't that right, Sarah?'

'You'll be going, then, Julian,' Clive said tonelessly.

'Yes, I will, since you ask, Clive.'

There was another silence while we sipped our tea and waited to see if they would start an argument.

It was broken by Amanda. 'Have you seen the way Tanya's shaved her head?'

'Yes, all up the sides, yuk.'

'Ah, now she'll be there.' Vivienne was acid. 'Demo-woman. Wind her up and send her off.'

'You just feel guilty, Viv, because you didn't go the last time. After all your pontificating you didn't stand up and be counted.'

'No, no!' said Vivienne, shaking back her hair. 'I sat down instead all last summer at Greenham and no one gave a shit. So I got disillusioned with political action.'

'Listen to that,' said Julian. 'She got disillusioned with political action.'

'No, but it's true! Whenever Tanya does anything it's like she invented the bloody wheel, just because you and Scott fancy her.'

'Miaow!'

'Well, OK, Amanda, it's bitchy, but do you know what she said when I told her that Dad had been made redundant? She said: "If you lived in the *Third World*, Vivienne, your father would probably be *dead*!"'

Everybody screamed with delight.

*

I decided to walk back to the Fruit and Veg with Clive before getting the bus. I thought I might be able to pick up my wages.

'You want to watch that Julian,' said Clive, abruptly.

'Hmm?'

'I think he's a bit of a bastard.'

We went into the back room. 'Why do you say that?' I asked him.

'Oh, I don't know . . .' He paused to shrug himself into his overall. 'It's just a feeling.'

I tucked the label down inside his collar. 'You're talking to his ex-girlfriend – one of them, anyway,' I said, grinning.

Clive turned round. 'You and Julian? Really?' he said.

'Come on, it's not that incredible!'

'No, I just mean I didn't know . . . I didn't mean it, what I said just now, Sarah,' and then, as I continued to smile, 'God, you could have told me!' He was actually blushing.

I was laughing by now. 'It's OK! We broke up ages ago. Anyway, I think you're probably right, he is a bastard. A bit of a bastard, didn't you say?'

'Look, I didn't mean it, it was just an idle thought!'

'Clive, you're so honourable.'

I helped him tip the Coxes into the boxes. I managed to coax a smile out of him as 'Sex Machine' came pulsing out of our tiny office. The boss was back.

It's going to be May soon. *In depraved May* – how does it go – *Came Christ the tiger* . . . You notice it first in the trees, not in the first green but in the second, the slightly later fuller beech-green which is warm and somehow naked. There will be caverns of it disturbed by the bus as it comes along the lane under a sky full of warm rain, an iron-grey sky which deepens the colour. It's as if the wood has its tongue out, panting. I always think depraved May, when I see this colour. I notice trees more these days, since we moved out of town four years ago. Each time a bit further away from the sea. There's no talk of another move. Perhaps they'll stay here, my mother and father . . . What am I saying, it's going to be May soon. It's not even April yet. The clocks only changed . . . when was it, last weekend?

Clive and Julian argue periodically, mainly about politics. They only met recently, through going to the Cadena with me at lunchtimes. It's always Julian who starts it. I think my disenchantment with Julian is almost complete.

I can still see why I was drawn to him, in the same detached way that I can see how he's still sexy for other people. I admired him, not for the way he behaved in the English class – ostentatiously reading Hunter S. Thompson instead of *Volpone* like the rest of us – but for his single-minded devotion to the king, the seer and sage, T. S. Eliot, a copy of whose *Selected Poems* he was never without. He even set them to music. He sang in a band which played in the Grapes for half an hour: 'Oh oh oh that Shakespeherian rag . . .' Not Eliot's finest moment, nor Julian's: the band had their own sound system but Julian's mike was wired to the PA so you either had the band with Julian mouthing, or Julian singing without the band, depending on where you were in the room. Either way it was a terrible mess. Everybody was bent double laughing but I felt sorry for him, even though – or especially as – we'd just split up. He was only trying to pay homage to the king.

But ever since he introduced me to Eliot May was depraved and I was fixated. Last summer I read nothing else but Eliot, during the exams, after the exams. I baked on the flat roof above the garage and kept the book open with my chin, grunting, as I unclipped my bikini top. I needed someone to fill the gap left by Ezra Pound, because after Genevieve died I couldn't read Ezra Pound any more. The first time I tried – it was ages later, I was at my second boarding-school – I read one poem and was gripped for a whole day by this unbearable sliding feeling I realized afterwards was fear. After that it was OK, but it made me sad, so I put the book up on my top shelf. I didn't throw it away because it had a photo of Naomi stuck inside the cover. Poppies and day's eyes. Weird, to be scared of Ezra Pound.

I should stop thinking about the past. I had an intimation last night that I was overheating it in a sort of red-alert, asbestos fashion. I was charging it up too much. I should leave it to cool, let it spool and stream . . .

God, they were mighty when we were kids, the ships, we used to go down and visit them when they were parked at Portsmouth. People everywhere and such a noise, a noise like a gigantic infernal hosing and scrubbing, and the radar swivelling *wing-wing-wing*; and the smell of hot metal, paint and fuel fumes, my mother hates it because his clothes always smelt like that just before he went away – you can't get that smell anywhere else. Well, sometimes a bus smells like that but not very often, not even a ferry smells quite like it.

I was going to say, spool and stream the way power-cables and fuel-lines do from a ship being fed.

I took my shoes off at the back door which always swings open with a crash because it is badly balanced and made largely of glass.

'Oh, sweetheart, did you get wet?' My mother was home before me, standing on tip-toe on the newly washed floor, sponging the kitchen surfaces.

'Not too bad. It's stopped now.' I nipped over the damp tiles in my socks to put the kettle on. 'Can I put my overalls in the machine?'

In the utility room next to the kitchen I saw a great load of white shirts on the clothes horse.

'I couldn't put those out,' said my mother from the kitchen, raising her voice slightly so that I could hear her, 'because I—'

'Because you keep thinking it's going to rain, yes, isn't it a pain.'

'Such a bore.'

'Why doesn't it bloody stop, I'm getting pissed off with being soaked the whole time.'

'I wish you wouldn't talk like that.'

'Any other bits and bobs to go in a hot wash?' I said, in a voice higher and louder than necessary, to show that I had ignored what she had just said. I raked through the laundry basket, throwing garments on the floor.

'There's some jeans, and my denim skirt, and the tea towels.'

'Right-oh!' I called, almost sang, as I put them in and slammed the door. 'Just going out for a fag,' I told her, skidding shoeless over the clean floor again to the back door, as the machine began to hum.

'What?'

'Just going out for a cigarette!' I almost shouted, climbing into my wellingtons before crashing the door shut behind me.

I stood in the tool-shed and smoked rapidly, *mmff-ahh, mmff-ahh, mmff-ahh*. (It's a convention that I don't smoke in the house: 'My own daughter, puffing away, I couldn't bear it,' Mum says, as if it's less carcinogenic to do it in the shed.) I gazed, as I usually do, at the two big wooden boards on the wall, set with hooks, hung with tools. Behind each tool was its painted silhouette – in red on one of the boards, for my father's set, and in black on the other, for Jonathan's. I saw several empty shapes, which should have indicated that my father was using a hacksaw and a claw hammer and Jonathan two pairs of pliers. Since neither of them were at home they must have done the unforgivable and failed to replace them.

They came back briefly at the weekend, Jonathan and my father. They went and varnished the dinghy together.

I lit one cigarette from another, which is something I do not usually do. I wanted Flora to come home quickly from her dancing. Flora was needed to pinch my mother's cheeks, and dance her a bit around the room, and demand cup-cakes from a mix or something. She's so good at that; I leave all that kind of thing to her these days. Anyway, I can't open my mouth to my mother because Genevieve's name has been stuck like a bone in my throat.

Yesterday morning, on the way to work, I saw her again. She was on the bus into town. She was sitting up at the front; I only realized it was her when she turned round in her seat, said something I couldn't catch, and winked. I was at the back, I tried to push through towards her but she was gone; and by 'gone' I mean she got off the bus. She didn't disappear as you would expect from a dead person.

The shed was dim. The tools gleamed. The rain started pattering again on the corrugated-iron roof above my head. I picked up a spanner and swung it in my hand. I wondered where the missing tools were, how long they had been gone, and was rewarded with a bizarre vision of my father locked in a brawl with the Argentinian I met in Spain. I pictured them lumbering about in my bedroom, stumbling over the boxes of books: my father older than the Argentinian, his head trapped in the crook of the man's arm as he tried to kill him, flailing with his hammer, slashing ineffectually with his hacksaw.

The sheets were out on the washing-line in the rain. I unstuck my tongue from the roof of my mouth and sprinted out across the grass to save them.

My mother had come out at exactly the same moment. She was feeling the sheets uncertainly.

'No, no, come on, let's bring them in,' I said, with a fist of pegs already, and we hauled them down in armfuls off the line.

It seems now that if it happens, he will go. If it happens. But it won't happen.

EIGHT

'They treat you like a child,' Julian said to me, the first time he came to my house.

'I am a child,' I replied unthinkingly. 'I'm still fifteen, actually.' Instantly I felt a fool. I opened my mouth to deny it and to tell him how much I resented his remark, but I was pre-empted by one of his tender looks.

'Ackshlee,' he said gently, before turning to the photographs on the landing. 'Royal Naval College,' he read. 'Which one is your dad? No, let me guess . . .'

'You won't be able to, he's too young. Shall we go down?' I could hear Flora banging cutlery down on the table, cross because I wasn't helping her.

'Look at this one, the missile going off. It's called – Sea Slug!' He burst into laughter. 'Why, does it go along very slowly, leaving a trail?' Then, before I could stop him, he unhooked a couple of wooden plaques from the wall. 'Aurora and Galatea. Who are they?'

'Ships,' I said shortly. 'I think lunch—'

'I didn't know they had crests like this. They look like they've been painted with the foot.'

'Julian, put them back.'

'I'm interested!'

'You're not. You're just making fun. Let's go down. Mummy must be dishing up.'

At that first meal my father took great delight in Julian's recently shaven head, testing it for intelligence bumps, showing Julian pictures from various illustrated books of Huron Indians and suchlike, suggesting future styles . . . I remember Julian's brown eyes, round already from this onslaught of attention, fairly popping when I told my father how interested he'd been in the photographs, how I'm sure he'd love to hear more . . . It was wicked, but nobody, least of all Julian who was my boyfriend, was going to laugh at me and at the things in my house.

Anyway he was the one who was childish, the way he read that stupid book in class, looking at me to see if I'd noticed. Distracting me so much that the teacher – not unkindly – asked for Miss Finney's full attention. 'Only when *Mr* Staples tears his from *Fear and Loathing in Las Vegas*, I said, which was a *very* sarky reply and the first time I'd opened my mouth in that class. Everyone giggled – at me, at Julian, and at the teacher who had ignored Julian's behaviour over several lessons. But I couldn't help it; in all my schools nobody would ever have read a book of their own in class, peeping it provocatively from behind the set text like that, certainly not after the age of eleven or twelve at the most!

I was twitchy from the beginning when it came to Julian. I wasn't even civil to him after that lesson, when we bought our first oxtail soups from the machine and swapped terse remarks on books and bands. I said I'd already read *Fear and Loathing*, thank you, when he offered to lend it to me – and then rushed to Smiths, but in vain; I had to resort to picking it up casually off his desk and leafing through, chuckling quietly as if at my favourite bits. It's pathetic, but he got under my skin, that is all I can say in my defence. And only when I sat at his desk trying not to laugh too loud did it occur to me that it would have been nice to apologize for the incident in the classroom. And then it occurred to me that he hadn't mentioned it, or even seemed offended by it.

We made love on a Saturday morning, when his house

was empty. For privacy only, not secrecy. Afterwards he read to me, shivering in a dressing-gown on a stool beside the bed. I said get back in, why don't you, but he said that if he did we'd want to do it again and there were no more Durex. '*Quis hic locus, quae regio, quae mundi plaga,*' he intoned instead, shivering, and I lay on my carefully placed towel and heard Eliot's *Marina* for the first time. The noise of traffic and children retreated before the thunder of the surf, and I lay there and pretended to be Hercules, washed up after the wreck.

It was short-lived. One day when I made a particularly caustic joke he said, 'That's not like you,' and I burst out: 'It is! It's exactly like me!' making him stare. 'What do you think I am, a schoolgirl?' And then about a month before we broke up he suddenly cried: 'Oh, Sarah, can't you get serious about anything?' with such pleading warmth that I was completely thrown. 'No, Jules, no, I'm sorry, I can't, not any more,' I replied, and to my horror I started to cry. He cuddled me remorsefully but it wasn't his fault, and anyway it was no good. Gradually we drifted into different circles. He gave up English for history and I hardly spoke to him until the exams. It was quite a surprise when he started coming a couple of months ago to the Cadena, a new, taller figure, lounging at our table, bitching. I wish he'd leave us alone. He doesn't even like Clive. He refers to him as Mr Spud when he's not there. When he's addressing me he calls him Spud–U–Like.

They lined the walls of our house, up the stairs and on the landing: they had done so in every house we'd ever lived in. I had thought they were beautiful when I was a child, the destroyers marking the open sea, the castles and rising suns which were the symbols of ships with beautiful names. 'Household gods': Julian's words, of course – crass, but he did want to know. I could have told him how I'd gazed at them as a kid, and all the rest, but I didn't. I let him make a fool of me and sent him downstairs for my father to look for genius in the shape of his head. What else could I have done? I had no heart now for protests. The last time I had risen up it had been with Genevieve and we had gone together into tragedy. Who was Julian to come along and taunt me for letting myself be babied? Who is he now, to jeer because I won't march in processions? If the boy had seen what I have seen . . . !

I meant to say, Genevieve had gone to tragedy. Not us together. Because of course it was just her, she went on her own. I didn't go with her.

The landscape changed to battleground. A cold, clear light shone from the sky. My childhood was left far behind.

I gazed at the hero who lay mortally wounded on the unblemished sward, his outstretched limbs balanced by an artless pyramid of weeping companions. The tattered standard was unfurled above his head against a ragged panorama of storm clouds. In the background, shrouded in rain or smoke, the armies clashed upon the plain. And from a break in the cloud, high up and far over the hills, came the light; the whole scene was back-lit by this rupture in the storm, every raindrop and bayonet glinted in it. It was terrible, this silvered, non-terrestrial light, it was cold: the hero was pointing at it, transfixed, as if he could see something his companions could not. I used to look at this as I did at the plaques and pictures at home, as an object to admire. Now I wondered what he saw.

The murmur of men's voices, the clink of cutlery, filled the room where the picture hung unmentioned on the wall and I sat straight-backed at my grandparents' dining-table. I didn't talk with my mouth full. I seldom looked up from my plate, and when I did it was to stare out of the window at the lawn which was the same deep green as the painted turf in the frame. Tall men out of uniform helped the women to serve the meal, standing with a carving-knife or corkscrew in their hands: 'Boys, have some more ham . . . Who's for another glass of wine?' Though they didn't drink much, the men, and the women even less; the day was long past when my grandmother had been disastrously plied by the young bloods of the gunners' mess, in India, before dinner in the viceregal presence. There was little excess, beneath that sober light, in that oak-panelled room.

A family, my paternal clan, gathering on a Sunday in the early spring. My grandparents, my uncles, their wives, my cousins. My brother Jonathan, ten years old, hands busy under the table, making a set of dentures out of orange-peel. My mother with a new short hair-cut her father-in-law didn't like, preferring her 'elegant chignon, Katharine, what have you done with it . . .' My sister Flora who was four, thundering up the corridor to race through the dining-room with the regularity of a comet. It was Flora whose turn it was to blow the bugle now, encouraged by our older cousins, the army-bound boys in ties and jackets seated opposite myself and Jonathan, permitted a glass of wine. My father, who not long afterwards would take Jonathan out to the greenhouse and discuss with him the merits of a career in the services; and 'Why the *greenhouse*?' was all Jonathan would say, ironically fingering his chin and frowning, but at present of the age to flash me a mouthful of pithy fangs, to be thrown a lightning glance of admonition by our mother . . . And myself at twelve, pale and straight-backed, lank light brown hair chin length, rolling my napkin-ring back and forth on the table, lost in thought.

The previous summer was long gone. Genevieve, her gun and her car had receded into the haze. It was a travesty, that car journey, of the one I had wanted to take. I knew that now. Instead of travelling for leagues to foreign lands we had blasted down to the Mediterranean coast and straight back again to a scene of ugly chaos. It was grotesque. And what about the gun? And the man? The *men*? There were two of them, remember, Palastrier and, just when I'd pinned him down, Genevieve had cried out Belar! and Naomi said: My father. I didn't know what was going on. I had come home to England possessed of one fact only. I knew what she did with the gun. Why she did it, I hadn't a clue.

No dashing headgear at Lucifer's. (We were forbidden to call it that but every girl in the school did.) No blue berets. I sat at that Sunday table, school-bound, in an off-white blouse with darts, a maroon tie and pullover, a grey tweed skirt and an adjustable belt with a clasp and a zip pocket for a very small amount of money. The skirt was too large at the waist; it came untucked from the belt and slid down to my hips so that the blouse stuck out at the back. The belt floated free around my waist underneath my pullover. If I wasn't careful I would earn myself a red girdle for bad deportment. This was the antithesis of a green girdle for good deportment, a long strip of material, a sash of shame, another thing to be rucked up around the waist. The fact that other girls had to wear even worse jumpers – lilac, mustard, poison-green according to their school house – was no consolation. I sat there uncomfortably constrained, alone with my secret – my exclusive secret, since not even Genevieve shared it with me. She hadn't seen me watching her outside the flat. Stupid girl, always hiding and hoarding! I should have challenged her. She might have told me about Belar immediately – she blurted it out quick enough when I asked the following summer – and then I'd have understood it all. Instead, I sat a whole year at Lucifer's in ignorance and prickly tweed.

I knew a woman who had a gun. I saw her point it at a man. What good was that now? I wasn't a child any more. A child would have been squirming with curiosity, but I sat very still. I had to watch my back. I was already marked out, rolling my napkin-ring slowly back and forth, already disgraced. It was penitently that I sat there beneath the cold, clear light of the new order.

There was a narrow flagstoned passage outside the chapel, a drainpipe beside the door, a dripping gutter. On choir practice days the door was left open all morning so that the green carpet grew soggy in the rain. They put the buns in the doorway at the end of the passage, where the music rooms were. Buns for break on choir days.

This term it was the Stabat Mater. I sang second soprano and alto. Sometimes on Sundays I switched to first soprano for the Agnus Dei, for the exhilaration of it, but when we practised the Stabat Mater I stayed in my division for the alto aria Eja Mater, where the 'Eja' was a poised sigh and the 'fons amoris' a sob genteelly controlled.

The Agnus Dei would be performed as part of the Sung Eucharist. The Communion wine was cooking sherry. It made my throat hot for the rest of the service. I sang the high Miserere Nobis which went up each time it was repeated, so that by the Dona Nobis Pacem we were shrieking. Because we didn't eat before this service I got a fizzy sensation in my nose and mouth when I sang this.

This was Lucifer's, and I was now in the second term of my first year.

The bun was damp in my mouth. I stuffed half of it in, tucking my errant blouse in with my other hand. I paid back the 25p I owed to one girl and borrowed 25p from another to buy a bar of chocolate from the tuck shop. I loitered with the other singers in the entrance to the courtyard, sheltering from the light rain. The singing went on in the chapel behind us.

'Flat,' someone announced thickly, mouth full of bun, and the rest of us went: 'Mm.'

It began to rain harder. Flutes took over from clarinets, with a scraping of chairs, in the music rooms above us. I glanced at my watch and then at my friend Paulina. 'Time for a quick half?' She nodded.

We split the cigarette behind the large wheeled dustbins outside the kitchens. Paulina loudly spat out shreds of tobacco and I flapped at her. 'They'll hear you!' I hissed. 'Are you going to London for the Exeat?'

'No, to the Paris flat,' replied Paulina, whose father was a doctor who worked in Bahrain.

'The Paris flat!' I sighed. 'I suppose you have a view of the Eiffel Tower.'

'Yes, we do, actually. 'Paulina gazed at me with her big green eyes, the type of eyes which made me think of grapes. 'Why don't you come? A long weekend in Paris, we could have fun. My brothers will be there.'

I rolled my eyes. 'It's my grandmother's birthday. There's going to be a huge Sunday lunch. And I've got to come back that afternoon and do weeding.'

'What?' Paulina widened the grape-eyes.

'For listening to the charts during Compline.'

Paulina gave a high scream of laughter. 'You fool! I bet you were jigging about. You've got to stand still!'

'Miss Pye saw the earpiece.'

'Honestly, Sarah, you are an idiot!'

I was laughing as well now. 'Do you know what she said?'

'No, what?'

I tried to school my lips into a crisp Edinburgh accent. '"There is a time and a place for the Led Zeppelin, Sarah"!'

'"The Led Zeppelin"!'

We stood there hooting, grinding out the stubs of the halved cigarette beneath our shoes. Then we set off round the courtyard, under the walls to keep out of the rain.

Outside the headmistress's office we parted. Paulina started to walk away, but turned.

'You can't go in there like that,' she said. At practised lightning speed we swapped skirts, her grey tweed for my blue games kilt. Then, before I knew it, she was tucking my blouse in properly for me, all the way round, settling the belt snugly over the waistband of the skirt, pulling the jersey down neatly over my hips. I held my arms up as if I were wading into cold water and turned my face away. 'Paulina, Paulina, for Christ's sake, this is too much,' I pleaded in a high voice, eyes heavenward.

The headmistress lived in a well of a room. You had to go down a flight of steps to reach her. She wore a black gown most of the time, always in chapel when she dealt out the Communion wine. 'The ber-lud of Chrrist' we'd say at breakfast afterwards, looming up on each other like Dracula with cups of tea.

She was writing. I waited for her to look up and say 'Ah, Sarah'. It was usually 'Ah, Sarah' this term.

But she began speaking while her head was still bowed over her desk. 'I expect your father,' she began, 'being a naval officer, has talked to you about authority before now.' Only then did she look up at me blandly through her glasses. Scribble scribble dot dot, went her signature.

I stared. 'What?'

'I expect your father talks to you about authority, when he discusses your behaviour with you.'

'Yes, he does.' I was still nonplussed. 'From time to time.'

'In which case he will have told you what is important about authority.'

I was accustomed to the light now. The woman's face was reflective, lined, sad. 'You have to obey it,' I volunteered.

'Yes, that's true' – on a rising note, as if she were encouraging a timid child. 'And why do you have to obey it?'

I opted for levity. 'Because if you don't, you have to weed the flower-beds.'

The headmistress rose to her feet and went to the window. She addressed the garden. 'Sarah, we obey authority, not out of fear of punishment, but out of understanding. Rules and regulations are made for an intelligible reason, which is that they provide the maximum freedom for everybody in the community. Since you're an intelligent girl, I can't see why you have such difficulty grasping this. Does it make sense to you? Does the idea make sense?'

'Yes, Madam, it makes sense.'

'Now, if we take the question of uniforms . . .'

We took the question of uniforms as I had known from the beginning that we would. We discussed it from every aspect, the social (equality, identity, cohesion). The economic (hard-wearing fabrics, laundry, growing girls, re-usability). The health (warmth in winter, ventilation, laundry again). We established beyond doubt that if one possessed two skirts, the first a short, thin kilt and the second a knee-length tweed skirt, then one would wear the former only for games and not at other times, and one would use the latter for normal day-wear during the winter months. One would not parade around in the former all day with striped socks and a sloppy Joe sweater – and neither would one stuff the latter down the back of a chest of drawers and pretend one had lost it! Not, that is, if one was a rational person! 'The question is, why, Sarah? I need to know why! You have ample opportunity to wear exactly what you like after tea and at weekends, and yet you persist in wearing your games kilt for whole days at a time! Why can't you bring yourself to wear your uniform correctly?'

'I am, I am now!'

'I would bet,' she said gently, 'that that skirt belongs to Paulina Ferens.'

I stared at the floor, blinking rapidly. 'It's ugly,' I said at last.

'It may not be to your taste, but it's really quite ordinary–looking.'

'It's too big! Well, mine is!'

'Good Heavens, my girl, you're not helpless! Take it to needlework! Miss Legg will help you make some tucks!'

I stared, chewing my lip.

'Will you do that?'

'Yes, Madam.'

'In your next lesson?'

'Yes, Madam.' I scuffed one foot on the floor.

The headmistress sat down at her desk. She put her hands together as if she were praying, forefingers against her mouth.

'What should I tell your parents about this behaviour?' she said at last. 'How should I explain it to your father, who, I would have thought, would be an example to you in this area?'

'How? Why? He doesn't have to wear the damn thing.'

'That's ill mannered,' said the headmistress. 'And wilfully obtuse.'

*

There was no point in changing into our own clothes – which were called 'mufti', I never knew why. We were all going to spend the rest of the day in the same place, together, doing the same things. After tea we would go to our dormitories and take off the mustard, green, lilac, maroon pullovers and matching ties and foul skirts and put on other skirts of a certain length and smartness, other cardigans or sweaters, other blouses, socks and tights, other shoes with a 1½ inch heel maximum. We would eat our white bread and jam and then go and change our clothes, and then we would go to needlework with our hair brushed and sit among the whirr of machines with our hands clean with the darkness outside and the rain, and we would pin and tack and baste and laugh and chat, last week somebody sewed on a puff-sleeve upside-down and everyone thought it was so funny, ha-ha-ha, I wanted to burn the place down.

'Ill mannered,' I raged, needle slipping in sweaty hands as I forced it through the grey tweed. 'Wilfully obtuse. I am so stupid, did you know, Paulina, that I can't see the point of doing this!'

'I'll help you when I've finished this row,' said Paulina quietly.

'God save us, you're doing smocking.'

'Yes, I'm making a top for the summer. Look, here's the pattern.'

'Separates for the Junior Miss, oh God, Paulina, how can you.'

'You're upsetting Miss Legg, saying God all the time.'

'Well really, look at it, with the bows, it's a garment for an idiot.'

'That's just silly.'

'You know I hate it. I hate it here.'

'What do you hate about it? Apart from needlework.'

'Just the way it is.' I ripped out the tuck I had made and drummed my heels on the ground. 'You know, I reckon my luck changed with this skirt.'

NINE

During my first lacrosse lesson ever I had caught the ball smack on the knee and this time it did turn black; I limped through my first term with a bruise the size of a saucer. 'I copped it on the knee, look, I can't bend my leg at all,' I said delightedly to my mother, who had exclaimed, 'Ooh my baby!' in front of all the teachers: and I was surprised at this lapse, that my mother should be unaware that it was right that my knee should be bruised, since this was not the soft holiday tennis-ball of the summer but a hard black rubber missile which came whack and made me say 'Jesus!' as the stick fell from my hands and the grass pitch, spreading for acres, seeped a shade greener as I quelled the pain.

I thought nothing of it at first – there was no time. We were taken away like yearlings, the smallest girls, to be weighed and measured, to be graded and marked, to have special lessons in singing that were for entertainment only, to break us in gently for the choir. We went in our 'mufti' after tea to the music sitting room, we gathered around the piano to learn the song 'Far far away, my pearly Adri-aatic' which had a chorus 'Chirri-birri-birri, I'm a sailor'; and I, who had a father bound for Iceland, sat there superiorly in my pinafore dress with my magnificent knee, knowing that it had nothing to do with pearly waves but instead with the command of massive machines which turned in the darkness against the powerful muscles of the Atlantic or the North Sea . . .

But the new era began, whack, on that first crisping September afternoon when the ball came into contact with my knee. Genevieve was tiny and distant in the hot haze. It was a cold clear autumn now and I didn't like the way it was; I began to smoke in the bushes, I grew an inch, I was shut up with my fellows like a hen in a coop in the chapel on Sunday evenings to sing 'Because there is none other that fighteth for us' with the groovy chords in the middle like a trumpet-call and then the small sad 'But only thaa-wo Lord'.

In Advent we were advised to go to candle-chapel and meditate, so in the evenings I sat and stared at the candles on the altar – we all sat there, or kneeled; those of the élite top sopranos whose voices went up to the lower heaven; those who carried the cross on Sundays, the sixteen-year-old sacristans tall and corn haired; those who spoke in tongues, which was a custom extirpated whenever discovered; those who ate only white food, being on the threshold of Confirmation. I meditated chiefly on 'Aladdin Sane'.

We were told to listen carefully to the Lesson when it was the parable of the talents; and I thought of buried treasure, and pondered how to hide the skirt.

I clapped as the prizes were distributed for Junior Cheerfulness and Senior Cheerfulness, and we were told that our school was famous for academic achievement, spiritual development and courtesy. This was after Mr Cockburn had given me a D in maths and I had said, 'Christ damn you, Mr Prickburn, it isn't bloody fair,' and he had heard me.

Christmas came and went, the first Exeat, the spring half-term. My grandfather told me not to kick against the pricks, darling, I was turning my mother grey, and there she was on her own so much. I was old enough to be a support to her now; and I thought of a pit-prop, and it chilled me, that word support, because it was used so often of my mother, of whom it was often said amongst all the grandparents that she was 'such a support to Robert in his career'. Then I was back under the crucified Christ again as we sang Eja Mater with a sigh in our voices and 'fons amoris' with a sob, and I squinted down the row at the raised heads, the uplifted chins, and I wondered how on earth they managed it, because I was sure they must be pretending.

The word 'support' used to make me think of support garments, which had made us snigger during our first term when we did 'lingerie' fashion shows at night with scarves and pillows and stockings – 'And this is for the mature woman with a simply *massive* bum' – and when, if we thought we heard a mistress lingering outside, we would sing the chorus 'Eavesdroppers hear no good of themselves' in a round with 'Fairy footsteps!' to the tune of the Messiah 'Hallelujah'; and even though we had just flung ourselves upon our beds racked with hysteria it was sweet and clear and in tune, because this was a musical school . . .

The knee mended. It was Easter. Suddenly I had been twelve for a long time, and I was about to go to France again, with my hair longer so that it went into bunches for games. I would arrive in France a little muddied from the fray, saying 'Oh, it's just a scratch,' breathing fast and laughing from the shock.

What did I remember from the previous summer? Naomi, of course. Naomi whom I met when I went down with Genevieve to Toulon and brought her back to Juliette's house. I remembered swift days, hurried and brilliant with sun as I recovered from fever and lolled under the trees in the garden or in the shadow of the chinoiserie room, Tante Juliette coming in and out, not speaking to me, as if I were to blame. This was after the great fight of the first evening when Naomi had screamed: 'Send them all away, send them all away,' and Genevieve had shouted at everyone – at Juliette, at Madame her mother, and at the man who had hammered on the door to be let in. He had come straight to Juliette's house after we left his building for the flat with no electricity.

He was waiting for us, in a fury, when we arrived home in the evening.

What next? My first proper conversation with Naomi. That took place in the garden of Tante Juliette's house the day after our return from Toulon, by the wall overlooking the valley. I hadn't noticed the trees yet. I wouldn't notice them for years, the trees which lined the river-banks, separate, small, straight, green. I would only ever see them clearly in my mind's eye, years later, by which time they had become sentinels of a more ancient land, shade and shelter for vagabonds limping, strumming, chewing sour fruit . . .

Naomi swung herself up on the wall that day and cried: 'Who are you!' with her black hair swinging forward over her face as she settled herself there, with her back to the view. I remembered her in mid-flight above me as she bounced and sprang and scrambled, turning her body to sit in the sun, blocking the view. 'Who are you!'

'I am Uncle Nicholas's niece.' Considering this the best way to start.

Naomi shut her eyes and said, from her great height: 'So am I.'

She leaned down to study me. She smiled a thin-lipped, sweet smile, her lips sticky from the gum she was chewing. It had a sickly odour; grape, perhaps, or orange. 'And why are you here?'

'To visit Tante Juliette, and Lucien and Katrine.'

'Oh-ho!' Naomi roared with laughter. 'Oh, you must have had fun! You had fun, did you? *Tu t'es bien amusée?*' She leaned down further and pinched my cheek. I jerked my head back. Naomi lost her balance and slid down off the wall to stand facing me. 'Why weren't you with them, if you came to visit them?' she demanded.

'I had sunstroke, I couldn't go.'

'You had sunstroke, you couldn't go!' Naomi whined. 'You look like you do, you pink pig, you little English girl. I don't know why you came with my mother. We could have gone back to Henri's house otherwise.'

'But you're going to live here now, not with Henri

Palastrier,' I blurted, regretting it immediately. Surely Genevieve had told her!

But she just said: 'How do you know?'

'Genevieve told me.'

'Ohh! Did she? She told you? I see! And who told you to call her "Genevieve"?'

'What else should I call her?' I leaned against the wall. My hands were trembling a little from nerves and fatigue.

Naomi came closer. Her eyes were as black as olives. 'I think,' she said, 'that I will be very glad when Uncle Nicholas comes back, because then everything will be settled. Maman and I can leave you to be teased by Lucien and go home instead of being stuck here in Juliette's house with a stupid English girl!' She began to cry. 'So you see!' she gasped. 'So you see!' And she ran back to the house, sobbing loudly. She took very small steps as she ran. I remembered how she'd hopped down the steps the day before in Toulon. She had some problem with her feet, a weakness of some kind in her ankles, which made her toddle as she ran.

Then us lying upstairs together in the bedroom.

No – then Nicholas's return.

No – first Genevieve coming out into the garden, to the wall where I was still standing. 'She keeps talking about going home to Mr Palastrier,' I said, panic-stricken. 'Haven't you told her yet! I said —'

'It's been arranged for weeks. She's just being enervating. She's tired now and so are you. And so am I.' Her eyes were watering, her hair scraped into a scarf. Her face had a scoured look. 'Juliette's giving me hell,' she said.

'You should really change your dress now. It's beyond a joke.'

'Help me with her, Sarah.' Meaning Naomi. 'Help me with her.'

Sitting in the red room. Airless. The family engaged in family things, in pretending everything was normal, and the visitors sitting alone, in quarantine. Naomi sat sullenly, cross-legged. Genevieve sprawled on a couch, half-on, half-off. I knelt in front of the table, pouring mineral water into glasses clinking with ice. We were all waiting for Nicholas to come back; he had some power, I presumed, to resolve the situation. Genevieve and Naomi didn't want to stay, but it was clear that there was nowhere else for them to go.

Naomi unfolded a leg and pushed me between the shoulder-blades as I poured, causing me to spill the water. 'I don't want any,' she said.

'That's lucky, yours has just gone all over the table.'

'Maman, can't we go back to Henri's now?'

Then at some point in the evening, at Genevieve's insistence, I opened the bedroom door to find the snuffling figure on the bed, mumbling, *'Fou le camp.'* The shutters were big and tall and beautiful; Naomi should have lived there, it was right for her. I think now that it would have been better if Genevieve had given in then and there, and let Naomi stay with Nicholas and Juliette. Naomi should have opened those shutters every day, in the morning or after the siesta, and seen that courtyard cut in half by sun and shadow. After all, she would end up there in the end.

'Fuck off, I said, didn't you hear?'

'Uncle Nicholas is back.'

We could hear him downstairs. This time there was no screaming, not like the previous night when it seemed that the river-valley had let loose a mad dog into the house to run wild up and down the stairs. This time there were only quiet English words. *Genevieve, sweetheart, I thought we'd got it all sorted out . . . Look at you, darling, I hate to see you like this . . . You can't . . . Let us take her off your hands for a little while . . .* I could hardly make out what he was saying.

'Did you know,' Naomi said suddenly, 'my mother is still married to my father?'

I looked at her. 'He's still her husband? But they aren't together.'

'No! No! But,' Naomi repeated significantly, 'they are still married. Do you know, we left him when I was four!'

'And he's called Belar?'

She grinned and nodded. 'That is our surname. His first name is Paul. And then after we left him we went to live with Henri, that is to say Henri Pa-las-tri-er, now are you satisfied, Miss Long Nose?'

We sat side by side on the bed. Downstairs Genevieve said: '*Nicholas, help me out, you're my only friend, you don't want this to happen, it's been cooked up by Juliette, she's always wanted to . . . ever since . . .*'

'Do you know,' Naomi said, 'I like visiting my father – except when Maman turns up and makes a scene like the other day. She wasn't supposed to come, you know. I was supposed to stay for another week. I don't know what she says that makes him so wild. Nobody knows. Tante Juliette says that he and Maman are one of life's mysteries. What are you staring at?'

I dropped my gaze and carefully unwrapped a Malabar chewing-gum. They came with transfers inside.

'I wouldn't mind living here either,' Naomi went on. 'I've stayed here so much recently. Henri is just like an uncle, more like an uncle than Nicholas, but all the same I wouldn't mind being here with my cousins. But I think Maman will make another plan.' She slapped a Malabar transfer on to her forearm. 'That's why she came down to Toulon when she wasn't supposed to, you know. To make everyone think again.'

I said helplessly, 'I expect she will,' as downstairs Nicholas said: *What more can I do, tell me . . . anything, anything . . . come to this . . . darling, we have to take her in . . .*'

Naomi looked at me, speculating and shrewd. 'I bet he's saying, "Oh, *chérie*, let us look after Naomi." Is he?'

'Yes, something like that.'

She chuckled. 'He can't fool me by speaking English!' She lay back on the pillow. 'He'll help her, though. He always does.' She began to comb long strands of hair through her fingers, repeating in a lazy sing-song: 'He always does . . .'

Later in the night, after we had chewed all the gum, talking but not giggling yet, Naomi had said: 'Will you be my friend, then?'

'I didn't know you met the little girl.' My mother, rummaging for grey thread in the sewing-basket which was always a mess because she hated sewing. It was like the guts of a creature in there, all hanging out whenever you grabbed anything. The events of that first summer were fading like a burn mark with the approach of Lucifer's.

'Yes. She's living – staying with Aunt Juliette now. Until Genevieve gets a place. Then she'll live with Genevieve again like she used to. And then I'll go and stay with them, she says.'

'Oh, will you, indeed!'

'She means it this time.'

'Well, I don't know about that . . .'

'She'll do it. You'll see.'

'What I don't see is you sewing on any of these flaming name-tapes, darling, do have a go, I can't face the lot.'

'Three brassières!' My father, chortling, reading from Lucifer's clothing list. 'What do you want with three brassières?'

'Ha ha ha. Anyway it says optional, Daddy, look.'

Genevieve did do it in the end. She came to live not far from Juliette and Nicholas. First she got a small flat in St-Cyprien, the town where Naomi, still staying with Juliette, was going to school with her cousins Lucien and Katrine. I went to Lucifer's and my father went to Iceland. I sat in the music sitting room and sang 'My pearly Adri-aatic' with all the other girls and thought of great machines moving out over the brine in the dark and bitter northern night. I had my first lacrosse lesson.

It wasn't until Easter that she wrote.

Dear Sarah, said the letter. *I have left the apartment now and found a house not far outside St-Cyprien, on the edge of a small village. I am restoring it with a friend. Please come and visit us, and help me and Naomi put the finishing touches to our new house. Come in the summer as you did before. The house has a tower. I hope you are enjoying your new school and Naomi promises that she will write . . .*

But Naomi hadn't written. Naomi wouldn't start writing until after that summer, after I had made my second visit to France.

I grew my hair longer and wore it in bunches at school. I held my twelfth birthday party in my dormitory. That summer term I failed the Divinity exam on purpose. I betrayed myself; I pretended I didn't know what a ziggurat was. My paternal godfather recited a poem which began 'Failed in Divinity' to amuse everyone, and my mother said: 'Sarah's going to stay with my brother Nicholas again . . . well actually with his sister-in-law, she's got a daughter Sarah's age. She lives a stone's throw from Nick.'

'Is that the hippy one who used to be an actress?' Jonathan asked.

Chuck the hook down, see what you get.

Poppies and day's eyes?

Not yet.

TEN

'This map,' Genevieve said to me, 'shows an old part of France, before France as a country existed. This part was called Langue d'Oc, which is the name of the language they spoke. Look, you see, it includes us, here.'

I stared, deciphered a few crabbed names, but couldn't see the name of the town or the village. I looked up at Genevieve for an explanation, but she was still staring at the map, her eyes closed, her lips pursed. She was fatter than last year, her hair less ragged. She looked more French.

'And this is a statue,' she continued, 'made of the tusk of an elephant. It represents Marie, the Blessed Virgin. It is one of the first statues ever carved which attempts to portray the human form as a living entity rather than a symbol. You can see how she is smiling, how she curves' – Genevieve indicated with her hand – 'to fit the tusk. In this old part of France which I showed you' – she pointed at the map – 'they revered women greatly and had a great love for the Virgin. She came to stand for all women. Have you heard of courtly love?'

I shook my head.

'This area is the birthplace of courtly love. While other parts of France slowly became more patriarchal, this place remained dedicated to the cult of the woman.'

'The cult of the woman,' I repeated. Genevieve looked sharply at me, her eyes bright with amusement. 'Do you know what that means?' she asked.

'We haven't studied France much yet,' I said defensively – which made her laugh, and call me a little savage, and tell me that I would have to read some books; to which I replied that I read a lot of books.

'I'm sure you do,' she said before turning away down the darkened passage to the kitchen.

'Where's Naomi?' I called after her.

'You'll find her somewhere outside, I expect.' There came a sound of vegetables being chopped. 'I never know exactly where she is. Put your case up in the loft first. You may find her in the woods.'

Dear Sarah, we are moving house and you must come and help us do our painting and restoration. Naomi is being very wild and she needs a grown-up girl like you to be her friend. Here is a telephone number so your mother can call me and we can make arrangements when the time comes. I will meet you at the same station as before. Yours, Genevieve. There had been not one but several letters, arriving ill addressed through the spring and early summer, read hurriedly and stuffed into the pocket of my jeans. I hadn't wanted to answer them at first, in spite of my certainty at the end of the previous summer that I would go back, that I wanted to go back. They were a little unnerving, these repeated exhortations to me and me alone, on lined paper, in different-coloured inks. Tante Juliette would never have done things that way.

'How funny that she should write to you and not to me,' my mother remarked, when I spilled the beans at last. She had thought they were from Naomi.

'She says it's a *ruine*,' – my mother again, doubtful, at the end of the summer term. 'But I suppose Juliette's just down the road. You and Naomi can stay with the other children if the roof falls in.'

'Oh, she's only joking,' I had replied.

Now that I was here, my suitcase still in my hand and one history-of-art lesson the better, I no longer felt so confident. I was suddenly reluctant to go and look for Naomi on my own. Reluctant also to say to the new fat Genevieve: 'Come with me, I don't want to get lost'; say it to this woman engrossed in cooking – which was something I would never have believed had I not seen it with my own eyes – and get her to come and help me. I would be laughed at again. Genevieve of course could not see the mud and the stripes, and even I didn't know they were there, not really.

The house was, in fact, almost a *ruine*. Out of the eight or so rooms only four were habitable. They had been made into the kitchen, the sitting room, a storage room full of plants and tools and other equipment, and a large bedroom upstairs with a double bed in it. I was to sleep with Naomi in the loft. There was an earth closet or privy in the back yard, and all washing was to be done in the kitchen. And 'habitable' meant simply that the floors were sound and the walls weren't falling in. There were no carpets or curtains. All the plates were of a different size and pattern. There was a plank bridge joining the main section of the house to a ruined tower which Genevieve said was nice for sitting in at sunset. 'It's a death-trap!' I muttered vehemently to myself, using a phrase of my mother's, as I made my way to the loft.

I climbed steps and followed passageways, sheepishly turning at every corner to be sure of the way back. Finally I reached the foot of the ladder which led up to the loft.

My suitcase was heavy. I couldn't drag it after me, since it made me lose my balance and my footing, so I held it up in front of me against my chest. I began to push it up the ladder, heaving myself up rung by rung, the dust thick in my mouth and on my palms. It wasn't the little blue case I had liked so much, but a larger, new one, bought for school, ugly, heavy even when it was empty.

I knew I had reached the top when the case fell forward into space and landed with a smack on the floorboards, clipping me under the chin. I pushed it away from the steps across the floor and clambered up after it to crouch at the top of the ladder, brushing the dust off my hands and face, breathing hard. The loft was dim. I could see the outline of the shutters, and the daylight coming in through the chinks between the roof-tiles. I put out a hand and touched the stones of the wall. They were large and square, dampish, gritty. I breathed in the smell of the house. It was not so dark, really. Just a question of one's eyes getting used to it.

There was only a second or two of silence. Then a scrape and a thump from the far corner. I thought at first it was an animal, but then there was another thump, this time of a heavy metal object being dropped, and a human curse. I froze.

'Who's that?' said a voice in French. I saw the large shape of a man, kneeling, holding something I couldn't see. 'The lamp! I want the lamp!' His voice was hoarse and urgent.

'*Non!*' I cried, and then I was gone, slithering backwards down the ladder and scraping my shins; '*Non!*' I gasped, and clattered away down the passage, only once taking a wrong turn, as he called: 'I'm coming down after you! I need it now!' His footsteps were on the boards above and I squealed as I took the last flight of stairs at a run and dashed down the corridor to the kitchen.

'Genevieve, Genevieve!' I panted. 'There's a man in my room!'

She looked up from the pot on the stove. 'Where?' she said; and then 'What?' Calmly, still stirring, with a faint look of surprise accentuated by recently plucked eyebrows which I noticed and hated in passing as I continued: 'Oh, God, Genevieve, he was in the attic, I think he might be an axe-murderer, he was up there yelling. Listen! Can't you hear him? He's coming down the stairs!'

Genevieve began laughing as the kitchen door opened. She grabbed my arm as I tore past towards the back door. 'It's Jean-René,' she said. 'Jean-René is our friend. He lives with us in the house. Jean-René, this is Sarah from England.'

I was still held in her firm grip, standing to my shame actually behind her, deeply embarrassed. 'Didn't I say in my letters?' she said next.

'Perhaps you did mention a friend,' I said stonily. 'I can't honestly remember.'

Genevieve laughed. 'She thought you were an axe-murderer, Jean-René.'

The man looked blank. 'Murderer!' she repeated, letting go of me to make a swinging motion with her arms and cackling.

The man smiled. 'I am sorry you were afraid because of me,' he said in English, uncertainly.

Slowly I raised my head. *'Ce n'est pas grave,'* I replied.

He wore glasses. As I glanced up at him he was cleaning them on the tail of his shirt. His eyes were pale blue and red-rimmed. He was smiling broadly; his teeth were uneven. He looked younger than Genevieve. He had a sallow, unfinished face.

'I was trying to put a light in the loft for the girls,' he continued in French to Genevieve. 'The dust up there is appalling.' He turned to me. *'Tu es venue d'Angleterre alors!'*

'Oui,' I said.

'And why do you come to stay with this *salope* who told you nothing about the house or about me?'

'Je ne sais pas.' I smiled shyly.

'Viens avec moi. On va chercher Naomi,' he said. I followed him outside.

She hadn't told me, merely asked meaningless questions. 'Where.' 'What.' She had continued stirring as if she had no idea what I was talking about. She didn't apologize for the fright. It was a reflex, of course, a flippant action, and I knew it; I saw, as Genevieve spoke, like a glint in her eye, that she was playing, although there was nothing so obvious as a glint in her eye; and to show that I had seen it, that I had spotted her underneath the calm cooking, I shot her a hard look as I went out of the door.

As if in answer Genevieve slit open a red pepper with a great grin on her face and winked at me. 'Supper in ten minutes!' she called after us, musically, and I said under my breath: *'Salope.'*

*

Jean-René led me down to the end of the field. There was a path at the bottom which meandered beside a stream through the trees. We walked along the path, the earth damp in the shade, the stream shallow and stony.

'She can usually be found down here,' said Jean-René. We strode on over the light-dappled ground, occasionally cutting across the undergrowth to rejoin the path. 'I am missing a bag of cement,' he said suddenly. I was puzzled by this remark.

We found Naomi in a clearing. She was squatting amongst half a dozen large stones and a heap of small ones, trying with her fingers to open a large grey full sack made of strong paper. I noticed that Jean-René's shoulders had sagged but he was smiling. 'Hello, Naomi,' he called.

She was no taller, just as thin as last year, her black hair longer than ever and her skin browner. At that moment her face, hair and clothes were covered in mud. There was a plastic container of water by her feet; clearly she had been mixing it with earth. She glanced up and grinned whitely.

'Hello,' she said. 'Are you going to help me with this sack?' She didn't look at Jean-René, her black eyes remained fixed piercingly on me. 'What funny trousers,' she remarked next.

'They're the fashion.'

'Oh really?' Naomi stood up and wiped her hands on her T-shirt. Then she formally shook hands with me and kissed me on both cheeks. 'This is how we greet people politely,' she said. '*Je te serre la main, et puis je te donne une bise, comme ça.* Tante Juliette told me.' She indicated the spot where she had been crouching. 'I'm building a house here.'

Jean-René took a step forward. 'It's time for supper, Naomi,' he said quietly.

She ignored him and kneeled again on the wet ground. 'This is where the foundations are going to be,' she said. 'I was just about to mix some cement. I didn't have any sand, but I reckon that mud will do just as well.' With tremendous energy she began to pour water into the muddy hollow she had dug. 'Come on, then – help me!'

'No – later,' I said. 'I'm hungry. I want to eat now.'

'You always think of your stomach,' Naomi replied annoyingly, as if she knew me well, grunting with the effort of lifting one of the large stones.

Jean-René spoke again. 'I need the cement, Naomi, for the house. I didn't buy it for fun.' He sounded more resigned than cross.

She darted a look at him. 'Oh, don't build anything for me! I am perfectly all right here. I can build my own house . . . and catch fish in the river, thank you very much.'

Jean-René smiled and thrust his hands into his pockets, turning round to look at the setting sun so that Naomi wouldn't see him smiling. 'It will soon be too dark to build anything,' he continued. 'If you want to use cement I can show you tomorrow – if you help me start on the wall. I can bring the bricks, and you could mix the cement.'

'I'm not building anything for you, you *sale Boche*,' Naomi said quickly, turning her back on him to get a better purchase on the rock.

'Oh well, in that case you can do without this,' he replied, and picked up the sack and hoisted it on to his shoulder.

Naomi was gasping now from her labours. She hadn't noticed that Jean-René had taken the sack. 'Come on, Sarah,' she said. 'Help me.' She turned to find me retreating, trailing behind Jean-René.

'Come on yourself, Naomi!' I called. I was already exasperated. 'Don't be such a fool! Come and have supper!'

'Give me back my sack! Oh, you pair of bastards! Give it back!' Her voice grew fainter as we reached the end of the path and began to cross the field to the house. Just as we reached the back door she caught up with us, running, silent, her muddy face streaked with tears. Neither I nor Jean-René said anything.

I was woken the following morning by a cock crowing. I thought it was early until I opened my eyes and saw through the chinks in the roof-tiles that the sun was shining brightly overhead. Naomi's mattress was empty. The house was silent.

I rolled over on to my front and pulled open the shutter. It made a loud scraping noise on the floorboards. I caterpil-lared forward in my sleeping-bag. I saw the tops of the trees by the stream, then the field, then the chicken-run in the yard below. I poked my head out and squinted up at the tower. There was a weathervane at the top, travelling against the light clouds. The cock crowed again; my head swam as I looked down. I shuffled in and began to dress.

I wondered where Naomi was. 'I'm going into town tomorrow in the van,' Genevieve had said the previous night. 'Keep her off Jean René's back for me, will you?' As I was expecting to be asked if I wanted to go with her, I had nodded unsmiling. Now I brushed my hair and with a sinking heart went down to the kitchen.

Jean-René was working outside. I lingered by the back door watching him. I saw that the van was already gone. Naomi was nowhere to be seen.

He straightened up when he realized that I was there. 'There is some bread and jam in the kitchen,' he said. 'Shall I make you a tartine?' He came over to me and ushered me indoors.

'I can do it, thank you.'

'How about some coffee? I will put some on the stove for you. Genevieve has gone to St-Cyprien. I expect she told you.'

'I can make it. You don't have to help me, it's OK.'

'No, I'll do it, this small gas burner is tricky, only the other day Genevieve burned herself.' He spoke slowly, with the occasional gesture, to make it easier for me to under-stand. 'Do you want strong, medium, or weak?'

'Oh, um, medium, please.' I thanked him solemnly as I took the cup, which made him laugh.

'You don't have to thank me!' he said. 'We do not thank each other very much here. We do not say please, either, very often. You will see.'

I sipped, knowing that he meant Naomi, and thinking, obscurely: Serve you right.

'She's down by the river again,' he said. He stared into space, his face suddenly very sad. 'She's building her house, I am sure. I gave her a bit of sand and a little bucket of lime.' He looked at me and smirked. 'You can help her build her wall, or help me build mine, as you wish. What do you think?'

Arrested by the sad look, then repelled by the unattractive, tooth-covering smile, I replied more vehemently than I had meant to. 'I don't want to build anything. If I have to, I will make my own wall. Then it will be fair!'

Jean-René began to laugh quietly. The colour rushed into my cheeks and I buried my face in my coffee cup. He laughed some more, and lit a cigarette. 'Genevieve wants you to be a policeman,' he said, still laughing. 'Between the two enemies!'

'Yes, I know. You don't need to tell me. I knew her when I was eight. I was with her last year as well, at my uncle's.'

'Yes, I understand. You were here first, little cousin. I see,' he said, and I blushed again, because I hadn't thought that I meant that. He stood up. 'You must know also how she likes to make people dance.' He waggled his fingers like a puppeteer, and then walked out into the yard, throwing the cigarette on the ground without stubbing it out.

When I came out he was busy again, slapping one brick down next to the previous one in a steady rhythm. I watched him. 'Are you a builder?' I said at last.

'No, I'm not. But I've worked for builders in the past. I'm a journalist.'

'Do you work on a newspaper here?'

'Yes, but not all the time. Would you fetch me some water from the kitchen, please? Use that bucket.'

When I returned I sat on the ground near the growing wall. 'Why did Naomi call you a *sale Boche*?' I asked next.

Jean-René, who was squinting at a spirit-level, did not immediately reply. 'My father's family came from Belgium. My family name is Oortmans. I suppose it sounds like a

German name to Naomi,' he said slowly. 'That is Naomi's excuse, anyway.'

'You know,' I said after a pause, 'you know, Genevieve doesn't make people dance; it's just that some of them are horrible to her like Juliette and – and so on.' Not wanting to mention the names that Naomi had told me last year, of the men. Perhaps Jean-René didn't know who they were.

He put the trowel down and looked at me wordlessly for a moment. Then he stood up and began to shift bricks from a large stack over to a smaller pile by the end of the wall.

'You might understand some day,' he said, breathing hard with the exertion, 'that sometimes you can get yourself into a trap, and it's difficult to get out of a trap especially if you're drinking as much as Genevieve has been drinking. If you drink, you can't think clearly enough to find the way out. And Genevieve has usually been horrible to people before they started doing it to her; though I don't know who you mean, since Paul Belar keeps wisely out of the way and Henri Palastrier has behaved like a saint throughout. Not that it's any of your business. Mix this for me, would you?' He handed me a spade before I could say anything. 'Put that sand with the lime and begin with a little water.'

Stiffly I obeyed, and for the next hour carried and mixed and wheeled the barrow until I was hot and tired. I was dazed by this rough down-pegging, its rudeness to me and to Genevieve. A lot you know, I thought darkly, smarting. He looked so vague, that was it, the way the sweat ran down his face as if his face were melting. I couldn't believe that he had said such sharp and categorical words.

'I do like working with my hands,' he announced now, rubbing them together to clean them. It was as if he had never mentioned Genevieve or the others. 'Don't you?'

'It depends,' I replied sombrely. 'If I can decide what to do it's OK. I don't much like being told, though. And if you don't mind,' I concluded, 'I think I heard the van just then, so I'll go and see if Genevieve is back.'

*

I was waylaid by Naomi who came running out of the woods like a savage, brandishing a sharp stick. 'Where are you going, you traitoress!' she began without preliminary.

'Just to see if Genevieve has come.'

Naomi waved the stick. It was very sharp. She must have spent hours whittling away at the end. 'And what have you been doing all morning?'

'Helping Jean-René—' I began, and just in time put out my hand to grab the end of the stick as it came towards me. Grasping it firmly, I managed to twist it from her grasp. 'Naomi!' I cried. 'You could have poked my eye out, you idiot! What is wrong with you!'

We stood very close, face to face. Naomi glared at me, the whites of her eyes clear and bright, her lips wet. She was covered in mud again, almost as if she had smeared it purposefully all over her face.

'What is wrong with me is that you have not spoken to me since you came, because you are too busy helping him build his precious bathroom!' she hissed. 'I suppose he showed you how to mix the cement, because you were a good girl and helped him with his little palace. Well, I don't need any lessons!' Her breathing became ragged in a way now familiar to me. 'I don't need a house at all! In fact, I'll just live in the woods!' She turned her head away suddenly; she had caught sight of Genevieve climbing down from the van. 'Maman!' she yelled. 'Maman! They've done it all without me! They didn't let me help at all! They left me down by the river all alooone!' She ran, sobbing, into her mother's arms, with the small steps which gave her the gait of a younger child. Stunned at this sudden volte-face I hated them all – Jean-René for his cleverness which was odious, and Naomi for her exasperating tantrums, and Genevieve for grinning now over the top of Naomi's head and calling, 'Have you had an enjoyable morning, Sarah?' and adding, 'Good!' before I had a chance to reply.

ELEVEN

I could leave directly. How long would it take me to walk to the station with my suitcase? It had all been a ghastly mistake. I should have stayed at home – or gone to Tante Juliette's house according to the original plan, to sit with Katrine in her bedroom and play with her fifty dolls. Even that would have been preferable.

Rubbish. I didn't mean a word of it. And I was too old for gallivanting about with suitcases. Flora was only nine when she did it, last year, but all that time ago I was already twelve. There's eight years between us; sometimes we seem to belong to different time zones, Flora and I.

'She attacked me, she actually launched herself at me with a stick, did you see her?' I cried. 'Honestly, Genevieve, she's uncontrollable!'

'Yes, I saw, and I'm sorry. I'm sure she's sorry —'

'You know I think I'd rather be at Lucifer's playing bloody lacrosse, it's safer!'

'Oh, darling, please stay with us. We need you. Naomi has so few friends . . .'

'I'm not surprised!'

The stone floor of the kitchen was cold under my bare feet. The windows and the back door were open, to make the air circulate, but it still smelt slightly musty in there. Genevieve said it was the old wooden cupboards – she and Jean-René were going to rip them out when they got round to doing the kitchen. I sat on the bench and rubbed my bare legs. It wasn't really warm enough for shorts.

She gave a little gasp. I looked up to see her trying to smile at me. 'She's had such an unsettled time recently.' Her voice was unsteady. 'She just seems to get worse and worse . . .' She was still holding the quavering smile. It was awful to see how much I had hurt her.

'I didn't mean that.' I heaved an exasperated sigh. 'You're so different now, from how you were, I don't know what to say to you!'

The quavering smile disappeared, her face cleared. 'Yes, I am, aren't I.'

'I don't know you like this! Cooking!' I accused.

She put a hand self-consciously against the back of her neck.

'And you're fatter. I bet you taste all the time when you cook.'

She roared with laughter. 'Oh, Sarah! Come here!'

I scrambled off the bench, giggling in spite of myself. She put her arm around my waist. 'And I hate your eyebrows,' I added. She shook with mirth against me.

'Look,' I said, 'I'm sure she'll like Jean-René in the end. I know she will. He's very – good.' The word popped out, taking me aback.

'Oh, I hope so, Sarah, I honestly do.'

She looked up at me. She was wearing a scarf on her head; it was the same wretched one she'd had on the previous summer, in Juliette's garden. It seemed so wrong in that big cool kitchen, that she should be beseeching in that wretched scarf.

I shivered. 'I'll give it a try with her, then.'

We sat at the table. I told her all about Lucifer's, the singing, the games. 'Sometimes I think I like it but then we have to go and do something absurd like learn "O Come All Ye Faithful" in Latin. I just don't get it. Everyone else –

practically everyone else – thinks it's great. They wear tights, voluntarily . . .' Poor Sarah, she said.

When she pulled off the scarf I said: 'And your hair, even, look, it's all neat, it's practically brown!'

I'm still your friend, though, she said.

Naomi built stolidly for two days. On the third she declared she would never finish it before the winter; she was suffering from an acute lack of resources. Besides, she thought that building walls and houses showed an urge to dominate people sexually. She said this at the table one evening, causing Jean-René to choke on a mouthful of food and run spluttering from the room, to return with eyes streaming and mouth covered with a handkerchief. Naomi spent the rest of the meal casting wide-eyed sideways glances at her mother and at me.

That evening it began to rain, and it continued throughout the following morning. Naomi and I tried to fish in the river but it was too wet to be any fun. In the afternoon Naomi took me to the café in the village, 'where I usually go to play cards'.

The village was about a mile from the house, a hamlet of grey-shuttered houses, a church with a high square tower, a shop, a café-bar. We walked together through a light drizzle broken by the cover of the walnut trees lining the road. I had brought no waterproof clothing and had borrowed a coat of Genevieve's, a plastic mackintosh, which almost fitted, to my surprise. Naomi, though she had a coat of her own, was wearing a battered oilskin belonging to Jean-René.

We walked silently past the dripping maize fields and the empty farmyards. I remembered the small woods from the previous year when I had got lost after the troglodyte village; how the trees were cut back and cut back until many thin branches sprang from a big stump. Now I told Naomi about my trip to the troglodyte village in the hope that she would laugh, but she didn't, although she had seemed before to enjoy the chance to insult Lucien. Tante Juliette's house lay over the other side of the hill, far away in the rain. It might have been in another country.

We bought Cokes with the money Genevieve had given us and sat down at a table near the bar. On the other side of the room three boys played an unbalanced game of table football, making a great deal of noise with their thundering feet and their shouting. Naomi greeted one of the boys, but didn't go to speak to him. 'They go to my school,' she said.

She taught me how to play vingt-et-un. We played for matches and then for ten centimes. Naomi kept winning.

'You're not concentrating!' she exclaimed. 'What's the matter?'

'I'm not very good at card games,' I replied, stifling a yawn.

There was a special smell in the café which I didn't immediately like; a mixture of old wine, old coffee, spillages, ashtrays, cigarette smoke. The fresh air gusting in brought other smells, those of rain and farms. The café proprietor looked over his newspaper at the boys from time to time but paid no attention to us.

'Why do you go to boarding-school?' Naomi asked suddenly.

'In case my father gets posted somewhere. We can't keep on and on changing schools. Lucifer's is my fifth school,' I added carelessly, tucking my hair behind my ear. 'Seventh if you count the kindergartens. I'm used to moving.'

Naomi shrugged. 'So am I,' she said. 'What sports do you do in England?' she asked next. 'Do you play football?'

'Only in the garden, or on the beach. At school I play lacrosse.' I described the game vividly but Naomi remained unimpressed.

'I thought everybody played football in England,' she persisted. Her face had assumed a sly, baiting expression.

'Well, they don't. Only men, and boys. Do you play pétanque, Naomi?'

'Do you eat fish and chips and rosbif, Sarah?' Naomi swept another ten centimes across the table and dealt the cards again. 'You are very soon going to be destitute,' she said, smiling, showing sharp teeth. Her eyes were as black as watermelon seeds.

'I used to play pétanque with Madelon, when we lived with Henri,' she continued. 'Madelon was our housekeeper. Oh yes, I was a boules champion. But I doubt whether the Boche knows how.'

'Jean-René isn't German. Even if he was, it's still very rude to call someone names like that!'

'Ohh!' Naomi pursed her lips and widened her eyes exactly the way her mother did. 'You are cross! Maybe you'd like him for a father then, if you think he is so nice.'

'I don't think he wants to be your father.'

'Ha! You know nothing! Henri never did the things that he does.'

'What things?'

'Oh, you are completely *débile*, honestly! Look what he does! How he worms his way in!' She made a brief snake-like motion with her hand before shooting it forward and burying it in my side, causing me to giggle helplessly. 'Henri never did that' she went on. 'We were always . . . it was nice, to be in his house. He never . . . it was as if this was his *petit coin*,' she patted her hands on one corner of the table, 'and that was Maman's,' and she patted the other corner. 'Henri didn't go about building walls and saying "*Genevieve*"' – she imitated Jean-René's slightly nasal tones – '"*Genevieve*, let's have our bathroom *here* and our bedroom *here* and our table and our fridge and our plant-pots *there*! And our van, hmm, yes, let's park it there in the summer *à l'ombre*, Genevieve!" As if she doesn't know to park a car in the shade!'

I shredded a match between my fingers. 'But you aren't with Henri Palastrier now,' I said slowly.

Naomi did not immediately reply. She shuffled the cards deliberately, tapping them on the table, endways, sideways, endways again.

'No,' she said. 'No, She . . . they started to have problems. But it was still the best!' she concluded. 'And I liked it there. Henri liked me, you see.' She tapped her chest meaningfully, and I was hard put not to laugh again, she was so theatrical with her gestures. 'I stayed with him on my own for a long time. It wasn't just because of her.'

'But the house is for you, too.' It sounded lame, even to me. 'He's doing it for both of you. It will be lovely when it's finished —'

'He's doing it for her, so that she will love him more than me. That is obvious to anyone who is not as dense as you are.'

I hung my head. I made a careful zigzag out of the matchsticks. 'He needs you to help him,' I said faintly.

'What – me help him so she loves him more?'

'You could both do it, you and him.'

Naomi merely snorted.

'You could surprise her with how quickly you did it.'

Her eyes flickered and she gave me a cold stare. Figuring that I had nothing to lose, I continued. 'He can't do it all on his own.'

'You could help him, then, if you're so keen.'

'I won't be there.'

'Well, Maman could. Then they could have great fun together all day. "*Genevieve*, pass me our hammer and our nails, *chérie*."' There was misery in her voice.

'Oh, you've seen her trying, you know she's no good,' I struggled on. 'She's always dropping things. She doesn't even know how to use the plumb line! Surely it's better to leave only the easy things to her . . .' By now Naomi was looking at me with something approaching hatred, so I tailed off into a shrug.

To my relief she didn't pursue the subject. We continued to play vingt-et-un, Naomi slapping the cards down with venom, refusing to smile even when she won two francs, pocketing the money with cold complacency.

Then we had a noisy and aggressive game of table football with two of the boys, during which Naomi swore and shouted a lot and my feet were jumped on. I found out that I was bloodly awful at that, as well. I didn't have the natural flick of the wrist. So Naomi told me, crowing. The boys said that I might improve if I had more practice.

On the way home, quite by surprise, she started to hop and jump around the road, taking her little steps and explaining to me about her feet. 'You know why I walk like this? Because of my ankles. You see – they are weak. When I was younger I could hardly run but I can now, you see, look!' She began to run to show me, moving her arms comically and laughing, and I started to laugh as well, as Naomi beetled from one side of the road to the other, waving her arms ludicrously and saying 'Hop!' when she reached the bank. She went on and on until I begged her to stop, I was nearly dying of it, I had a stitch, and Naomi said, 'I can't help it Sarah, this is the way it is – Hop! – look, even my arms – Hop! – I can't stop them . . .' Then when we were nearly home she stood panting and grinning by the river-bank, surrounded by the wet greenery, for me to take a photograph of her.

'Poppies and day's eyes in the green email,' she said suddenly in English, all in a rush like a spell.

I brought the camera down from my eye. 'What did you say?'

'Poppies and day's eyes in the green email,' Naomi repeated, a little shyly. 'Is it wrong?'

'I don't know. I haven't heard it before. It's funny to hear you say something like that, in English.'

'It's a poem. Whenever we go past the river here, Maman recites this poem, or at least this line.'

'Let me take the photo now. Ready?'

'Poppies . . .'

'Oh, Naomi, please let me.'

'OK.'

'Ready! *Un, deux —*'

'Poppies —'

'Naomee, *je t'en pris!* . . .'

The way it had come out like a bird call, bubbling out of her mouth, and her mouth moving in an unaccustomed way as she said the words, into a silence that was suddenly singing; I recorded it on my film, the mouth talking and smiling at once, the green . . .

When it wasn't raining we plastered and painted. When it rained, we swam in the river. Jean-René fitted a water-heater in the new bathroom in an atmosphere of great drama, announcing the beginning of each new stage as if he were an astronaut leaving a capsule. Naomi and I daily promised fish for supper and daily failed to produce any.

The weather grew brighter again, though it never reached the shocking temperatures of the previous year. Genevieve took her pictures down and dusted them; she didn't dust anything else. There was nothing else to dust. Jean-René remarked that the cult of the woman was alive and well in this house; it consisted of him doing all the work while we sat in the field and teased the chickens, and yelled for cold drinks whenever we saw him going towards the house. One day Jean-René bought Naomi an individual greengage tart in a box from the *pâtisserie* in town, for her alone since nobody else liked them, and Naomi said '*Je vous remercie*' in a loud voice before running away and snivelling in the loft. My game of table football improved.

I developed little red lumps on the palms of my hands. When they grew bigger – aggravated, no doubt, by the manual labour and the sports – I showed them to Genevieve.

Her forehead creased in lines of worry. 'Undoubtedly you have a dreadful infection,' she said. 'Are you insured?'

Though I thought she was being a little premature I had to admit that I wasn't.

'I've got some cream' she said, taking me by the hand and leading me upstairs to her bedroom.

They had made it nice. There was a large white counterpane on the bed and a straw mat on the floor. The walls were white and the floorboards stained dark brown. Genevieve produced a battered plastic bag and tipped the contents out on to the bed. I saw innumerable jars of cosmetics, among them an old, almost empty pot of deep red. Bottles of perfume, powders, oils, cards of kirby-grips, all with very feminine, very French names. I averted my eyes hurriedly from certain items obviously connected with contraception. I hoped she hadn't seen me look at them. She might quiz me ruthlessly about my embarrassment, or even – perish the thought – tell me how they were used. There were other medicines; pill bottles, tubes, droppers, all scattered about. There were items of jewellery, necklaces and rings, and bangles and brooches and earrings. And earrings.

I picked up the single heavy false-diamond stud and turned it in the air at eye-level. It made slivers of whiter light on the white walls.

'I lost mine in Dartmouth,' I said. 'Ages ago.'

There was a silence, broken only by the slight movement of Genevieve's body on the bed. Then, my eyes still fixed on the diamond, I said: 'Why do you keep it, Genevieve?'

'Ohh . . . why should I throw it away?' The woman's voice was calm. 'An old earring, it doesn't take up much room.' She glanced up to see that I had buried the stud in my fist like a nut I was trying to crack; and she knew that I meant the gun, because I was looking at it now where it lay in the bottom of the bag.

TWELVE

'That?' said Genevieve. 'You know my old gun. You – you kept it for me in London, do you remember, in your case? I'd forgotten I had it. I told you, it doesn't work.' She sighed as if she were relaxed and reminiscing. 'What a long time ago that was! I don't suppose you remember the flat.'

'I remember the drawing room,' I said, 'where you had that row with Juliette and shouted at my dad.' We were sitting completely still, the bag on the bed between us. The sunlit room was stuffy.

'Oh, yes! I . . . we were quarrelling about Henri Palastrier, she always hated him. But wasn't it an incredible place? Just like a hotel. Your uncle Nicholas is a rich man. I stayed in a hotel like that once, you know, Sarah. With Naomi and Palastrier. It was in winter, just like that winter in London, the weather was the same.'

It was the first New Year they were together, she said. Naomi was four and ran about in the foyer. She herself wore a fur coat. Palastrier signed the register for them like a papa. She talked on and on, hectically now, about 'the winter of diamonds and freedom' as she called it, and her eyes began to glisten with tears.

I tried to picture the hotel but I could only see Nicholas's flat. The big window and the red velvet curtains. I shivered, feeling eight again for a minute, as if we were sitting together on the floor in that drawing room. But I soon stopped listening. I couldn't care less about Palastrier now.

I bounced the earring like a jacks-ball, from knuckle to palm and back again. 'Diamonds,' I said scornfully.

'Yes,' Genevieve said. She smiled at me damply. 'There were diamonds in London too, weren't there, my darling.'

'And a gun.'

'Ah, forget the gun, child, it's not important. Palastrier and I drifted apart. We were together for four years, you know. Then afterwards I – I got into trouble, but . . . but along came Jean-René and now we are free and easy and very happy. And it's all over.' Genevieve sat up. She sniffed, smiled again, more brightly this time. She held out her hand for the earring.

I closed my hand over it. 'Did Palastrier find out about it?' I asked. 'Is that why you split up?'

'Find out about what?'

'About the gun, of course!'

'What is it with you and this gun!' Genevieve exclaimed. 'You can't leave it alone, can you? Palastrier has nothing to do with the gun! Nothing!' She spat the words out, her lips trembling. Reaching into the bag, she tossed it into my lap. 'There!' she said. 'Reacquaint yourself, why not, since you're so interested!'

I wriggled backwards, joggling it off my knees as if it were a snake.

'Go on. Pick it up. You picked it up before!' Her voice was harsh. 'Don't be a coward now!'

I did as I was told. It was as black as ever, a little bit heavier than you'd think, just like before.

Genevieve chuckled. 'Hold it properly. Point it at me if you like. It's safe, it isn't loaded.'

I jerked my head up. 'You said it didn't work before,' I said softly.

'That's what I meant. I meant, it doesn't work. It's not possible to load it.'

'But you said "isn't loaded" just now.' I kneeled up on the bed, raised the gun, and aimed squinting at the window. The setting sun dropped like a coin into my open eye.

'I could have loaded it, you know,' I went on. 'I could have come up here when you went to St-Cyprien and loaded it.' I listened for a moment to Genevieve's breathing behind me. 'Or maybe I didn't. Maybe I didn't know it was there. But maybe I did.' Half-blind, I swung it round to point at her. 'Does Belar think it doesn't work?'

Her eyes widened.

'He seemed pretty scared when you did this to him last summer in Toulon. I could see his hands. Warding you off.'

She shook her head, formed her lips for a word. It made a dry sound.

I held her there for a moment before lowering the gun. 'Oh, you're probably right.' I sighed. 'It doesn't work. It can't, can it, or Belar would have told your family. Nicholas or Juliette. He'd have said: "Genevieve's gone mad, she pointed a gun at me." And I can't believe he said that, because I don't think they'd have left you in peace if he had. I don't think I'd be here, either.'

'It was just a game,' Genevieve protested faintly. 'The gun doesn't work.'

'Huh! Funny game! What kind of a game could it be!' I was contemptuous. 'Well, I didn't mention it, anyway. Obviously.' I laughed. 'Gosh, though, you were in such a panic that time in London, when you thought Juliette had it!'

'Yes!' Genevieve, swallowing, began to recover herself. 'What a fuss about nothing —'

'Fuss about nothing,' I chimed in, stuffing the reclaimed earring into my jeans pocket. 'Do you think Jean-René is back yet?' I giggled at the thought. 'Maybe he'd like to have a go with this old broken gun!'

'Sarah! Stop it!' She reached out, but I wasn't in a mood for giving things back. 'OK,' she said. 'Actually I use it for self-defence. Paul can be violent.'

'Who is Paul?'

'Belar.'

'Oh, yes.'

'Sometimes he can get very angry and try to hit people. Do you remember how he came chasing up to your room at Juliette's house and banged on the door?' She licked her lips. 'He has no self-control. I prefer not to risk it when I am with him.'

'So it's not a game.'

'No – you see, my family never discovered he was violent. In fact, he has never hurt Naomi. But if he knew, they'd be worried about Naomi visiting him.'

'But that's why you left him, because he was violent?'

'Yes.'

'Then how come you're still married to him?'

'Because – I am tired of questions, Sarah! I don't want to remarry – I don't want to marry anyone! Neither does he, so we don't need a divorce. Think of the scandal, the trauma for Naomi! I could not stay with him, that is all! I could not stay with him! How could I!'

She was lying through her teeth, that was obvious to me. I always knew when she was lying. She was losing her temper too; she tried to snatch the gun back but I was too quick for her. I leapt backwards out of range, I said: 'No, I'm not ready, I want to play with it. Show me how you load it. Show me how you unload it. Show me . . .'

At last I tired of tormenting her. I surrendered it. She put it away. I got up from the bed and rubbed my tingling calves.

The white light in the room had been superseded by a penetrating twilight. I went over to the window and Genevieve came to stand behind me.

'Will you look at that sky!' she breathed, her arms around my neck. 'You wouldn't believe it could be so pale and still so blue!' She rested her chin lightly on the top of my head.

'I never thought I'd see a sky like that so far from the sea. That is the only thing I miss from the coast. Skies like that. We're lucky tonight.'

'Genevieve, why do you have it really?'

She tightened her embrace. 'Ahh, Sarah' – her voice was husky – 'don't ask me again: I cannot tell you.' She gave a high laugh, as if to say: *the very idea*. 'I cannot!'

I clasped her strong forearms and leaned back against her. I contented myself with the warmth of her body. I looked out at the peaceful evening and let her ramble on, laughing huskily from time to time, about the years she spent with Belar.

The truth came out in the middle of it all like an arrow, steady and straight.

It hit me almost before I recognized it, but when it hit me I comprehended everything from the beginning.

It's like the facts of life, I thought slowly. Once you find out, you realize that you always knew.

She was drawing breath to continue but I pulled away and turned to face her. 'You said you weren't going to tell,' I said, 'you said you wouldn't and then you did, you just told me why!'

She stood silently, holding her hand in a loose fist against her lips.

'You didn't need to make up stories about violence,' I said. 'Not with me. I understand! You just had to, didn't you!'

She drew her hand away. Her lips parted. It must have been the shock of saying it which had made her dumb. I'm sure she hadn't meant to.

'You had to teach him a lesson!'

She began to laugh helplessly, shoulders shaking. She sat down on the bed and hooted.

Splinters, of course, hardly visible except on close examination. Jean-René removed them expertly with the aid of a sterilized needle. I sat squirming on the kitchen chair, lips pressed together, and Jean-René did not say 'There, there,' or 'Nearly finished now,' or any of the usual things people say on these occasions. He just peered silently at my hand, bending my fingers back ruthlessly.

Naomi entered the kitchen with a basket of shopping. 'Ooh! What have we here!' she exclaimed. 'A bit of fortune telling?' She craned this way and that, exaggeratedly intrigued. 'Where is Maman? They had no powdered sugar, only granulated.'

'I expect we'll survive,' Jean-René murmured. Naomi came closer and looked over his shoulder. She watched the operation without speaking.

'I think they're from the ladder to the attic,' I managed from between clenched teeth.

'I'll sandpaper it down,' Jean-René replied absently. He removed the last one, and straightened up. He smiled at me. 'You must have a special way of going up and down the ladder!' We laughed.

Naomi was loitering, as she loitered so often, with her burning gaze, biting her lip or chewing her hair, watching. Then she sat down on the chair. Jean-René turned and looked at her expectantly.

'I've got one too,' she said.

'You've got what?'

'A splinter. In my hand. From the ladder.' She showed him what appeared to be an unblemished palm.

Obediently he took her hand. She whimpered as the needle probed her skin, writhing as if she were being filmed and saying: 'Aie! Aie!'

'Keep still,' he said, and then: 'I can't see anything.'

'It's there, I swear, I swear.'

'There's nothing . . . perhaps it was a little scratch, or a bite.'

'I know there is one!' Naomi sat stock-still, tears filling her eyes. 'It hurts!'

Jean-René looked at her questioningly.

Her chin trembled. 'Find it!' she commanded.

Finally, after a long examination, he drew out a minute speck of wood on the tip of the needle. Naomi wept silently. 'It was very small,' he said. 'So small I could hardly see it.'

'*C'est parce que tu es myope*,' Naomi replied, but her tears continued unabated. 'My father can see for miles, you know.

He doesn't need glasses or binoculars or anything. He can see as far away as anything . . .' She sniffed hugely, and sat there gulping air and saying, '*Mon père, tu sais, mon père,*' at intervals and getting no further. She did not withdraw her hand from Jean-René's. It was as if she had forgotten it existed.

'I had a splinter,' she said later to her mother, who commented on her red eyes and blotchy face. 'It was tiny, but Jean-René said that the smallest ones are often the most painful.'

'Really, Jean-René?' Genevieve was incredulous.

'It is often the case,' Jean-René said gravely.

On my last afternoon Genevieve took Naomi and me up to the road which ran along the back of the hill above the village. For our education she told us about Arnaut Daniel. He was a poet, she said, a singer; what they call a troubadour or jongleur. He used to sing love songs at the courts of certain great ladies who lived in the castles hereabouts. This was a long time ago, when the English fought here. This is too romantic for you, Sarah, I can see that. There's no need to say 'Oh, yuk,' though. Yes, Naomi, I will tell about Ezra Pound in a minute.

Arnaut and others like him used to tramp from town to town, playing their lutes in taverns and squares, hoping to be paid in money or food. They had hard times as well, you see; they weren't always in favour with the great ladies or their husbands. No – Ezra Pound wasn't another jongleur. He was an American poet, a modern man, who wrote about Arnaut. He walked along this road, I am almost sure, trying to follow the route of Arnaut. Maybe he sheltered from the rain under this tree as we are doing now. Maybe they both did, he and Arnaut, at different times. I know of a play where they meet under a tree like this. Think of it. They might have had sore feet. They might have been hungry, unlike you two fat girls. They might have been thrown out of a village where the people were even hungrier than they were. Unlikely in Ezra's case, I admit, since he was a modern man, but all too possible in Arnaut's. Some of these jongleurs became outlaws, you know, they lived from hand to mouth. People hounded them out of their villages in the cold weather. Not so romantic after all, is it, Sarah. Later I will show you Ezra's book. You can recite for us and earn your keep.

Where has Naomi gone? Bored, was she? Well, she has heard it all before.

Yes. I met your mother in London. We were both studying literature. Katharine Whelan, she was then. Your cousin Katrine was named after her, did you know? She was born the year your mother married. One Katharine Whelan ended and another began. No, I wouldn't say that we were friends now. You now how time passes. I don't dislike her; oh, please don't think that. Really I admire her and I'm glad that she's so happy with all her beautiful children – there are three of you, aren't there? – and her lovely husband. But we used to be so close, back when she came to Nicholas's wedding at Juliette's house. Oh, we had such fun! We ran away and climbed a tree – just over the hill there. We'd had such a lot of champagne . . . She told you? Oh.

Yes, of course I brought it with me! I knew you'd want to play.

No one will hear. I've got a thing to make it silent.

Quick! Pretend the villagers are after us! Into the woods before anyone sees us!

Here – you can hold it if you like. Now run . . . !

It was nothing to do with luck. It was on purpose that they were pushing me down, down on to my bottom or my knees where I would stay because other people would stand on me and other people would stand on them. I would die before I became 'courteous'. I couldn't escape to the hills and I had no gun, but I had the heart of a gun-woman. I would just have to try and be an outlaw anyway. It was my only hope.

The autumn came, the winter. At Lucifer's I got letters

from Naomi telling me how they were doing up the tower, it was something fantastic to see, and I must come and visit again in the summer. I railed away in the choir-stalls in honour of the impending Birth of Our Lord. Paulina refused to cover for me any more and I committed so many crimes of apparel that Miss Pye took away my blue kilt and made me sign for it before games.

I beat the spring as usual and turned thirteen at the end of February. I went to my grandmother's birthday lunch. When I served him with pudding my senior uncle asked me 'How's the black sheep?' but I just smiled. I could probably outshoot him. Imagine if they'd seen me in the woods, these tall sons in their Sunday 'mufti'! Their passports read: Civil Servant, to protect them from people like me. The terrible light from the battle painting shone down on us: it shone down on my mother who looked briefly at me. A little grey spark came and went in her eye.

We all walked on the lawn for a bit and then we left for our army HQs and navy HQs and schools. Tall grey imposing places where people clipped hedges and cut the grass and cleaned birdshit off the statues. All of us except my mother and Flora; they went home.

During the journey back to school my father said that he was so tired of all this stupidity, that when he came back in June he expected a better report from the staff. That he wished I could supply him with some reasonable explanation. 'It's just so boring there,' I replied, to which my mother remarked that in her experience only boring people were bored.

'You must be rigid, then.'

'Sarah!' Both parents in unison; and I went back to school.

On that last evening in France Genevieve had found the book and made me recite as the light faded from the room, and I filled the room with the English words: 'Bewildering spring, and by the Auvezere Poppies and day's eyes in the green email rose over us.' As I read it out, the low flooded land squared out with poplars and the broken bundle of mirrors, I saw Naomi sit down between the other two. I looked at her mother and saw that the earth still caked our shoes.

Blue was a brave, clean colour but I wasn't allowed it any more. I was consigned to wear grey and moan the Stabat Mater in a sodden Gormenghast where the Virgin had never smiled in her life. To bleat for someone to defend me from the darkness, to sit down under it like a wave coming in from the Channel.

We shrieked like hens in the hen-coop of hell when the devil gets in like a dog-fox and makes havoc among them and they are much affrighted: *Agnus Dei!* we shrieked, and even in our terror came in bang like a hammer-blow, and the Communion was dealt out.

Miserere Nobis! I choked on a mouthful of the wine and spat it out.

Miserere Nobis! I ripped the grey skirt down the seam.

Dona Nobis Pacem! I set fire to it out in the bracken, and half the common went up with it.

THIRTEEN

A-roads and B-roads, interchanges, lights; the past grows the way a city spreads along the coast. Ribbon development, conurbation, hinterland, lacuna; slow, fast, sidestep, leap, like a crystal, like something without a mind. A city which is the same wherever it is, north, south, England or France; it cheats you with grey days in winter and in summer threatens to take off like a gas-balloon into air saturated with a light of the palest blue imaginable, it is a roaring road with the sea a bright margin, a sword, a sunderer; even on grey days the sea is a Crusader's weapon, leaden, almost too heavy to swing above your head, a neck-breaking thing . . .

The past is like those big cities on the coast, the way it ravels and sprawls, the way it changes colour. It is like those places where both Genevieve and I have lived in our time. It is so untrustworthy.

There are so many ways you can go, factory, round-about, dockyard, Base, it seems you will never get out; and then suddenly you stamp on the gas and go rocketing down a side-road like a green tunnel, bumping down into a field where the engine cuts and there is stillness and silence broken only by the engine ticking and the rain pattering on the roof. You can sit there, humming, staring, tapping your fingers on the wheel; you can turn the radio on, turn the radio off again. Feed the chickens as Genevieve learned to do with a young serious man from a distant province who wears glasses, who is determined to get some small things in life and for you to have them too. You can roll up your sleeves as she did and get yourself a job; you can type the letters at the school your daughter attends and your daughter scolds you for the amount of wine you drink. You can watch her grow strong and listen to her accent change . . .

The sky doesn't go all hot and pale here. At least, only occasionally. You can sit at home and make lentil soup on Sundays, you're not a star any more with brassy hair and sunglasses, there's nobody to impress. You can grow older.

'Genevieve?'

No answer. Rain on the leaves.

'Genevieve.'

Silence. Green caverns disturbed under the trees.

After she died I called her and heard no answer. In the beginning I used to think I could hear her voice, now and again, but I was never sure; I became less and less sure as time passed. Then the photograph of Naomi was all I had left, the black-haired child by the river, making a mouth like a kiss – stuck into the book of poems I didn't want to look at. It went on for a long time, this pattering, ticking peace, but I have learned as she did that you can't stay in the gloaming for ever. Something happens to hook you out. Just when everything is mashing and clicking along nicely the clutch goes, the zip breaks, you lose the corkscrew.

Genevieve has come back. She's roaming around out there, waving at docksides and jumping off buses. It took me ages to work out what it was she said to me as she got off that bus, but I did it in the end. She said: *Not long now*.

Yesterday morning Flora told me that I had woken her up in the middle of the night and asked her if she'd seen my passport. It was my scrabbling in her dressing-table drawers which had woken her. I have no recollection of having done this.

Her room used to be mine.

Yesterday I took my driving test and passed. I passed without Graham Stilgo. When I went into the office at half-past eight there was another, unfamiliar man waiting for me, moustached like a walrus, who told me that Graham had flu and that he, walrus, would be taking me for my pre-test lesson. We drove around in near silence for an hour before he handed me over at the test-centre to the examiner. My emergency stop was about fifty foot long and I muddled two road-signs, but I passed anyway. I wished Graham had been there.

I went round to the Fruit and Veg in the afternoon. In the event I was early. Clive congratulated me by smiling a lot and saying: 'I knew you'd do it,' several times, and making me a Camp coffee with milk and sugar. The boss would be very happy, he said, since now I could drive the van for him.

I grinned at the thought. 'We could go joy-riding. Or even better, I could take it to the demo tomorrow. You could lean out of the window with a megaphone, what do you think? Clive?'

Clive had gone brick-red. Even his neck was red. In fact, his neck was all I could see, because he had turned his back to me.

'What's up?' I said, and it took a moment for him to reply.

'I suppose Julian put you up to it,' he muttered at last, giving me a quick red glance before going into the back room. Since there was a lull I followed him. I think I would have followed him even if the shop had been packed, I was so angry.

'What do you mean by that?' I began. 'Clive? What do you mean, he put me up to it?'

He began to rip the string out of packs of paper bags with a knife, flipping through the bags with his thumb to separate them. I never bother to do this, preferring to tear each one off the string as I need it, even though I often end up with half a bag. When Clive comes across a stack of my unprepared bags behind the counter he huffs and puffs.

'Do you think I can't make up my own mind?' I said. 'I mean, I know you think he's a prat, but —'

'He's so bloody pathetic!' Clive burst out. 'It makes me sick, the way he goes on, always calling it the Malvinas instead of the Falklands – look how he went on in the café, frigging about with that newspaper and talking about the Armada!'

'So he's pretentious. That doesn't mean nobody else is allowed to have an opinion.' I tried to keep my voice level.

'Yeah, that's how he's so clever. Arsing around and manipulating on the sly.'

'So you think he manipulated me? You think if it wasn't for him I wouldn't be going? I'd sit at home? Twiddle my thumbs?'

'He challenged you,' Clive ploughed on. 'He challenged you to go on this protest, even though —'

'Even though what? What?'

He looked at me, blushing even more with anger and embarrassment because I had shouted at him.

'Look, Sarah,' he said, 'you don't have to do all this brave face stuff with me. You remember Matthew, Suzanne's fiancé? He's in the navy, you know, and it looks like he'll be going. It's a madhouse at home, Suzanne's been creating about it all day, Mum sent her to the doctor's in the end.' He came towards me. 'What I'm saying is, you don't have to put up a front with me . . . and you don't have to prove anything to a pillock like Julian. I mean, everyone's against war, you know, it's just that some of us —'

'Some of us what? Have a job to do? Know where our duty lies? Oh, God, don't start giving me that *crap*, Clive!' Everyone in the shop could hear us now, I was sure, but I didn't care. 'Don't even start! You're dead right, I've got nothing to prove. And there's something you haven't realized, which is that war hasn't been declared yet. Were you aware of that? No one has actually said there's going to be a war. So we don't need to hear any of this *crap*, OK?'

'So how come you're demonstrating against it if there's no chance of it happening, Sarah?'

'Because . . .' I was crying, of all stupidities. 'Because I shall do what I damn well please.' I breathed in noisily through my nose. 'You've cut your finger,' I added.

'So I have.'

'Is it deep?'

'No, it'll stop in a minute. Sarah . . .'

'You'd better have a plaster anyway.'

'No, I'll get out front,' he said, but he didn't move.

I wiped my eyes with the heel of my hand. 'Nobody knows what's going to happen,' I said.

'No. You're right. I'm sorry. You can do what you like.'

'I'm just upset because Graham didn't turn up this morning.'

'Your driving instructor?'

'Yes, he said he'd be there, to, to come with me and he wasn't.' The thought of Graham not being there just made me start crying even harder.

Clive put his arms around me. He said that it didn't matter because I had passed anyway, because I was a really smart girl; that when Graham was back we could go and see him, that he would take me there on his bike after work, and that above all everything was going to be all right. I hung on to him, punctuating my weeping with profanities.

Last night I lay in bed and silently yelled for her, begged her to leave me alone, bellowed for her again. The thought of seeing her once more made me gibber with fear but I couldn't conceive of another day without her. I'm through with you, I cried. Begone! Back with you to whatever trench in limbo-land you stuck your head out of, you hell-cat, you misery – take yourself off! I spent years lamenting you and now you have the gall to come and freak me on street corners; you know I walk with my head down, Genevieve, for fear I might see you – and yet I walk, and I walk, and I catch myself craning, seeking . . . It wasn't me who charged it all up again, Genevieve. I didn't want to remember it. You did it. You pushed up some lever deep inside it and shot yourself out . . .

I got tired of ranting. I pictured my mother as she had been that evening – a lifetime ago now – when I said: 'Mum. Down by the docks. I think I saw someone who looked like Genevieve.' She had been sitting on the sofa with her whisky and water in one hand and her menthol cigarette in the other, her feet with their pearlized toes in their sandals. What was it she had said in reply? 'It's enough,' she had said, 'without you risking your neck in these . . . capers.' She had looked young, for a minute, and then she had gone upstairs.

You'd have to say 'fair' about them both, as well as 'blue-eyed', but they weren't the least bit alike – except for near identical feet, I suppose. Two girls, tipsily unaware of their odd shoes until the flash-bulb popped at Juliette's wedding. A pink girl and a lemon girl, a fair girl and a honey one, climbing a tree. Eighteen, were they? Twenty? I picture their toes, white where they pressed and slid against the lichen and bark, their forearms bare where the coat-sleeve rode up, tensed to heave them with a great crack and a creaking and a squeal into the branches: 'Genevieve!' 'Katharine!' Or *Genevieve, Katrine*. Not Kate. Had anyone ever called her Kate?

I want to be safe and young in the house on the heath. I want to run out past the white washing on the line, down over the dunes to the sea. I wish I'd never met her. I wish I'd never got in her car and driven with her to Toulon.

Something at the end has disappeared. There are no images for the end.

No, I only went to Toulon once, when the ship turned on the water.

I go and look in the photo album and I see that Genevieve is laughing but Katharine's face is shadowed, and when I peer closely I can see how Katharine is trying to turn her head away from the camera and that she looks pale and tearful and sick.

This morning I received two phone calls as I was getting ready for work. The first was Clive, at home on his day off, who invited me to go and see a band at the Art School. The second was Vivienne, who asked me if I was coming to the demonstration. 'Julian says he'll pick you up.'

I told both of them I'd call them back when I got to the Fruit and Veg. I didn't have time to think about it right now. There would never be time to fix it with the boss, not now.

Flora came into the kitchen, wearing a leotard striped like a bee and eating a banana. 'Sarah, you'll never get the bus!'

'You don't look exactly ready yourself,' I replied indistinctly without turning from the mirror, my kohl pencil poised over my lower lid.

'Mum's taking me today. Oh, she wants you to get some tights.'

'What?'

'Tights, for tomorrow. She knows you haven't got any.'

I turned round. 'What about tomorrow?'

'Grandma and Grandpa's do.'

'I didn't know there was a do.'

'Well, there is. Just a lunch. Just us. Jonathan's coming home tonight. Do the other eye, it's making me feel weird, you staring at me all lopsided.'

My mother appeared in the doorway with her bag of school-books. 'Flora, up you go and change, I'm leaving in ten minutes,' she said. Flora ducked past her to thump her way up the stairs. 'That child! You'd never believe she could dance a step . . . Sarah, shouldn't you be gone?'

'I have to get tights, then,' I said.

'Yes, I think your grandmother would be a bit put out if you wore trousers this time.' She put her bag down on the table. 'Come on, Sarah, lovely,' she said gently, 'don't get in a state, not now . . .'

I turned away from her to the mirror and began to make the first of several tiny plaits in my hair. 'So we'll all be in our pretty dresses, will we?' I said in a tight, level voice. 'Super.' Behind me I heard my mother take a deep breath.

'Sarah, this is not the time,' she began, and her voice shook. 'This is not the time to make a fuss about—'

'It's not the clothes! You know what it is!' I swung round to face her. 'It's why we're all gathering now like this!'

'Oh, Sarah, for Heaven's sake.' She was trying to remain calm, but we were both trembling, and I couldn't stop.

'Huh? Why now? Because you think he might be gone after the weekend, don't you! Of course you do! So you've arranged a little party, just in case!'

'Sarah, will you keep your voice down!' Her face was now pale with anger. 'I am not having Flora upset! Try to remember that she is much younger than you! Take some notice of her needs for once!'

'That's the whole point! What good is it for her needs, or any of our needs for that matter, to go through with some bloody ra-ra send-off! Because that's what it'll be! It's disgusting! Christ,' I said, and I was shouting now, 'you know what it'll be like! You know how much you'll hate it! Think about it! We'll probably toast the bloody Queen!'

There was a pause while we both breathed in and out, shook, and stared at each other, appalled. We were both crying. Flora ran down the stairs and banged the front door behind her.

My mother reached for the kitchen roll and tore off two sheets. I thought she was going to dry her eyes but she came towards me with it. Gently she blotted my face as I gasped for air.

'Do you think I care what we do, Sarah, my love?' Her voice was a little thin thread. 'Do you honestly think I care whether we toast the Queen . . .' She gave a tiny scratch of a laugh. 'Or whether we drink to the Argentine Air Force?'

We stood stock-still. In the silence I heard the dog barking in the road. I thought: Damn, I bet she's after a rabbit, I'll have to catch her before I go for the bus. Time passed.

Finally I gulped snot. 'That's obscene,' I said. 'That's an obscene thing to say.'

'Oh, I know.' She wiped her red eyes, blinking, looking at me. 'But if we did that, do you think it would make one bit of difference to what happened?'

When I didn't answer she turned away, groping in her handbag for her car-keys. 'What's the matter?' she asked, her voice beginning to rise. 'Aren't I allowed to say what I think?' I thought she was about to start weeping again, but she strode out of the front door and nearly slammed it off its hinges.

I followed her outside. Flora was waiting in the car, looking straight in front of her, her chubby cheeks grey. My mother climbed in beside her and started the engine. I began to run after the car as it pulled away. I followed it for fifty yards down the road in the rain.

'Mummy!' I screamed hoarsely, weeping as I ran. I couldn't keep up with her. 'Mummy!' I screamed. 'Come back!'

About an hour later I picked up the phone and dialled, still snivelling.

'Julian?' I said. 'Jules?' I was almost incoherent. 'Pick me up this afternoon. Not from the Fruit and Veg, OK? I'll be at the bus-stop.'

FOURTEEN

They did an operation on me after she died. I didn't know they'd done it until afterwards. They took out the heart I had fought with so that I had no heart for fighting. I wonder now if perhaps I secretly let them do it. I could have. She was dead, and I never thought there would come a time when I'd need it again.

The excision took place at the end of the summer when I was thirteen. The operating-theatre reminded me of the room at my maternal grandmother's house referred to always as 'Katharine's room'; there were the same dried flowers, rose-covered cushions and chair-covers, dust turning in the light, and books. The woman in this room was older than my mother, though; she had horny bare feet in Roman sandals, glasses on a chain around her neck, a battered folder against her bosom. She was called Miss Dupree. She was my new headmistress, and this was my new school.

There had been a battle but it was over now. The tattered standard slapped against the pole in the fitful breeze, the birds hopped and cheeped undisturbed over the dung and the tangled harness of fallen horses. The sun shone impartially down on the acres of turf and glinting guns, and the smoke curled blue from the thatch of pillaged farms. We sat there in the quiet.

'We go to the church in town here, Sarah, those of us who are C of E,' said Miss Dupree. 'I do hope you won't spit out the Communion wine in front of everyone. I wouldn't know what to say to the vicar.'

I looked up at her and saw that she was smiling. I could feel our long conversation drawing to a close, but I didn't want to leave. It was so restful that I felt I could go to sleep, sitting there.

'I promise I won't,' I replied; and my nose started to bleed, suddenly and copiously, without any warning at all, dripping fast like a tap so that I gasped in shock. The woman said calmly, 'Oh, Sarah,' and gave me a man-sized box of paper hankies to staunch the bright oxygenated blood pattering on to my shirt. Only when I was drained of all that scarlet blood did I say to Miss Dupree: 'She's dead, Genevieve, my . . . she was my aunt. She died,' and only after that did I find that my outlaw's heart had been excised as swiftly and painlessly as if they had used a laser-beam.

I saw Naomi the following summer, but it was a mistake. She was living at last with Nicholas and Juliette. I found her at fourteen heavy-faced and sisterly with Katrine, beloved of Nicholas who took us three girls on the river in his little boat. Naomi clutched the side and said she was frightened; I knew that she wasn't but that downriver lay the other house, and Nicholas realized his mistake and rowed us to the shore.

Naomi told me that Jean-René came to visit from time to time, as did Henri Palastrier: 'You see how lucky I am, with my pile of stepfathers!' she said with a loud laugh, tilting her head towards Nicholas with a hint of the old, black wide-eyed glare. I said once, 'Genevieve —' and Naomi said: 'No. No, Sarah. Mention her to me as *ta mère*, if you must mention her at all.' I looked at the ground in grief, but Naomi's eyes were dry.

We had nothing to say; we actually quarrelled once, briefly, about the correct pronunciation of Latin, *via* and *vita* versus *wia* and *wita*. One day I walked alone up the hill road towards the other house but turned back half-way. On my return I found Naomi sitting on the wall of Juliette's garden, swinging her legs, watching me.

That afternoon I started to feel very odd, weak and sick all the time, as if my innards were sliding away somewhere. When I started actually throwing up we decided I should go home. They said it was my glands.

I went to make quiches in my cookery class at my second boarding-school. I took my exams. At fifteen I kissed Miss Dupree goodbye and went to sixth form college, and not once after the operation did I dream I'd have any use for a heart like that, since Genevieve was no longer there to be fought for and we lived in a green leafy place far from the sea.

Police horses, all bay, all shiny. I wondered if they had been chosen to match. They trotted up and down on the edge of the crowd, the riders wooden beneath their helmets, walkie-talkies clipped to their collars. Other policemen in yellow jackets lined the street on each side of the procession. People with loud hailers were urging the newcomers to move down to the back and not to try to break into the march from the side. The surrounding streets were closed off with railings. From the front of the procession there came the sound of drumming.

Julian gripped me by the upper arm and steered me ahead of him, against the flow of people making their way to the back. 'What are you doing, Julian, let go, where are the others!' We were due to meet Vivienne and Scott in ten minutes.

'We'll find them. I want to get up to the front,' he said calmly, ignoring the calls of those around us to stop pushing the wrong way.

'They should let them start off at the front. There are too many people here!'

'Don't panic, Sarah. Look, hold this.'

' "Socialist Workers say No to War in the South Atlantic",
I'm not bloody carrying that.'

'What would you like it to say? "Convent Girls want their
Daddies to Stay at Home?"'

'You shit. Let go of my arm, you shit.'

Julian laughed, and let go of me. 'See you at the front.'

'Fuck you,' I said, as he disappeared illegally over a
barrier into the crowd.

In the event I had no time to get to the back before the
march moved off. I was able to sidle in between two policemen. I went slowly along, standing on tiptoe from time to
time, thinking that I might catch sight of Vivienne or Scott,
although I was beginning to realize it was useless. I wished
I'd joined them at the beginning instead of coming with
Julian.

'Bit late, aren't you!' The voice came from above us, from
a fat, smiling man in glasses at a window overlooking the
street. He was answered by a barrage of hostile shouts and
calls from below. Never too late to do something completely
pointless, I thought. It seemed to be getting more crowded
instead of less; there seemed to be a lack of progress ahead,
but the people behind us didn't understand. Then there came
a sudden push in the small of my back and I was forced
forward, stumbling, against a woman in front of me. The
chanting and the drumming seemed to be coming down the
procession towards us.

'It's no good shoving,' I said over my shoulder; there
wasn't enough room for me to turn round. Others joined in.
'We can't move on! We can't budge up here!' The shouts
came first from ahead and then from all around me. I could
see people beginning to crane to the right and the left and
realized that I was doing the same thing; we were all starting
to look for a way out, but there were no side-streets. 'Jesus,'
I said, and a man next to me laughed nervously and muttered
something, but I didn't hear what it was because I was
propelled violently forward again. This time I fell to my

knees and someone trod on my leg. I yelped and was tugged up by my elbow. The third time it happened I caught hold of a jacket sleeve but others were not so lucky. Several fell over and some screamed. There was no chanting now, and the sound instead was a frightened murmur, getting louder all the time, interspersed by cries to stop pushing.

'Sarah!'

I stared around me.

'Over here!' It was Clive, ten yards from me against the wall. He was head and shoulders above everybody else, he looked quite bizarre. He was waving at me frantically.

'I'll never get there!'

'Come on!'

I fought my way to the edge. The crowd had swept me on downstream by the time I made it. Clive struggled up behind me.

'There's a big set-to up ahead,' he said, 'that's why we're all stuck here.'

'You mean a – a riot?'

'Yeah, a real riot!' He laughed.

'What are you doing here?' I was puffing, laughing in relief. 'And how come you had such a good view!'

'I was standing on a copper's head.' He laughed again, a bit hysterically. 'An orange box. I thought I'd be out of the way there so I could look out for you lot, but you knocked over the barriers and things got a bit close for comfort.'

'I didn't knock over any bloody barriers! God, let's get out of here.'

'Where?'

'Look, I can see from here, this is just a bottleneck. If we go with the crowd we'll get to the corner, look, and then we can get out. Clive?' I gazed wildly around, but he had gone.

'Clive!' I called, and then there was a new noise, a sort of groan, and I was borne forward again. This time a lot of people were tumbled and I trod on someone's hand as I was carried along, I heard them cry out but I couldn't help it. I tried to yell his name again, but by now I was hardly touching the ground, I could hardly get my breath with the pressure on my back and chest. 'Clive!' I gasped, but he had gone.

'They broke his collar-bone. They had a piece of pipe, metal pipe. He just stood there, he couldn't get away, and they bashed him.' Vivienne stirred three sugars into her tea and lifted the cup to her trembling lips. She had a cut on her eyebrow and the tears streamed down her face. She had been crying ever since I found her and took her to the Cadena Cafeteria.

'Who bashed him?'

'A couple of blokes. I didn't see. They've taken him to hospital. God, Sarah,' she said, 'it was insane up there, people just went insane, it was bloody havoc!' She leaned against my shoulder and sobbed.

I put my arm round her and squeezed her. 'He was only there watching. He was on his day off!' I said bitterly.

'I thought he came with you!'

'No, he thought it was a stupid idea. I came with Julian.' I sighed. 'I should have been at work. I've probably been sacked.'

'What a mess. We do our bit for peace and look what happens.'

'Oh, Viv, don't cry! Clive will be all right!'

I glanced up at the café window. Julian was standing outside, his hands in his pockets. Vivienne saw him at the same moment and tapped on the glass. He came in and sat down. I left the table to get another cup of coffee without speaking to him.

Vivienne was telling him about Clive when I returned. He was listening in silence.

'Not a scratch on you, I see,' I remarked, stupidly, before I could stop myself.

'I didn't come here to fight,' he replied.

'Do you suppose Clive did?'

'Your friend has been known to mix it a bit, shall we say.'

'Julian, I saw what happened!' Vivienne was aghast. 'He didn't lift a finger!'

'You saw the end of what happened,' he said after a pause.

'Are you suggesting he provoked it?' I asked. 'And how do you mean, she saw the end? Were you there? Did you watch it?'

Julian said nothing.

'Did you, Julian?' I swallowed.

'I didn't come here to fight,' he repeated.

I narrowed my eyes. 'You stood and watched him get beaten up, and you did nothing. You shit.'

'Oh, call me something else, Sarah, for variety's sake at least.'

'Why? It's what you are,' I heard myself say. 'You wouldn't even stand by a friend. I don't think I like you at all.'

'Stop it, you two, will you?' Vivienne was crying again.

'I don't like you, either,' Julian said, laughing. '"Stand by a friend,"' he whined. 'Listen to yourself.' He turned to Vivienne. 'Do you know what Sarah is?' he said conversationally. 'She's a peace-time pacifist. I always thought so.' He looked at me with contempt. 'Blood will out,' he said.

I felt myself lifting up off the seat. I was filling up with a buoyant rage. 'What is that supposed to mean?'

Julian was rising to his feet along with me. 'You and the brave boys in blue, or khaki, or whatever it is they wear. Your tribe.'

I brought my face closer to his. I spoke slowly and clearly. 'At least they've got guts,' I said.

Vivienne buried her face in her hands.

Julian stared down at me in silence for a moment, his mouth twisted, lips pressed together.

'It's your kind,' he hissed, 'who get us into this, time – and – time – *again*!' And he pushed past me and strode out of the door.

Vivienne was saying something to me but I couldn't hear her, Vivienne was talking but she seemed to have gone, I couldn't see her; the café was suddenly very full of people, all crowding around the small tables, rising, seating themselves, bringing steaming cups of tea. The murmur was deafening, the windows were misted up. It was getting gloomier in there by the second. The hubbub echoed in my ears like in a swimming-pool. People passed in front of me as blurred shapes. I yawned, blinked, frowned; and then I saw – was it her again? Could it be her? I looked again, and my blood drained away.

She smiled back at me as our eyes met. She was just the same as ever, with her deep red lips, her black clothes, her diamonds in her ears, smiling her old, wicked smile; it was her, sitting there waiting for me.

I walked slowly over to her table. I sat down carefully so as not to jog the image.

'So it is you,' I said. 'I knew you were back!'

Genevieve grasped my hand and kissed it.

'Look at you, so pretty now!' she said. 'Well? What are we waiting for? Let's go!'

FIFTEEN

We ran fast down the path, so fast in the heat, first one ahead, then the other, first in bright sunlight and then plunging into the deep shade of the river-bank, panting and gasping and laughing, chasing and chasing, swinging my baggage between us; incredible to be back, after all the yelling and the brawling; incredible to be shot of Lucifer's and still to feel fine and hard and free, to run with Naomi all the way back from the station – two miles we had covered before reaching the river, over the fields and along the hill road with the valley below and the poplar trees standing straight, green, faithful, small. 'Naomi, Naomee, you're pulling my arm off!'

'Cause you're not – fit, you can't – run!'

Laughing, slowing down, Naomi took her sandals off by the river-bank, glanced up at me through licks of long black hair, panting hard. I stood on one foot, hopping, pulling off my gym shoe. 'What are we going to do?' Naomi said. 'Go for a swim in the river?'

'If you like . . . I could throw you in!'

'Or I could throw you in!'

'We could throw each other in!'

'They threw each other in the river and were never seen

again!' We capered barefoot by the river-bank, giggling. 'Just feel the earth beneath your feet,' Naomi said. 'Isn't it nice?'

'Oh, yes, it's so . . . exquisite!'

We wriggled our toes in the mud. I sat down on a stone and dropped my head for a moment between my knees to get my breath. Then I looked around me. 'Isn't this where you tried to build your house?'

'I think so.' Naomi was a bit shamefaced. 'The foundations are on the other side of the path there.'

'The foundations!'

'It was a long time ago!'

'It was last year!'

'A year is a long time!'

'Tu es débile, tu sais?'

'Don't laugh at me!' Naomi pleaded, laughing herself. 'You don't know what it was like! I was young!'

'Hmm . . .' I began to roll up my trousers, and a thought occurred to me. 'Do you think we're too old to play table football now?'

Naomi smirked and looked at the ground. Then she said: 'Do you remember Olivier?'

'The fat one . . . ? No! Naomi, really? Your boyfriend!'

'He's not fat now! He's very nice!'

'Olivier!'

'Sarah!' She was blushing.

'I'm very happy for you. I suppose you do your homework together?'

'Sometimes.'

'And then he takes you down to the café and jumps on your feet?'

'Oh! How can you be so cruel!' Naomi pretended to sob. I leaped up to embrace her in mock remorse, she slipped and screamed, I found myself sliding with her and then suddenly we were standing calf-deep in the water, speechless, convulsed. We hugged each other fiercely. 'I've missed you,' I said.

'Me too.'

'I've been expelled.'

Naomi stepped backwards, her arms outstretched to rest on my shoulders. '*Ça!*' she said, open-mouthed. 'Why?'

'I'll tell you later. Genevieve is bound to ask about my life, you know how nosy she is, your mother. You're getting shorter.'

Naomi hadn't noticed that she was sinking. The water was now up to her knees and her dress-hem was drenched. '*Putain!*' she screeched. 'Come on, no time to waste. Let's go home and see what our mother has got for our tea, yes, jolly ho?'

'Oh, yes, jolly ho!'

The pictures in the house are in the same place, hanging together by the stairs. I can make out the names on the map now. Siorac, Beynac, St-Cyprien. The Virgin lilts in her ivory draperies: she is smiling. In one hand she is holding a little pear.

Langue d'Oc, Aquitaine, Guyenne, Perigord. Overlapping places, different names for different times. I understand that now. I am thirteen. I understand everything.

The house is cleaner. Everything is finished. The windows are shining and the shutters mended. The kitchen is complete with a batterie de cuisine; Jean-René is as good a cook as Genevieve. There are some new chairs in the sitting room, and the veranda floorboards are safe; we can sit out and watch the sun go down through the trees in the evening. And the tower room, as Naomi promised, is magnificent to see, with big windows and a proper stairway. There is a vegetable plot in the field, and even the chickens are fatter and more numerous.

It is nice, isn't it. But the winters have been hard, they have eaten up all their strength and nearly all their savings. Genevieve has kept her car against Jean-René's urgings but the rest of her jewels are gone. But now that they are both working, they are breaking even – though Genevieve was frowned upon at the school when they discovered she was 'living in sin', and Naomi suffered because of it, having her there behind the typewriter in the office; and it was her cousin Lucien who defended Naomi against the remarks of the other boys and girls . . .

There was quite a freeze this winter, ten days or more. On the morning of the thaw Genevieve sat up in bed and said: 'My God, I can't see my breath, Jean-René, you must have put too much wood in the stove and the chimney's caught . . .'

But they keep themselves now, in their renovated house. The two of them and their growing girl.

Genevieve says: 'You silly child, why did you have to fight all the time! Only fit for a Spartan camp, you are, tormenting your poor mother, not enough style to act the holy débutante, not enough style to carry it off, ha ha . . .' She teases, she says, 'I can imagine it.'

Naomi and I are like David and Jonathan, lords of the land. Blackberries go spat in our hands from the tugged briars, weed at the river bottom slides over our feet. Under the walnut trees the earth which was turned in the spring is tufted now with dry grass, and up on the heights the ground threatens to parch again as we walk, the two girls, or the girls and the woman, or sometimes the girls and the woman and the man (it is not Jean-René's holiday, he has to work every day), along the hill paths or in the meadows beneath other ruins.

We dance one evening in the field, all holding hands, round and round. Naomi and I, dancing in a circle, Naomi and Genevieve together, Naomi turning under her arm; and then me with Genevieve: I can see her jump, the woman, her head go back, her mouth open and eyes close – hair flying upwards as she comes down, lips curving into a smile – and as she touches the ground again her eyes open and focus on me and she reaches out towards me, her hand brushing my cheek, I am her height now; and I step back, grinning, shaking myself free to approach once more and our upper arms meet, slide together as I put my hands around Genevieve's waist, and Genevieve joins her hands behind my back —

Who did I say were David and Jonathan?

Her daughter is so unlike her physically, there does not seem to be a grain of her in Naomi, it must be all from Belar – though they do say that Madame had hair like that, when she was young. Her daughter is different with men and boys, too; Genevieve would never have behaved as primly at thirteen as Naomi does with Olivier, Genevieve always liked a rumpus. But Naomi is becoming almost sedate at times; she queens it a bit with Jean-René in a way Palastrier never allowed her to, he was such a dig gruff uncle. But Jean-René is several years younger than her mother, he can be more of a . . . more of a prince to her. A prince to her princess.

He does things for Naomi, like bringing her her shoes if she leaves them somewhere and cannot find them. He notices where she has left them. Genevieve sits and lights a cigarette and lets her dry hot gaze rake over him as he does this, and says something, something honeyed, something cutting, something witty which makes us all laugh. Jean-René weeps when he laughs.

The sharp images are coming to an end. They have been slowing down and now there are very few left. Now all I can see is our two bodies as the sun goes down to leave dusk behind in the field: the one skinny with no tits at all yet, the other smallish and strong, she would be stocky if she grew any heavier, she has a stocky shape . . .

The past has come. It has sped along submarine through time to burst up bam! through the floor of the Cadena Cafeteria, knocking tables through the plate-glass, spouting weed and small fish and icy brine over the floor-tiles, scattering the occupants! God knows what they mean, these acronyms and figures stamped on its metal flank, I've never been this close before, I never knew how big they were – Ooh, fuck, I said, you only just missed me! She just laughed; she was just like she'd been in the beginning, the spit-image of herself in the post-zoo café on that lowering winter afternoon with her velvet and her fur and the hundreds-and-thousands still multicoloured in her gut, *My God, Genevieve, you look just the same!*

Come on, she said, there's no time to lose. Jean-René

and Naomi are waiting for us; you remember how we were all dancing in the field? They will be wondering where we've gone soon!'

'But look at you,' I said, 'you're young, you haven't met Jean-René yet, I don't understand;' but she said, 'Never mind, you will, soon enough. Now come *on*!'

Vivienne was slapping my face but I said: 'Leave off, I've got to get after her,' and dashed outside. My cash-point spewed out money – not surprising, I had been saving for this – and my passport was in my bag. I grabbed a taxi and made for the station.

At the port I bought my ticket in a trice. Genevieve was already up on deck. She shouted something rude at the ships parked in the Base and several people looked at us. She threw her hat over the side and we drank duty-free whisky from the bottle. We found a dark place to sit because I felt closer to her in the dark.

She started to change when we got to Paris – I mean, change her clothes, though her face changed a bit each time as well. Between dozes I watched her; I didn't mind. She had a long way to go, after all, in time to be like she was five years ago when I was thirteen and we danced in the field. In the train south of Paris she put on her sweat-soaked orange dress; 'Do you remember? Do you remember?' she said, displaying her dry tanned arms as if she were showing off gold bangles. And then her fatter Frenchness, briefly head-scarfed, her secretive smile and plucked eyebrows in Limoges, making me giggle. She bobbed ahead of me in the crowd, carrying a basket of food. After Limoges she became – for a short moment – the woman smoking on the train: I said: 'No, that was the year before, and how did you know about her?' She uttered: *'Qu'est-ce que tu as?'* in reply, in a voice made of brushed wool, and laughed gutturally so that her words came out with smoke. I demanded food like a twelve-year-old, I was hungry, and she got out her knife and slit open a red pepper with a great grin on her face: she handed me a tartine, 'Jean-René made this,' she said, 'he remembered you liked lots of jam . . .'

I wanted to talk all the time; I talked endlessly, though I was very sleepy and she didn't encourage me. I wanted to ask her so many questions but she kept giving me the gimlet eyes and smiling. Finally she took the scarf off her head and shook out her hair, closed her eyes, stretched, opened her eyes again. She sat there in an old shirt and jeans now, freckle-armed, a wiry grey hair at her parting. 'Sleep now my darling,' she said. 'I'll wake you when we arrive. It won't be long,' she said, and I tried to keep my eyes open, I really did.

At Siorac I woke up and she was gone.

The train pulled in and I got off, stretching my legs and shivering. The station was deserted. I slipped through the building like a criminal, passing my younger self who was standing somewhere in the shadows crying, waiting for Tante Juliette. I wished I could have stopped to wipe Sarah's tears away with my thumb.

The sun was low. I walked for miles before realizing that it was lying the wrong side of me. I was travelling away from the house, not towards it as I had intended. I cut across a field. The dew soaked my leather boots. The pack on my back was heavy. Passing a vineyard the road at last became familiar; it was almost dark now. I was hungry again, so I picked a small handful of grapes to stay myself. Their sourness banished the spit from my mouth.

Some rhythm was called for to steady my pace; my left foot was blistered and I feared I would soon start to limp. Though I had broken a string in St-Vincent I thought I could accompany myself. My saliva announced its return with a glandular pang in my jowl: I began to sing.

She rejoined me on the hill road. She was hardly visible in the dusk, so we held hands and walked together in step.

'We'll be home soon,' she said as she let go. In ecstasy I said: 'It hasn't changed!' as I saw the small fields lying emerald in the last light, the fences and the coppice-woods, the valley as gentle and deep as ever in the evening light, in the air which smelled so different, which smelled the same. I glimpsed her ahead of me beneath the walnut trees at the bend in the road, calling me and laughing.

When I reached her she said: 'No, we will not go to the house, not yet. Let us go up into the woods.'

I said: 'But we didn't go into the woods this year. Only the year before. Anyway I should be holding the gun if we do – you gave it to me, remember?'

She had the gun in one hand and the fat black cylinder in the other.

She said: 'Yes. You were the only other person who held it. I never let him hold it . . . But I think I will hold it this time.'

She did a big smile.

I said: 'No. We didn't play, not this year. We got in the car and it wasn't a game.'

She said: 'Both of us?'

I said: 'Both of us.'

She said: 'And where did we go?'

I said: 'To the sea.'

She said: 'I didn't leave you behind at the station, did I.'

She was screwing the fat black cylinder on to the barrel of the gun.

I said: 'Hey, Genevieve, I won't tell.'

She said: 'I think you will if you are given half a chance.'

She said: 'I – think – it – is – time – we – went – into – the – woods.'

I hurried swiftly and silently along the road in the twilight. Soon I would reach the field and the house. She hurried swiftly and silently behind me. I plunged through the gap in the fence and down through the orchard towards the field.

'*Attention! C'est interdit aux jongleurs-terroristes!*' The voice spoke from the branches above my head; bird-like, a voice like Naomi's if Naomi were a bird. '*C'est interdit aux putains-criminelles!*'

'Naomi!' I cried. 'Please! It wasn't my fault! Let me get to the house before she finds me!' The sun was going down afire, abandoning the small fields, the coppices, the shadowed stone of the farms. Dark soon, dark now.

I'm running faster than ever but I can hear a click-click behind me, a click-click and a curse.

Just down through the trees and I'll reach the house.

Who is that in the field coming towards me?

Who is that calling my name?

JEAN-RENÉ

SIXTEEN

Unless you engage yourself to a schoolfriend at twenty-one (which I did) and marry her at twenty-five (which I did not) you must expect the person you find in the end, the one you intend to spend your life with, to have a history of some kind. It is only natural. Few of us, in this modern age, settle for our first loves. We pride ourselves on growing out of them.

Genevieve Belar was thirty-two when I met her, and there had been a lover before me and a husband before him. The husband, Paul Belar, was a remnant from a dizzy youth – still married to her, but time had done all the work of a divorce except for the formalities themselves. The lover, Henri Palastrier, was a closer, more fleshly figure who seemed more of a father to Genevieve's daughter Naomi than the father himself. Naomi never mentioned Belar, not even after she had been to visit him, but she and her mother spoke from time to time about Palastrier. These were the two men who had once shared my lover's life; the young husband and the middle-aged companion, the distant, featureless Belar and the more accessible Palastrier. I expected nothing more than to become acquainted with them at second-hand. I certainly never considered either of them for long. Belar I never met, and I did not begin my friendship with Henri Palastrier until after Genevieve's death.

I think it must have been Nicholas Whelan, Naomi's uncle, who mentioned shortly after Genevieve died that Palastrier might call on me. The news prompted me to speculate increasingly on my fellow-in-mourning. To beguile my loneliness as much as anything else I began to form an image of him based less on what Genevieve had told me than on my native preconceptions – prejudices, perhaps – regarding him. By the time we met I was determined that we should be antithetical: as a fugitive from a northern city, educated son of parents who were themselves fugitives from the northern countryside, I had created a Palastrier who was a waterfront man with a natural *contrebandier*'s contempt for the peasantry and their surroundings. I imagined him sitting in his southern lair, looking at his southern hills, his shining roads, everything right in his world. He made things, did things, I decided, whereas I – in a very small way – attempted to describe what people make and do. But antitheses are not men, they tend to collapse in front of men; indeed, when it comes to manual work it is years since Palastrier put down his spade (he made good young) while I have since put a good many stones together, measured, lifted, smoothed them off with my palm.

He watched me, standing ankle-deep in the wet grass as I checked my wall for frost damage. My wall was then two years and three months old. His shoes were thin, the wind whipped his trouser-legs; he shifted from foot to foot, whistling through his teeth. 'It looks sound to me,' he said.

'But I have to make sure,' I protested. I didn't know then that walls were his trade. 'My bathroom is on the other side,' – and my saying 'bathroom' made him shudder, the idea that I should stand naked under water on the other side of that thin north-facing construction.

It would be more accurate to say that I was checking the repairs I had made after previous frost damage, for it was only November and a mild one at that. It was the winter before which had done the harm. That winter had been the coldest in living memory; and when I say 'living' I mean the memory of those who had grown up speaking patois, those to whom French was a second language. I think they are all dead now, the patois-speakers; the last to go in this commune was M. Pasquier, whose family owns the farm bordering my land. I remember when I first came down here I heard him in the byre, hectoring the veal-calves in a tongue I took to be Spanish until Genevieve put me right. Old Pasquier could remember a winter of his youth when there were 19 degrees of frost but the winter in question (his last, incidentally) surpassed it; the thermometer by his barn door registered minus 23 degrees. The frost went deep into the ground and burst both the mains water-pipes and the local supply from the water-tower on the hill. Neither did the sewerage escape; many people around me had cracked drains, shattered lavatory bowls. I was spared that at least, sitting smugly (as smugly as one can in those conditions) on the wooden seat of my earth closet, but my pipes went, including the thin copper ones to my shower water-heater which split myriad times in places undiscovered until the spring. I carried ice up from the stream and boiled it. I tended my wood-burning stove like a Neanderthal. I washed very seldom. That winter I stood out in the plum orchard and felt the frost on my eyelashes. That winter was the one immediately after Genevieve's death.

When I told him, that day out in the field, Palastrier seemed to brush my remark aside. 'Last year it went down to twenty-three below,' I said, and he merely lifted his chin. I assumed that he was indifferent. Well, I reasoned, he has never experienced it himself. Nothing outside his little periphery concerns him. On the coast they never have such frosts, so what could possibly be the purpose in telling him? I wondered if my worries over my bathroom were of equally little moment to him, perhaps comically northern, at any rate not quite manly – yes, that was the crucial element in my stereotype of Palastrier, his idea of the correct behaviour of *men* – because he said: 'I will send one of my people,' closing the matter with a wave of his broad hand. Good Heavens, I thought on that damp afternoon, where I come from such attitudes no longer exist – we're border people, I suppose, we can't afford prejudice . . . I was right enough in that, at least. We can't afford prejudice.

The first winter we lived in that house, when Naomi was twelve, there were a few days of frost and the following summer was rainy. The second winter, when Naomi was thirteen, it was quite sharply colder and the following summer was hot and dry. Genevieve shot her husband and then herself, Naomi went to live with her uncle and aunt. And then the first winter after her death: minus 23, myself alone in the house, unwashed, the following summer hot and dry. The second winter after she died: mild, but by then I was wary, carefully checking my walls, and Palastrier came to see me. These are my own personal annals. It may seem odd to count off the events of my life along with the weather-patterns, but I find it restful. Not that I am trying to detect a causal relationship between winter and summer weather, nor even between weather as a whole and tragedy. I read the newspapers – I write them, in fact – and I am aware that not a week passes without a barrage of gunshots exploding like a rash across France regardless of cloud-cover or sunshine. No, it is nothing more than a litany; now, five years after her death, I count off the seasons along with the events they contain in the hope of making the events seem as distant as those long gone seasons and therefore bearable. It does not work, of course, not even after all these lessons in time and distance, but as I said, it is restful.

Genevieve fifteen months in the ground (and that is a story in itself, her interment) and her former lover appeared in my field. Over a year had passed since Nicholas Whelan mentioned him to me and I had long since ceased to expect him in the flesh. It turned out later that Naomi had tried to call me but, ignorant of that fact and having spoken to no one for four days, I was startled enough for my heart-rate palpably to increase. I repeated his name like an old man presented with a prodigal nephew – farcically, since Palastrier was a generation older than me: 'Palastrier? Henri Palastrier?'

He nodded without smiling but his face was friendly, unusually so for a first meeting. I was to discover that he seldom smiled; that he joked with friends and conversed with strangers with the same permanent, disarming, mildly surprised expression which dispensed with a smile on his part, caused a smile on the part of others. At the time of the handshake, however, I merely stammered and turned away from him almost immediately, babbling about my wall, how the frost had damaged it last year and might again. I did not ask him why he had come because, at this late stage, I could not conceive of a reason for his visit. I told him how cold it had been.

He dismissed my concern. He would send one of his men, he said, as if I were his bookish incompetent old uncle. At last I led him inside. It had been churlish to make him stand out in the wind, but he did not seem put out. Perhaps he expected that from a clog-wearer, a hacker of potatoes from the ground, I thought grimly. I offered him nothing.

As we began hesitantly to converse I felt suddenly as filthy as I had been that freezing winter of my initial bereavement, my hair as lank, my nails as clogged. I felt as if my reeling progress towards equilibrium, a progress as chancy as that of a drunk towards his porch-lamp, had been revealed as a journey in the wrong direction, the lamp a river-reflected moon, my foot an inch from the bank. He made me feel stupid. He made me angry. Here was a man who had the gall to present himself, over a year after her death, as an emissary from a dead woman. For what else did we have in common except Genevieve?

Genevieve killed her husband and then herself. One August evening in 1977 she went, at his bidding, to his apartment in Toulon. He was drunk; there was a violent quarrel; he threatened her with a gun. In the struggle to defend herself she shot him dead. Then, deranged by her own deed, she took his gun down to the sea-front and dispatched herself with it. The two deaths were spaced by a number of hours, according to the police. According to the police, Genevieve could well have been alive when they discovered her husband's body. The police, theatrical in their reconstructions, are really quite remorseless when it comes to speculation.

Naomi was thirteen at the time, and I had lived with Genevieve for two years. This puts me last on the list, behind Palastrier (four years) and the dead husband himself, Paul Belar (five years). Behind Naomi also, of course. She beat us all.

Before the week was out she had gone. Naomi, I mean. She left the day after the death of her mother and father. She departed the house stiffly, her face the colour of putty, the first two suitcases in her hands – she would not let me or her uncle Nicholas carry them. Her parents had died in a distant city, but for Naomi it was the same as if they had been carried from our house, swathed in sheets like Egyptian king and queen (succumbed to plague, spirited from the palace); as if they had left behind them shattered windows, bullet-pocked plaster, stained floorboards. The house made her sick, and she had to leave. I am not saying she should have stayed; no one in their right mind could have denied her the comfort of her remaining family. It was simply the shocking urgency of it, the way she had to go then and there, taking as much as she could with her: she sat, shivering on the doorstep, while her aunt packed her things, rising every few minutes to retch, assisted by her red-eyed English uncle, into the brambles. This place makes me sick, she said.

One Sunday morning; coffee, reheated bread, loud girls' chatter – Naomi's English cousin was staying with us – hangovers for myself and Genevieve, the radio. A morning of leisure, of sundry small expectations each as unassuming and innocently pleasurable as a little cake from the oven: you eat it, you eat its neighbour, it is unimportant. I forwent the discussion I wanted to have with Genevieve about the van battery, the lack of egg-boxes for our customers, the dilapidation of the roof which was proving to be our cross and curse, which was exhausting our wealth like a sky-god, which might eventually have forced us to move, I think. I can tolerate the dilapidation now. I no longer use that part of the house. Our bedroom can grow mushrooms. Our bedroom can rot . . .

One Sunday morning passed in that manner and on the next the house was empty of Naomi and her belongings and Genevieve was being lowered into the ground. Extraordinary to think of it in such terms, as two Sundays which had she not gone to see her husband would have probably been so similar as to be blurred with time, and we would disagree afterwards about what we did when . . . I rose with my hangover to the sound of three voices in the kitchen and the smell of coffee; I rose a week later to silence and desolation. I looked out at the first hint of autumn in the blue of the sky, and she was being buried.

I did not know the precise day of her burial until much later. It was Palastrier who told me. He went to the funeral and I did not. Naomi, apparently, had wanted them to be buried together under a dungheap; 'a pile of shit' were her exact words. Juliette refused to entertain the idea of Genevieve's body in the family grave. Murderess, suicide, adulteress, it would be impermissible. She would not even discuss it with the priest. She suggested that Belar's body remain where it was to be dealt with by his relatives – if he had any: he and Genevieve had married scandalously alone in Toulon. Surely, she said, there was a detective service they could use to trace them – covertly, in case they proved to be untouchables. At that final piece of snobbishness her husband had blown his famous cool and roared at his wife in front of the entire family, but temper solved nothing. It was not an internal matter this time. It involved the soul of his sister-in-law and therefore the Church. Perhaps a small mausoleum on their own land? It had been done before. Naomi says she will get some dynamite and blow it up? Perhaps not, in that case.

Surprisingly it was Madame, mother to Juliette and her

fallen sister, who said that God would forgive them both
even if the family did not, and that they should simply
consign the couple to the newly consecrated ground outside
the old churchyard wall known as the 'back seats' and
universally disliked. After all, she added, it would fill up in
time, it had to, and their bodies would come to lie amongst
scores of the shriven in the end, certainly before the Day of
Judgement. You should never deny the bad the company of
the good, she said. Not even in death.

All this was told me, with great energy, by Henri Palastrier. He had been regaled with it by Madame, in tones of
acerbic detachment, as they filed down the path to the
church. 'So,' he concluded, nose shining, finger wagging,
'that is exactly what they did. Belar turned out to be an only
child, without cousins, whose mother at the time of his death
was committed to an institution. There was some talk of a
woman, but if she existed she wanted nothing to do with a
corpse. So they put the two of them together into the new
ground. The village priest would not do it on the Sabbath –
too busy preparing for Mass, ha! – so with his permission
they imported an old acquaintance of Madame's. We did it
there in the morning, in bright daylight, for anyone to see
who wanted. By the first bell for Mass we had covered them
up. On the orders of Madame we all went – bar the imported
priest – into the church with the bell clanging away and the
earth still on our shoes . . . !'

I did not go to the funeral. I was not invited. Had I been
invited I think I would have declined. Their blood was on my
hands. It was I who had sat idly in ignorance as she went
alone to this brute to have him drunkenly wave his gun at
her and, in the struggle for her life, to deal him his fatal
injury. That night she went down to the water and put his
gun to her head while I sat bleating to Naomi about the
irresponsibility of her mother. How could I walk with Naomi
to the graveside when I had had no notion of Genevieve's
whereabouts until the police knocked on my door?

I saw none of them for at least a month. Once or twice
Nicholas came driving up the lane but I hid from him in the

field and he went away. It never occurred to me that Naomi might want to see me. I was convinced that she would never want to speak to me again. Nor did it cross my mind that her uncle and aunt might think my elusiveness strange, not to say rude. I was only behaving as a guilty man should towards innocents. A period of quarantine was necessary.

It ended when I found Naomi's pan-pipes in a cupboard. I took them to her without a second's hesitation.

It was quickly apparent, however, that my visit was a mistake.

Directly she saw me she began to scream and cry. I tried to calm her down. I said: 'It's me, Jean-René,' as if I had changed beyond recognition. Finally she sat with Juliette for five or ten minutes, silent in the face of my diffident questions, before going to sleep with her head in Juliette's lap.

By now it was October. 'She has not been to school this term,' Juliette said to me as she stroked Naomi's hair. I noticed that Naomi was sucking her thumb. 'She tries to do Katrine's studies here at home, but whenever she puts pen to paper the words come out backwards, jumbled up . . . She had this problem as a little girl, I believe, and now the shock has brought it back to her. Also she falls asleep at odd times, as you can see. Tell me, Jean-René,' said Juliette Whelan, 'did it not occur to you to telephone or write a little letter to ask if you might come and visit her?'

I blinked, opened my mouth, anchored my fingers in the roots of my hair.

'It did not occur to me,' I said at last, 'that I needed permission.'

'Oh! Well,' she said, and I felt the trap close. 'Since you were under that impression, and Naomi is so dear to you, then what has kept you from us for two long months?'

My words followed each other tentatively. 'I suppose I felt that I—'

'That you should have known?'

I bowed my head.

'That is what we concluded.' I looked up to see her nodding calmly, sadly. 'But it is also what we had assumed from the beginning. Goodness,' she said, 'we did not expect *you* to know.'

I swallowed. 'You mean that you yourself knew he had asked her to visit him?'

'No, no. I was speaking in a more general sense,' Juliette replied. She continued to stroke Naomi's hair, and sighed. 'These things are mysterious, Jean-René. We have always felt, knowing her as we did, that there was something bad in that marriage. It gave her a . . . doomed quality which she never lost after she left him. I used to feel that it had a life of its own, that if they tried to end it – God knows, they left it long enough – it would drag them down with it.' She gave a small tired smile. 'And it did.'

I was floundering now. 'Madame,' I said, 'I do not understand you. Firstly I do not believe that marriages have a life independent of the communion of their two partners. Genevieve had no contact with her husband all the time that I knew her – she had no marriage to speak of. Secondly, I perceived no doomed quality in your sister. She was many things but she was not doomed!'

'Hush, you'll wake Naomi. You knew her for such a very short time, Jean-René. Of course you perceived nothing. As I said, nobody expected that you would . . .'

'I perceived nothing,' I expostulated, 'because there was nothing there to be perceived! When I said "I should have known", I meant simply, known where she had gone, nothing more! There was nothing more! She married a brute, long ago. She confronted him when he was in a drunken frenzy and there was a dreadful accident. Alone and unhinged by shock and remorse, she ended her life!' Naomi murmured in her sleep, but I continued. 'If there had been any suggestion that she might visit him God knows I would have tried to dissuade her, suggested your husband accompany her, gone myself if she had insisted – anything, but I did not know! I repeat, I did not know where she was! That is the only point at issue here! If I had known . . . !' I stopped, gasping, feeling the blood suffuse my face.

'Jean-René,' said Juliette Whelan. 'I will make myself as

clear as I can. Nobody holds you responsible for my sister's death. We, her family, who have always been aware of her circumstances – we feel that nobody could have stopped what happened. It is dreadful, I agree, but there has always been something dreadful there. One cannot stop these things.' Naomi whimpered again, and Juliette slid the child's sleeping head on to a cushion before rising to her feet. 'That is all I can say,' she concluded. Then, bleakly: 'Because that is all I know.'

My visit ended then. I stood up. 'What you have said disgusts me, Madame. Really, it makes me sick to hear it.' I turned and made my way unaccompanied to the front door, staggering slightly from the shock.

She came out as I was climbing into the van. 'What do you think you could have done, Jean-René?' she called. 'What difference would it have made?' She raised her voice as I started the engine. 'You were never her keeper!' she cried, as I drove away down the tree-lined road.

I went into a bar in St-Cyprien, one I do not usually visit. I had a great number of beers – God knows why I had no desire for anything stronger, but my taste was for beer, beer until I had a gutful.

Naomi had never been mine to care for. All the time I had been with Genevieve they had hardly noticed I was there. Oh, they had kept a weary half-eye on us as we played houses but it was only because they were waiting for our house to fall down. Then they picked their way in as they always knew they would have to do. Gingerly they stepped in, holding their noses, to salvage, from the squalor and stink created by the mother, the daughter who had always belonged to them. Dear God, I had wanted Juliette's blame so much. I had wanted her to rail at me, to shriek: Why didn't you *stop* her! so that I could rail back, declare myself deceived, tragic, noble, exonerated; with Juliette I could have conducted the dialogue of my grief. But Juliette was not interested. Juliette *knew* that no one could have stopped her because she was *doomed*. And it was I and not she who had uttered it, the telling phrase. 'God knows I would have tried to dissuade her, *suggested your husband accompany her*, gone myself if she had insisted . . .' The moment came for my hot defence and I put myself obediently behind Nicholas Whelan. I had never taken my rightful place at Genevieve's side: I had conceded to all of them, her daughter, the men in her past, her family. No wonder they considered that they owned her. I should be grateful they remembered my name.

How had that happened? I only knew it when she died. I had loved her so much: why was I, still and always, last on the list? This was not a question Juliette could answer. No, my grief was to be a soliloquy, a closed circle of barren speculation which revolved faster with the shortening days and left me giddily addressing the sinking winter sun.

Oh, the winter was long. The temperature dropped, and dropped again. The pipes burst. I brought water from the stream, I did not wash. I expected that the cold would ease off at the end of January as it had done during the previous two years, and in December I was still revelling in it, standing out at night in the plum orchard, daring myself to stay longer and longer. Then as the New Year wore on it began to frighten me: I had never experienced cold like this, not alone in the country like this. All January it sat there. In February a thaw was forecast but it never reached us in our hills. The sky stayed as clear as glass. My fingers cracked open so that I could not manhandle logs and maintain the van. I became lazy.

One bright morning my lingering toothache flared into life, my last gas-bottle ran out, I could not start the van. I stumbled over ruts of rock to the farm, my eyes running with the sunlight and the pain of the abcess. Mme Pasquier, the old man's daughter-in-law, lent me her car. When I returned, salved and drilled and provisioned, she held out a lidded tin and a covered dish. I thanked her with half my mouth and offered her as always my plumbing skills if she should ever need (she never did) and made my way home.

In the tin I found leek and potato soup, coarsely mashed; in the dish a baked custard. I heated up the soup on the strong new blue gas-jet. I crammed my wood-stove with logs until it roared. I took the first spoonful of soup. I blew on it, filled my mouth – and felt Genevieve sitting there on the bench with me, hunkering down closely the way she used to so that our thighs and shoulders pressed together. She used to untuck my shirt sometimes as I sat there on that bench, seated beside me or standing behind me with her chin on my shoulder. She would pull my shirt out of my belt and wrap her arms around my naked back and stomach, kneading my flanks and saying 'Ooh yum yum, this is my favourite, favourite bit of you,' and I would pretend to be ruffled: 'Favourite? My sides?' Or she would actually grab my hand so that I couldn't eat and had to listen to what she had to say, which was an action so exquisitely annoying that I would cry out like a man in pain. I sat there and ate my soup and felt her warm and firm and shifting beside me. By the time I started on the custard I was blubbering.

'*Et moi aussi*,' said Palastrier, raising his already raised eyebrows in surprise at my ruefulness, when I told him. 'Some months after she died I suddenly bellowed. I loved that woman. There was nobody like her . . . By God' – grasping my wrist on the table – 'I do believe I too was eating a custard at the time! Madelon had made it for me – she used to prepare it for Naomi and me, to cheer us up after a hard day. We'd eat it with little coffee-spoons' – miming the action. 'Nothing like it for getting out your griefs!'

The winter ended. I woke one morning to the sound of pissing. Water, mild melted water, was being expelled at high speed through the rents in my shower-piping. I wrote what I swore would be my last weather article for the paper; I had written nothing else for three months. First I had reported snow accidents, then ice accidents, then every industrial, agricultural, social, even cultural disaster which could be related to the extreme conditions. I called my editor who offered me other work at the price of a couple of flood-pieces, and I agreed. I went to see Naomi again.

I refused as a point of honour to telephone beforehand, or 'write a little letter'. What a farcical idea! I could deliver it by hand in fifteen minutes! I arrived at the house and went straight in through the front door. I half expected to find them ranged like the Spanish Bourbons in the *salon*, but there seemed to be no one about, nor any smell of cooking, and it was midday. I called for Juliette, but there was no reply. Perhaps they were all upstairs sleeping? Unlikely so early in the day, even in high summer: on a brisk April forenoon impossible.

Eventually the girl, Katrine, came downstairs on tiptoe. 'My mother is out,' she said.

'I only wanted to see Naomi.'

'*Elle se repose.*' This was rapped out stiffly, as if she and Naomi were a couple of dowagers. She was a pasty girl, with a look of flakes in her hair, I could not discern from where I stood. No expression at all in her face.

'Why? Is she ill? Please tell her I would like to see her.'

Katrine retreated up the stairs and I followed her. At the top she turned and said: '*Attendez!*' She went away down the passage, knocked officiously on the door before opening. A muffled exchange; Naomi's sleepy interrogative tones. Then she was saying '*Mais oui,*' through a yawn, '*Mais oui* – I won't go down, tell him to come here . . .' I brushed past Katrine before she had time to deliver her invitation and entered the bedroom.

Naomi was lying in day clothes on the bed, partially covered by a quilt. As I entered she swung herself gracefully to her feet. She was taller by about five centimetres.

'Ah, my girl! How you've grown!' I exclaimed.

She shrugged, with a little smile. 'About time.'

I went to her and enveloped her in my arms.

She returned my embrace with warmth. Also obedience. A warm obedience. I let her go and sat down on her dressing-table stool to look at her. She threw herself once more on to the bed and lounged there pushing her hair off her face. She was pale.

'So,' she said.

'So!' I echoed, and we both laughed uneasily.

I laced my fingers and stared at them. Then I straightened up and glanced out of the window, rubbed my knee. 'Katrine didn't want to let me in,' I remarked, looking out at the courtyard. I was as nervous as I had been the first time I met her. I had been nervous then because by that time I already knew that her mother was the only woman for me.

Naomi laughed now. 'Katrine doesn't have much excitement in her life. Unlike me!' She stretched and turned on her side the better to look at me. 'How are you, Jean-René? Are you well?'

I couldn't hold her gaze for long. It was a bold, bright, curious stare, one I had never seen from her. I looked at the floor. 'I'm—' I began, and swallowed. 'I'm . . .' The floor heaved like toffee. I fumbled for a handkerchief and buried my face in it.

'Oh, surely you've stopped crying!' she exclaimed, in a voice which made me go cold. 'I stopped months ago! I'm better now. I go to school, I have fun with my cousins. Everything is fine!'

'Shut up, Naomi, please shut up,' I pleaded through the handkerchief.

'I'm sorry. What would you like me to say?'

'That you're glad to see me?' I quavered, hating myself.

'OK. I'm glad to see you.'

I crumpled the handkerchief in my hand. 'I'm glad to see you too, Naomi. Except that I really am. I'm not play-acting.'

Naomi snorted, began idly to plait a lock of her hair. The sleeves of her pullover were too long: they came down over her hands.

'You know,' I said next, 'I almost preferred it when you screamed.'

'I didn't.' She shook out the plait she had made. 'I went through hell,' she added casually.

'And now you're torturing me for it!'

'No, I'm not.' She sighed. 'You came in here looking like an undertaker, I tried to brighten you up, that's all.'

I scrubbed vexedly at my eyes. 'It's only because of seeing you, I'm sorry! It's because you've grown!' I accused her.

But she just said, 'You should have come back sooner, got it over with.'

'Ha! How could I?' I croaked. 'Juliette practically barred me from the house!'

'No! She did not!' Naomi was firm, staring at me intently. 'I know she never did that. And you're a grown-up man, aren't you? Even if she had, you could have refused to take no for an answer!'

'No, Naomi, I am not a man! Not any more! If I were a man I'd have . . . Oh, God, Naomi, if I could have done anything—'

'*Ah, non!*' she cried, in a loud voice. 'Not that! You cannot have thought you could come here and say *that*!'

I was silent. I watched her speak again through pale lips. Her eyes were lustreless. 'Everything is – over now,' she said. 'I don't think you've taken that in. If you had, you wouldn't come here and say what you said.

'I'm not saying this just to be nasty,' she continued after a pause. 'But I have to say, "It's finished," because it *is* finished, and because – because' – on a great expulsion of breath – 'it's the only way for me to, ah, to continue my life, you see.' She breathed in slowly to balance herself, to emphasize her message. 'I don't think I'll ever go to the house. But I want you to come and see me again. Now that we've had this talk it'll be better, I promise.'

There was a long silence. I sat nodding, sniffing. Out in the courtyard a bucket rolled on the cobbles. Shadows harried the sunshine across the walls under a fast April sky. I thought over all the things I had planned to say to her, and said none of them. She was right. There was no point any more.

Presently I cleared my throat.

'Don't mention her again, for God's sake,' she said quickly.

I almost laughed. 'I was only going to ask you why you're in bed on a nice day like this. Are you ill? I asked Katrine but she didn't say.'

'I have my monthly pains. Katrine would *never* tell a man about that!'

'Shall I make you a tisane?'

'You can't. This isn't your house.' Again the calm, bald stare, but she was smiling now. 'Katrine will do it, if she dares. The only tisane in the house is for Grand'mère, not for us children.'

'You're not a child. You're a woman. You always used to take tisane!'

'Tante Juliette doesn't agree with it.'

This made me angrier than anything else about Juliette Whelan. I realized at that moment that I had always disliked her. I wanted to shake her. I wanted to shake Naomi as well, jolt her out of this dogged tranquillity and make her cry along with me, but I had seen her in her affliction and I had no right to visit that on her again. No one did.

I said: 'I'll be back,' kissed her on the forehead, and left.

I no longer thought of blame. The question seemed irrelevant, a self-indulgence on my part when compared to the monstrous extent of her pain. I left that part of it alone. I ceased to wonder whether she would come to love Juliette more than her mother. I merely offered her myself in any way I thought would help her. Over the next half-year I saw her frequently. She would call me and I would meet her after school and take her for a hot chocolate in St-Cyprien. We sat talking about schoolwork, cousins, nothing in particular, setting a pattern to our relationship which has deepened but never changed. Then in November, the second winter after Genevieve's death, Henri Palastrier turned up in my field.

He came into my small life largely, inoffensively, like an ox into a parlour. He did not try to absolve me, as Juliette had done so cruelly; neither did he order the strict repression that Naomi dealt out to herself like morphine as many times a day as she needed. He offered me certain facts as he understood them. That is all he did. That is all he was: a man in possession of certain facts. He began to save me, I think.

SEVENTEEN

I looked up to see her looking down at me.

A pretty brown face, chin on bare brown forearm. Naughty eyes. *'Oh-oh,'* she called softly. *'Tu as chaud, hein?'*

I shielded my eyes from the sun, felt the sweat run down my neck as I tilted my head.

'I've been walking since daybreak,' I replied. The window was only a few feet above me, the street silent and deserted at three in the afternoon. I hardly needed to raise my voice. 'And it's a hot day!'

She vanished to reappear an instant later at the door: opening it a crack, peering round.

'Are you lost?' she asked.

'No.'

'You looked lost!' She was smiling now. She had a gap between her front teeth.

I put down my pack. 'To be lost,' I said, smiling back, 'you need a destination.'

She opened the door wider. She invited me in with a little jerk of her head.

'You were striding down the street like a troubadour!' she would say later, giggling. So tall and strong with your hat on. I couldn't resist!'

She took me upstairs and sat me down in a little worn velvet armchair. She brought up a tray set with coffee-cups, coffee-pot, two bottles of beer, two slices of melon. She kneeled down on the floor in front of me and offered me the things one after the other: the slice of melon, the cup of coffee, the bottle of beer. Slowly and carefully she fed me. She took no interest in the food and drink herself, so that I had second helpings of everything. I badly wanted to laugh, but I managed – at least at first – to refrain. I found that I couldn't help but go along with her, in whatever game it was she turned out to be playing. Besides, I was thirsty.

The curtains were lace. She had unhooked them so that they fell across the window and made patterns on the bed and the carpet and on her face.

'Where have you come from?' she asked me.

'Marseilles.' I wondered if she were a prostitute. If she were, I hoped my saying 'Marseilles' would put her off, because I had no money.

'Not on foot!' was all she said in reply, with a chuckle.

'No, not all the way on foot!'

'But you aren't from Marseilles.'

'No. I'm from Lille – that is, my family comes originally from a small place near Arras, but I grew up in Lille . . .'

'You've come a long way, then.' Eyes full of fun, lips on the brink of laughter. So I amused her too. I didn't mind.

'I've stopped at many places in between,' I replied after a pause. 'It's taken me, oh, over a year.'

'Tell me all the places you've been.'

'No!' Then I laughed out loud; I had to. 'I can't be bothered! I'm tired! And I want to hear about you now!'

'Oh, no, not yet, I haven't finished. Where were you going when I saw you?'

'I hadn't decided. I was just looking for somewhere to rest.' I bit into my second slice of melon, glanced at her rapt face, snorted again with laughter. 'Is that it? No more questions?'

'Yes, oh, please, one more!' she pleaded in delight. 'What do you do for a living? How do you survive?'

'I sing for my supper! Tell me, do you do this to every passer-by?'

Her eyes were almost green in the dim room. There was a rosette of light on her cheek. As she moved her head it shifted down on to her neck. A snowflake: I wanted to chase it with my tongue.

'Ooh, Palastrier,' she said once. 'Lovely man, but he wanted marriage in the end . . . you know it was his ring that fooled me, he had a big fat opal, a bachelor's ring. I never thought he'd want to take it off for a wedding band.' She told me how he took her to a grand hotel for the New Year, she said, gave her a fur coat, gave her diamonds – in fact I remember her calling her first winter with him 'the winter of diamonds and freedom', in a lyrical fashion. The diamonds she had remaining from that winter were gone long before she died, the last of them converted to beams and roof-tiles for our house. She was left with paste replicas and I would never have been able to restore even one of the originals to her. As for the freedom, I used to assume she meant simply 'no marriage'. 'Promise me, sweetheart, you won't ever propose, I've had enough marriage in my life!' And what about us – were we free, Henri and I? Was I free even then, at the beginning?

I camped by the river on the edge of town, half a mile from her house – her room, I should say; the rest of the building belonged to the owner of the dress shop on the ground floor. Every afternoon for five days I knocked at her door. Every afternoon for five days she appeared, led me upstairs, gave me coffee, fruits, beer. We talked, that is all we did, until sunset, and then I would leave. This was an unspoken routine. I assumed naturally that she had a life to lead and that these hours were convenient to her: discreetly I did not question. Will you come tomorrow? she would say, and I would shrug, and return at the same time.

I was a city boy. My father, when his father died, had sold the family farm and moved to Lille when I was still a

babe in arms. He sold toys for a living. I helped him in the
school holidays. Then when I left school I worked, from age
eighteen to twenty-five, in an insurance office. I grew into a
bright, diligent, methodical person (typical only child, typical
son of self-made man): I kept up and developed my many
hobbies. In my twenties I was still going out in the evenings
and on Sundays, taking photographs of people, incidents.
Even now I have files of these photographs: a dog barking at
a car on fire; a crashed milk lorry flooding the road, a child
in front of it ankle-deep in the white river; two shopping
women in the same hat, quizzing each other . . . I sold them
to newspapers and magazines, I wrote captions, I elaborated
the captions into amusing stories. I began – with a secret
smile – to call myself a freelance photo-journalist.

I was thrifty. I was engaged at twenty-one and from that
moment had saved nearly everything for my marriage, our
house. My betrothed and I set our wedding for one September and in July she ran off to Reims with an air-traffic
controller. When I had recovered from the shock – the shock
of relief, that is – I put my cameras in my bag and left my
gold in the bank; I took a couple of thousand francs with me
– the rest I intended to earn – and headed off south with the
idea of seeing how far I'd get. Now here I was, twenty-seven
years old, sitting every evening beneath the restless trees on
the river-bank, poking my fire with a stick, visiting a woman
in the afternoons.

Now I can hardly remember what it felt like to be that
boy who knew nothing. I have to tell myself, I have to restate
in my mind, that yes, there was a time when I didn't even
know her name, when I knew only that she existed, that she
lived in a small room above a dress shop on the main street
of a country town in the south-west of France. That she was
slightly older than I had originally thought (older than me, at
least), and that she wore a wedding ring (she didn't talk
about it, and I was the last one to ask her). I didn't know
about her sister, her English brother-in-law, her imposing
mother, her deceased respected father. I wouldn't even ask
her until my first week in her house, after I was overtaken by

a weaving van on the river road, two wild boys from the town inside: 'Ho!' they yelled as they passed. 'What's it like to fuck the judge's daughter?' and roared away.

I had no plans to stay. I was on my way up from the Mediterranean coast at the time; I think I was heading for Paris, but I remember also entertaining a wild notion of returning in the winter to Marseilles and boarding a ship. Certainly I had no intention of remaining in the area more than a fortnight. I had to get to a city sooner or later and take some casual work. Here in the country – I could see, I hardly had to ask – there would be nothing in the autumn and winter and it was already mid-September when I strode down that main street for the first time. I could imagine what they would be like in the winter, these hillsides: each little house with its stack of wood the size of another little house, its plume of blue smoke, its big black dog. Shut up tight till the spring.

On the fifth day, I asked her her name.

We were playing cards. She had made a fan of her cards and was hiding her face behind it. When I spoke she straightened her shoulders, inclined her neck, and bent her wrist to bring the cards gracefully down to her waist in a flamenco gesture. 'Mercedes!' She pronounced it, frowning theatrically, with a Spanish lisp.

'You've shown me your hand, Mercedes,' I said. 'Now tell me your real name.'

'Tell me yours!' she rejoined, fluttering with her fan.

I refused. I was not going to be beaten like this. I might have let it go had she not challenged me in turn. Even now I'm not sure how much, at that stage, I really wanted her to tell me. But after that retort I pressed her, I demanded to know her name, she demanded to know mine; we both began to guess through the alphabet, each shaking our heads and chuckling as we went from *A* to *B* to *C* without success.

She uncrossed her legs and spread them in a vee to encompass me. She stopped playing, but made me continue. With each wrong guess I made she shuffled a tiny bit towards me. I listed all the *D*s I could think of, and then all the *E*s, and she came slowly towards me on her bottom, nearer and nearer until she had to lift her knees over mine. She was smiling, silent, shutting her eyes to mean *wrong*.

'Françoise,' I said, and slid my hand underneath her skirt along the top of her thigh.

She grasped it and pushed it down between her legs.

'Aah,' I said.

She rolled her body forwards and took a deep breath. Try again, she whispered, her arms around me. 'You're so near.'

Open-mouthed I kissed her neck. 'Fernande,' I mumbled, after a long, confused interval.

'*Idiot!*' she hissed in my ear. 'Next letter!'

'Germaine,' I said at last, when I could next speak, and then I ran out of inspiration. We had to make love nameless.

On the sixth day her greeting changed. This time there was no fruit, coffee, beer, armchairs. No card games. For all the succeeding days there were none of these things. Instead she pulled me roughly in and planted her mouth on mine like a sea anemone; instead she tore open my jeans and plunged her small brown square-knuckled hand down inside, she said, *Ooh, quickly quickly, I've been waiting all day.* It was all I could do to stagger to her room. Day followed day. Each evening I would swear to leave the town in the morning. Each noon would find me on my river-bank, waiting.

After a fortnight I packed up my little tent and went jolting all the way to Bordeaux in the train, and from Bordeaux I went home.

For a while I helped my father with his business. I managed to sell a story on bull-fighting festivals in the villages of the Landes region to a local newspaper. I did not tell my parents about Genevieve (how we had laughed, when she had finally divulged). Only after three weeks, when my father suddenly said: 'You've come home to arrange your affairs, then,' did I realize that I was not going to stay. I told him I had met a woman – in agony I told him, fearing that I would have to reveal how little I knew about her, but he just nodded, harrumphed, said, 'Don't let time pass too quickly for you.' They never met her, my parents.

Still I refused to acknowledge that I had made any kind of decision about her. I bought a van and drove back down to the south-west. I went to St-Cyprien telling myself I was simply passing through. I parked beside the shop and knocked on the door. A dark-haired woman in her fifties appeared, pursed her mouth, said that she had paid the rent and left.

I went into a small supermarket on the main street, one that I had used in the summer. On my way in I bumped into a small dark-haired girl in a woollen dress who ran out past me, shouting, 'Maman, you said Choco-BN biscuits! Choco-BN!' before scampering away down the street.

She was standing with her back to me, feet apart, reading the label on a jar of jam. Her wire basket was heavily loaded: as I watched she bent to put it on the floor beside her. She swivelled one high heel, debated, replaced the jam on the shelf. She turned as the black-haired child came back into the shop whimpering, saying, 'Maman, I turned my ankle.' She opened her arms to receive the little girl.

I watched her comfort the child, buy her the coveted biscuits and pay for her goods. I did not approach them. Only after they had gone did I select my few things. Waiting for my change I looked up to see them go past, the mother and daughter, roaring down the main street in a dirty white convertible.

'She's living out of town now,' said the shopkeeper.

I started. His face was impassive, but I saw the glimmer deep in his dark eyes. I thought: He saw me during the summer. Then I thought: He thinks she's contemptible. I felt the anger heat my skin like a blush. 'Where,' I said sharply.

He raised his eyebrows and gave a deep, insulting sniff. 'Couldn't say. Go, quickly – jump into your new bus and follow her, why not.'

Instead of cursing him I did as he said. I followed her out on to the river road, across the bridge and up over the hill, down into a village. Just beyond the village she turned sharp left down a stony track and I let her go. I drove on up the next hill. Perhaps I would be able to see her house from the top.

I saw trees, a stream. A patch of open land. A roof, a tower, a white car.

I watched her come out with a bucket. She threw grain on the ground. Two, three, four hens appeared. The child came out, pulling a red jersey over her head, pretending to get her head stuck, waving her arms around.

I had to go down there. I had no fixed notion that my destiny lay there: on the contrary, faced with the evidence of it, I was reeling for the first time at the full extent of my ignorance. All my instincts were shot: if there was a daughter, who was to say there wouldn't be a husband after all? I stood there, cursing myself.

All the same I had to go down there. I knew it now. Why else had I returned if not to see her again? Tomorrow I would go. In the morning, when the girl was at school. Yes. That is what I would do. If there was a husband present, I would think of a pretext. I was good at making up stories . . .

'I happened to be wearing a reptilian old leather jacket, the day I finally plucked up courage to do it,' I said. 'And my hair was much longer. I think she was a bit shocked by my appearance.'

'Hardly the way a suitor should look,' Palastrier agreed.

We were sitting, comfortably sprawled, in the drawing room of his house. It was my first visit to his villa, two years ago now.

'A suitor!' I exclaimed.

'That is what you intended, wasn't it? To ask for the hand of the lady in the castle?' He refilled my glass and leaned back to consider me through half-closed eyes. 'If you wanted anything less you would have approached her in the shop, or perhaps followed her straight to her house. Which was the greater obstacle – Naomi, or the wedding ring?'

I sighed. 'The ring didn't make any difference to me. My

God, if everyone with a wedding ring were unavailable! I took no notice of it.'

'What? You must have thought about it. Or maybe you removed it in your mind, such was your desire to marry her yourself.'

'I never wanted to marry her! That was your obsession!'

We roared with laughter. 'I admit,' said Palastrier, wiping his eyes, 'that Naomi in her younger days would be enough in herself to put anyone off!'

He loved to talk about Naomi. I think we talked as much about Naomi as we did about Genevieve. I didn't understand at first; Naomi had only just left my house, I was still shy of her, Genevieve's death overshadowed that loss for me. But I came to realize that Palastrier, who had watched her grow up in his house, had only really begun to miss her when Genevieve died; as if her death, by closing off that period in his life, made Naomi's absence keener. Since he had no one except me to reminisce with, my company afforded him the luxury of recalling the years spent not only with Genevieve but with her daughter.

It was round about this time – my first visit to his house, I mean – that Naomi became aware that there was a friendship developing between her two stepfathers (self-styled stepfathers, I should say). Sixteen, she must have been, when she began to awaken sufficiently from her own trauma to look at me and say: 'You see a lot of each other, don't you, you and Henri! What on earth can you find to talk about?' Bright-eyed, knowing and not knowing, daring me to say. Now she is a smart and beautiful eighteen-year-old, working for her *baccalauréat* 'until my fingers bleed' as she puts it. Learning to drive, too; Nicholas Whelan lets her practise in his car between lessons. (This is illegal of course but he is an Englishman with a mind of his own; even after all these years he refuses to surrender entirely to the French state.) I've passed her several times on the road with him – grins, waves. She always calls me after these chance encounters and arranges to meet me the next time I am in Sarlat. (She studies there now, and my newspaper offices are in the main street.)

We go to a bar and she cajoles me. Serious, firm, she says, 'Jean-René, you should think about moving. The time has come, Jean-René. What is there for you here? Think about it at least . . .' She's changed so much – naturally – that I find her quite frightening, feeling as I do that I am the same, still . . .

But Palastrier's house! I had known for years about his villa down on the Mediterranean coast, the house he had built – not with his hands, needless to say, but with his construction company. 'Juliette hated that place,' Genevieve had said. 'She visited once – once only. Do you know what she said afterwards? "If proof were needed" – she said that, "if proof were needed"! – "the lamentable vulgarity of M. Palastrier's home testifies to his low origins." Hee, hee! If proof were needed, that proves what a bitch she is, my sister . . .'

I had laughed, but I confess I became sick of hearing about this palace as we dug and scrubbed and painted and shivered our way through the first winter in the ruin. Naomi was prey to thunderous moods which her mother could only dispel by doing imitations of Mme Boulas, who hastened wobbling up the main street on Fridays to the bread van calling for '*t-rrrois ficelles pour mon beau-f-rreyre*' in a voice so piercing that the echo rang off the church bells. Genevieve added a lopsided grin to her impression which made poor Mme Boulas seem quite demented but which broke Naomi every time. But even Genevieve was tight-lipped at times, and by the end of the winter they had almost persuaded me it was I who had forced them to live here. Now, the actual sight of their former home made me ashamed of my past irritation. They couldn't have had an inkling of what it would be like, to renovate an old rural dwelling and live in it at the same time.

It really was a villa – a real villa, just outside Toulon; a modern, white-walled house with ornate wooden shutters, grilles, verandas, balconies. At night it was floodlit with soft gold lamps set like scattered tiger's-eyes into the terrace tiles. (I could picture Juliette wincing at the floodlights.) By day it sat, magnificently shaded with palm-trees, high on its scrubby hill overlooking the sea. Palastrier led me inside and I stood open-mouthed in a vast room the size and feel of a swimming-pool, glass sculptures reflecting a watery light on to pale green walls, low tables made of a matt black stone I wanted to run my fingers over, deep leather couches and armchairs. I gaped similarly in the shadowed bedrooms, the Olympian bathrooms: satin, marble, velvet, mirror-glass. I gasped at the blue cube of a real swimming-pool outside with its retractable roof, at the oasis-garden (with parakeets? No – I have supplied the parakeets in my imagination). I shook the hand of Madelon whose name Naomi had made familiar: a stately woman in black dress and court shoes whom I could not imagine playing with Naomi until she smiled and spoke. This was extraordinary. The Romans of Provence must have lived like this. It was the opulence of it, the feeling of establishment, of home. 'My God,' I said to Palastrier on that first visit, 'she must have been in a desperate condition!' and he understood too quickly, too thoroughly, what I meant.

'Indeed she was,' he returned. 'She was in a "desperate" condition, as you say, after she left me. It was a wretched interlude for her, I think, that time before she met you. I saw her enough to know, though by that time I could do nothing to help her. Certainly she must have been "desperate" to disregard Nicholas Whelan's advice and buy that millstone of a village house!'

Something harsh in his tone, the bleakness of the little joke, made me look at him. Seeing my anxiety he softened.

'You've done a good job on that place, Jean-René, I didn't mean to offend you.'

'No, of course not.'

'It was her choice!' he went on more firmly. 'That is what I was trying to say. She did it. She cast herself into that state!'

I turned away and walked out of the room. I went swiftly down an undiscovered corridor and – feeling rather foolish now – found myself in a glass-roofed steamy jungle full of hanging foliage and tropical fruits of all kinds. I felt Palastrier's heavy hand on my shoulder.

'Come on, come on,' he grumbled. 'Now that you're here at last, let's have a drink. Unless you'd prefer a mango?'

I said that he was a man in possession of certain facts. I said also that he began to save me. But what was of value to me from the point of view of salvation was the faith he had, the depth of his understanding of the facts, rather than the facts themselves. My salvation is a complex story, for it is not due to Palastrier alone.

I had berated him the day he appeared in my field. Genevieve a year or more in the ground and he had the – the face to wander into my life like an ox, like a tame bear in his film director's coat and his expensive shoes, darting gentle implications from those lugubrious eyes, loading a challenge into every inoffensive remark! All right, I admit now: I put the challenges and the implications there. I was neck-deep in paranoia at the time. When I wasn't actually engaged in work I saw no one; as I said, I had spoken to no one for four days when he came. I had so much to say and only walls and trees and animals to address. I used to laugh at Genevieve for talking to the chickens: now I did it all the time. 'You seem quite isolated here,' Palastrier had said mildly, referring simply to the secluded situation of the house, but that was enough to do it: out popped the bung and my anger flooded into my kitchen to crash against the walls. Of course I am alone, I raged: Juliette has taken Naomi away, Juliette has infected my girl with her own repellent fatalism and turned her into a little zombie, Juliette has denied us the chance to grieve together. Juliette, lastly, has looked down her snub nose at me as if I were a hired boy! 'She said to me, "Oh, you weren't her keeper, you were never her keeper!"' I cried. 'She *disgusts* me!'

Palastrier thrust his hands into the sleeves of his coat – the kitchen was unheated, I had offered nothing to warm him – and gazed wordlessly up at me from where he sat perched on a small stool. Had I made him sit on that or had he chosen it?

'She was ignorant!' I went on, as loud as before. 'She acted as though she had been waiting all the time for our lives here to be ruined – as though she'd known all along, and yet she knew nothing about Genevieve's . . . Genevieve's mind!'

'Did you know what was going on in Genevieve's mind?' Palastrier asked.

I took a deep breath. When I spoke again it was as quietly as him. 'No,' I said finally. 'No. I thought I did, but obviously she kept certain things from me. She didn't tell me that Belar had summoned her. Do you think I'd have let it happen if I had known? But at least I didn't *pretend* that I knew!'

'And that is what Juliette did? She pretended to know?'

Again I had to breathe. 'She said . . . ah, she said: "These things are mysteries, Jean-René. We, her family, understood her circumstances." She talked about doom, for Heaven's sake! She exonerated herself and in the same breath claimed a superior intimation! Implicitly I was the ignorant one . . . !' I was weary now. I put my head in my hands. I felt that we were stumbling about in ordure to no purpose at all.

Palastrier spoke. 'There is an implicit claim only that she wasn't as surprised as you. That is not so disgusting, is it? You were shattered: she was merely horrified and grief-stricken. She was grief-stricken you know. I was there at the funeral. I saw her.'

He sighed. 'Perhaps what Juliette was trying to put into words was that she had suspected, with perhaps only an inch of her mind, that her sister – always neurotic, you cannot deny that – would one day, somehow, lay herself open to danger from that man. And then her sister died. But what exactly are you saying she pretended to "know"? She only ever talked about feelings to me, never knowledge. What can one *know* in these situations? My friend,' he concluded, 'on my way here I passed a very comfortable-looking hotel with a bar. As you have offered me nothing, I suggest we go there before my feet freeze to the floor.'

So we began. We repaired to the bar, I drank too much,

he drank too much. I offered him a bed for the night: politely he declined, preferring to stay at the hotel.

'Who did it?' he said suddenly, rhetorically, towards the end of the evening, startling me out of a cognac reverie. 'Juliette didn't do it. Juliette didn't fire the gun. It was your lover, Jean-René, your lover and mine. We may not have known it was going to happen, but that does not mean that fate brought this grief upon us all. Genevieve invited it. Accidents have a cause, and it was perhaps her rashly undertaken encounter with a violent man, as much as anything else, which caused this one. Look at it this way.' He leaned forward so that his face was close to mine. 'Forget doom, if it makes you angry; I am not fond of it myself. Think of actions. She and him together. Say that he did it, why not. But she went there. If anybody knew him she did. It was of their *making*.'

So we began. I was safe with him. However far and fast I fell, he would be waiting at the bottom. I could say anything and he would not so much as frown. He would drive up from the coast, visit Naomi, call on me – usually without warning. Once I returned to find him sitting patiently in my kitchen on the same small stool. We would drink in the hotel bar and he would pay. We would talk about Genevieve: regularly, once on each of these evenings, I would ask 'What happened there!' and he would say: 'We haven't got the answer to that, Jean René, not because of fate but because the only other person who knew is dead along with her.' This response seemed natural, sensible, extremely comforting. Never at any point did it occur to me that he was being evasive.

We met like this, once every couple of months, for a year. Then there was a long gap. Naomi when I asked her told me that he had gone to Mexico. Brightly she remarked on our growing friendship, she said: 'What do you find to talk about!' Then in the summer he returned, swarthy in a pink shirt.

'I've got a new car,' he announced. 'I want to show it off

to you. Come, drive with me to Toulon!' So off we went; he showed me round his villa, called my house a millstone and told me the same old home truth – 'It was of her *doing*!' – and I found myself discomfited among his tropical fruits.

And then drink in hand I stretched my legs in his swimming-pool *salon*, mollified, listening to the leather creak, raising my glass to him. I sighed, reflection following our laughter about Naomi's early antics.

'It's strange to think now,' I remarked, 'that there was a time when I didn't know Naomi existed. Or Belar, or Nicholas, or Juliette. Or you, for that matter. When it was just me and her, and I didn't know her name.'

'Innocence, innocence!' Palastrier rolled his eyes. 'Hard to remember that innocence, let alone recapture it.' He began to chat away, and I leaned back, lulled.

No. It never seemed that he was being evasive. I would swear he wasn't even doing it consciously in the beginning. I dare say in my turn I was equally unconscious, for it never occurred to me that I was interrogating when first I gently prompted these reminiscences. But the appetite comes with eating, and soon I would start to wonder how much longer I could hold back, under the cover of genial interlocutor, from saying to him: Enough of these titbits. You know something. What is it that you know and have not told me, Henri Palastrier?

'Innocence!' he sighed, and began. It was three years after her death and I would soon be hungry, but he did not give me my fill that time. It would be a long time before he gave me that.

EIGHTEEN

She was beautiful when she was young, that is the first thing I discovered from Henri. Far more beautiful than her sister Juliette – although by the time I met her I would say that Juliette was the prettier. I had never allowed prettiness of Juliette Whelan before, but seeing Genevieve when she was young has made it easier for me to acknowledge that Juliette today has a very appealing face, very good skin, and that seven years ago, when I met them both, Juliette looked better than her sister. Genevieve at that time was thirty-two and striking, but there was already a dullness to her complexion, the beginnings of a drinker's face, now I think of it: in fact I am sure of it, because that first year we were together I barred spirits from the house and the blood sang again in her cheeks, proof that her looks had ebbed because of the drinking and the stress of the previous two years. But it was clear to me, when I looked at Palastrier's photographs, that she would never again have been as she was at twenty-six, twenty-seven, for she was gorgeous then, she had an apricot bloom, a skin which was one vital tone duskier than her pale eyes demanded; and the drink seemed to feed the bloom and not kill it, when she was young . . .

Why should she be as she was then? Even if I'd seen her

as she was – she had no photographs of herself – I wouldn't have wanted her like that. I wanted the woman who announced her first grey hair with a squawk, who came to me with it in her hand and I swore it was blonde but to no avail. Thereafter she let them grow, though they never came in great number. I could never see them, I had to search for them and pull them out; *myope*, she said when I missed them. One afternoon M. Pasquier came by when we were sitting like apes on the veranda, my fingers raking through her hair. 'Frightful attack of fleas!' she had called. 'We think they're from the bedding!' The following day the old man's daughter-in-law called with some medicated shampoo, *'pour . . . Madame.'* Would she be grey now? I will be grey before my time, I know. I already have a small plantation of them at my temples like rogue oats in corn: they are strangers, they have a different texture. I can understand her initial revulsion. She visited my grey hairs on me, I think, now that I am the age she was when she died. I wondered, flipping through Palastrier's photographs, listening to him talk, what we'd be like together, Genevieve and I, in a fictitious living future: I used to dwell on this, but not any more. I no longer want her back – though it is not because she turned me grey before my time. I am not as petty as that.

The first photograph I saw on my first visit. A print in a silver frame, sharpe black-and-white in the gloom of the master bedroom of masterful Palastrier. Her face like a bright star, big smile and eyes glowing, young, young, young. Moved, I did not draw attention to it, but Palastrier, who was pulling on the curtain-cord to usher in the light, remarked: 'She was twenty-six in that one' – without looking at me, staring up at the pelmet as if he detected trouble with the mechanism. 'I've plenty of others . . . do you want to see?'

He pulled them out of a desk drawer, small buff envelopes stuffed so tight that the flaps pointed up in the air. Not all the photographs were of her. He eased them out of their flimsy casings and pretended, with a twinkle, to shuffle them before dealing Genevieve out on to the black stone table-top.

'Never sorted them,' he grunted. 'This is the quickest way.'
As he dealt, he talked. We did not look at all of them on my
first visit, nor on my second. Each time we met, we devoted
a little time to the photographs and his story – not too long:
we were careful not to become obsessed.

The one by my bed is the first one, he said, taken in
May, though she came in the winter. It took a long time for
her to settle in. Naomi was much quicker; Naomi thought it
all a great joke and apart from an unnerving belief in her
own power to walk on water (special swimming-pool meas-
ures had to be taken) speedily got on with the events of her
tumultuous life. One day in January – they had only just
arrived – Palastrier was awoken from an afternoon nap by
Naomi in her nightdress.

'Maman has taken Madelon shopping,' she announced,
'and I need to know how to flush the lavatories here. They're
all different, and none of them have normal handles.'

Palastrier took her all round the house and she flushed
every single lavatory except the one in the downstairs cloak-
room which had an old-fashioned high cistern and a chain
she could not reach. He had been obliged to lengthen it with
a piece of string.

'Of course I'd thought about what it would be like,' he
said to me, 'having a small girl in the house. But I didn't
know what it was going to be like, do you see what I mean?'
with a great burst of laughter as I sympathized! But however
intractable she proved later, Palastrier never forgot walking
with that four-year-old child through his darkened house on
that January afternoon, how the house was strange to her
and she was not afraid . . .

Genevieve was not so quick. Genevieve who had – with
Palastrier's fervent consent – desired and instigated and
arranged the whole menage, Genevieve kept her coat on for
weeks. On the first night she did not take it off until they
went upstairs to bed. She did not even put her bag down
until she had given Naomi her supper, until she was sure
what Naomi would eat in the morning. Palastrier asked her
if she was cold but she shook her head and laughed, shifting

from foot to foot and shoving her hands deeper into the fur. One afternoon he came home unusually early and heard laughter from upstairs. Going up, he found her alone in a bedroom, in her coat, laughing. He laughed as well, he was so entertained, and they undressed immediately.

At least I think they did. Palastrier did not say so, but the manner of his telling, the warmth in his face, his abrupt conclusion of the tale, made me think that they did. Or had Genevieve herself told me what happened next? I remember thinking as he spoke, This must have been just after their first New Year, and picturing acres of marble foyer, lights dancing from a huge chandelier. On this subject it is difficult to separate their voices, Genevieve's and Henri's . . .

He was too sensible to push her. The coat business did not worry him. It wasn't accompanied by melancholy silences, unexplained absences, or anything else that might signify regret. (Time enough for that later.) No: apart from the coat she seemed perfectly happy if a little stiff, and anyway it all passed along with the winter. Spring came, summer: she shed her coat and basked. She sat in her robe with the butterknife in her hand (The *silk* robe for every day! The *silver* butterknife!) and made tartines for her daughter. She sprinkled chocolate powder on the buttered slice and wiped her face, she left a faint dusting of dark powder on that fantastic scented ephemeral skin and Palastrier nearly fell over his feet with desire. Sometimes I hear people say, 'He'd have given her anything she wanted,' and generally I want to remonstrate, incredulous, but it was true for him. He would have. He tried to give her too much in the end.

The sky turned a pale, hot blue. She turned over in bed and mumbled to him, Henri, Henri, but he would always be gone before she woke. He would return to her early in the evening and grab her gently, bearishly, Henri, Henri. She was a beast, she painted and pampered, she bought clothes, a car, she revelled in everything including the courtship of his friends. So much so that Palastrier wondered whether it was the sheer luxury of his life which had made her so stiff and shivery in the beginning, and which was now turning her head. He had known all about her from the moment they met, the kind of good family she came from, the kind of disapproved marriage she had made which had taken her so far from home. Then he began to wonder whether perhaps she was acting as if it had turned her head in order to test him. In order to find out, by making use of the wealth he had so unashamedly on show, what kind of mistress he wanted her to be. He said nothing.

He need not have been concerned. She basked, she slumbered, she lived like a seal, but seals are equipped only with flippers and there were too many things to do, experiences to grab, for her to live like that for long. She ceased to roll over: Henri, she said, climbing into her stockings, I have to get changed now, the guests will be arriving, read Naomi a story instead: and he would roar with laughter and protest, It won't be the same thing at all! She ceased to be idle. She went in her new open-top car to her morning tennis lesson, she went to the market and bought food for dinner. She and Madelon would make vichyssoise for thirty in the kitchen, their hair in scarves. (A week after the first of these banquets Genevieve ordered the installation of a complete modern kitchen. 'Never will we scrub at that stone sink again!' she said to Madelon.) In the hot afternoon – the afternoons stay hot down there in the summer – she drove out, Henri's right-hand man, to the sites of villas, gîtes, hotels, to have terse discussions with the foreman. The men could not fool her. She knew what they were thinking. They watched her climb out of her open-top car and take off her sunglasses, and they looked at each other and kept their opinions to themselves. She was Mme Genevieve, with her small girl inseparable from the doll which was the only grimy thing in the house. Happy and rich she was, strong, wife but not wife: she thrived on it. Her big sports watch was white against her tan. The booze gave a sheen to her skin. Henri, she said at night, take off your bloody half-moons and come to bed . . .

'Years!' I exclaimed. 'She spent years with you!' It sounded absurd, if not rude, the moment I said it, but Palastrier did not take it amiss. Rather the contrary, if I could trust his shy smile. I detected pride there, in the smile and the lift of the chin. *Of course she did*, he meant, and I was abashed even though he had not taken offence. He had made her happy and was still proud of it. That is the mark of the man: knowing what he knew, he could still keep the good memories. He had the strength to hold them uncontaminated above that knowledge.

Installed, established years. Naomi's great problems at school, her strange ankles which sent her grieving to the physiotherapist on sports afternoons, her reading and writing difficulties. That child – he has pictures of her too, with her heavy hanks of black hair, her flip-flop feet – fighting to conquer her dyslexia, face dark with egg-laying concentration as she persisted in having *arivocaire* or even *avirocaire* for supper however hard she tried to do otherwise. Palastrier told her, 'It doesn't matter now. You can have your *arivocaire* and we'll have our *haricots verts*, and tomorrow we'll go, you and I, to see the lady who will help you with words like these.' Palastrier spent a mint of money on Genevieve's girl so that she could speak and spell. Palastrier sat reading with her, his voice a deep murmur which penetrated the whole house.

He had crises himself, in business and health. There were meetings which went on until the small hours: Genevieve sat with the tense-faced men at two in the morning making telephone calls, discussing possible solutions. She sat with him in hospital after his heart attack, making him laugh until he got tired. She bought great heaps of flowers when Madelon's mother died and stood beside Henri at the funeral. She was the one who found out about the business of Xavier and the teak doors, for Xavier was a crook and wanted by the police in Spain, and it was Genevieve who realized in the nick of time that he had stolen the doors, and so she drove after him like a fury almost to Perpignan and stopped him single-handed on the road . . .

Really, I cannot blame Palastrier for asking her to marry him.

Was she acting her way through those years? She might
have performed a bit in the beginning. I think Palastrier was
right to suspect that sybaritic coquette of those early months,
but only because what came after was so genuine in comparison. Why should she want to act? She had a big rich fun life,
but it wasn't as if he stood between her and the streets. And
anyway it wasn't all staunch and steadfast; she was as
inconsistent as the next human being. As Palastrier put it:
'She'd float off for days at a time. I'd find her alone making
cow-eyes at the window in the evenings. I'd go to see what
she was looking at, but it was always damn all.' But there
was an unexpected bitterness, as when he had described
'that millstone of a village house', almost a brutality of tone
which made me look up at him and reply rather coldly, 'You
sound as if you're describing a stupid woman.'

Immediately he retracted, saying simply that it made him
a little impatient, that was all, unjustifiably. 'We get these
splendid twilights here, I expect you've noticed, it's the sea
light. I've grown up with them, I perhaps forgot that for her
they were special . . .'

Sitting in his house I imagined her there alone. I saw her
alone in one of those vast dusks with a drink, with a cigarette,
Naomi at a schoolfriend's house or involved in a solitary
drama in the garden. I imagined her collecting that big
ashtray, that lighter set in a lump of quartz, her long
cigarettes and her tall pale drink, in order to sit down at that
dining-table by the window. She would not answer the
telephone if it rang during those moments. She would just
sit and stare. She looked through the window overlooking
the garden, though she could not see the garden from where
she sat. She could only see the hot pallor of the sky.

What was it about that blue, appearing even when she
was beautiful, long before the colour went from her skin?
Did the drink make her see it? Did the light make her drink?
There was a breath-held quality about such evenings, as if
they heralded the final ignition of the cosmos. Something
was going wrong; did Henri know what it was? He was so

uncharacteristically bitter. He would have pooh-poohed it if I had said, but it was almost as if in that sky, in her looking at that sky, he had focused all his misgivings.

His bellow of mirth jerked me out of my ruminations. 'Don't you start doing it as well!' he roared. 'Hold out your glass . . .'

It was so strange to see you young. *Oh! chérie, te voilà. Je te croyais partie* . . . And yet it wasn't you, not exactly, it was a young, smart girl, a sophisticated, shiny person younger than me. Look at you in that one, what an expensive suede skirt, what tanned calves and little ankles and high black heels. Jungle-print shirt, silk, open to the cleavage; I could see you were pushing your bosom out for the photo, you vain kid, sitting on the leather couch with your knees slightly parted, your blonde hair short and shiny – what a grin! What had Henri said to make you smile like that? The smile reassured me simply because in the midst of all that gloss it was the dead spit of the smile I knew. And you were sitting . . . the window was just behind you, so . . . you had been sitting where I was sitting then. That discovery made me go hot and cold.

I had to reconstruct. I had no choice. I had to make sense, in my own mind, of his story. If I were still convinced that Henri and I were antithetical in every way I'd have been gratified by the contrast in our recollections. He was more than capable of telling a good story, but when he spoke about his life with Genevieve it was diffidently, and his diffidence made me blush. I had been so glib, so self-indulgent in my descriptions of grief in the plum orchard, so regrettably over-emotional in my account of our life together. He, however, was artless, laboured, aware of his sudden lamentable deficit in narrative skill. Gone was the raconteur who had given me a pain in my side with his tale of the funeral. Instead I listened to a lover who stumbled, repeated himself, lost the thread, took five minutes to make a simple point. A hurt man telling the truth. I had given him mawkish melodrama and he paid me back with a small tragedy.

Of course the reconstruction was necessary, I told myself. I felt at times that it was almost noble on my part to work so hard in the interests of understanding, of truth. I told myself that I was merely unjumbling it into chronological sequence; that if I had added my own speculations here and there, they were only the disinterested interpolations of a biographer. I flattered myself that I might provide a few insights, perhaps help to dispel any remaining confusions Palastrier might have about Genevieve. I was the one who barred hard drink from the house, remember, and brought some of the colour back into her face. I was simply taking charge in each case. Going unerringly to the heart of the matter. Clever Jean-René!

By this time we had entered what I call the middle phase of our relationship, Henri and I. The final phase consisted of one meeting, our last, which took place five months ago, November of last year. But the middle phase lasted over a year, from summer to summer. We met perhaps half a dozen times, always at his house now, always at his invitation. (I must stress this: he was the instigator. I did not prey on him. The discrepancy in our incomes alone, apart from anything else, prompts me to clarify this.) My primary pain had long been dulled by time and booze of high quality and prolonged conversation. I had been given soothing maxims to digest, morsels which stayed me for the time being. Life was tolerable.

Naomi rolled her eyes in exasperation. I had become accustomed to her attitude by now. My first visit to her after Genevieve's death had taken on the quality of a child's bad dream, less painful and more detailed with time. The slow, odd, widowed brother François had been in the courtyard, cutting down the last dead sunflowers, when I arrived on that October morning, Naomi's pan-pipes in my hand. I remembered that suddenly, later: remembered also how she had been produced, a little white unsunned creature with lots of dull black hair over her face, for me to look at. Only then, after a minute, had she burst into a scream. A bad dream, darling, all over, all gone . . .

'You and Henri,' she said now, during our middle phase, a big girl of sixteen or seventeen. 'Honestly!' I rejoiced for her, for her strength, but began to suspect that she was getting a little impatient with me. Not that she said anything outright at that stage, but she already began subtly to chivvy me, I don't know how . . . she would purse her mouth and look at me, and there was grief, pity, love, exasperation, all mixed swiftly in one bright glance, quickly gone. 'Jean-René,' she would say, 'Jean-René, what shall we do with you!' and I glimpsed the adult she would become. I never wanted to hurt her but I think that in myself, simply in the way I was, I reminded her of the last days of her mother's life . . .

One time our conversation touched on Sarah, her cousin, Nicholas's sister's child.

'Oh yes. She did come again, you know, to us here,' she said. Then she referred to her as *cette fille*, and this shocked me.

'I'd have liked to see her again. Why didn't you call me?' I protested.

'What? For a reunion?' Naomi gave a scornful laugh. 'I'm sorry. I didn't know you were so attached . . . She set off one day to your house,' she said, remembering. 'She thought I didn't know where she was going. She never made it, she came back after ten minutes. She didn't have the guts. Like me, like me, like me . . .'

'Naomi . . .'

'Ah, Jean-René, I'm teasing! What shall we do with you! Get you together with Sarah maybe, to talk about old times . . . Though it was a long time ago I saw her. We were only fourteen. She shouldn't have come. She really shouldn't have come back.'

Walking over smooth sand in the shallows you catch a sea-urchin in the soft skin of your instep. That's what it felt like, listening to her.

I went instead to Palastrier. He told me what I wanted to

hear. Naomi never came with us, though he invited her countless times, and bussed her forgivingly on the forehead when she (rather rudely, in my opinion) refused.

We leaned back in our seats, soaking up liquor. This was the second thing we had in common, Genevieve being the first: our love of aniseed alcohol on a hot summer's day. During the heatwave we went out along the coast to patronize bars Palastrier would never have entered alone, places I remembered from my wanderings years ago. We ate seafood with near-green white wine, cracking the shells and sucking our fingers as we looked at the sea's blaze.

'How did you meet?' I asked him.

'By chance,' he replied. 'She was working at the town hall in the afternoons. I had some business there and I saw her a couple of times. I don't think we exchanged a word, but I noticed her and she noticed me. One day shortly afterwards I was driving home and there she was out on the road, on the other side, sticking her thumb out for a lift into town. I turned and picked her up. She was all wet and bedraggled, as if she'd fallen over . . .' He looked lost, for a moment, before concluding in a brighter tone. 'She wouldn't let me take her home, and I wasn't surprised!'

'No!' I chuckled. 'Unlike me, you notice wedding rings.'

He looked startled for a moment. He ruminatively licked his thumb, glanced across at me. 'You're a clever boy,' he remarked.

I raised my eyebrows to mean: Am I?

He was silent. Then he exclaimed abruptly: 'Ah, but he was a scorpion, that Belar!'

The nerves jumped in my belly. I tried to look nonplussed, as if I were a bit drunk by this stage.

'I mean to say,' he went on, 'I have no reason to defame him. I am the one she left him for, not vice versa.'

It was coming now. The main course. 'I didn't know you'd met him,' I said.

I realized that I was lying.

'Oh, yes. Oh, yes. Just the one time. Just a formality, really. After she made the break with him. We thought it would be best if we knew who we were, so to speak, as well as where we stood. Oh! I didn't like him at all!' He gave his deep rumbling laugh, stacked his shells and pulled the napkin with a flourish from his neck as if to change the subject.

'Of course he was a scorpion,' I said slowly, in what I hoped was a mystified fashion. 'He lunged at her with a revolver!'

'Of course. He was poison.'

'However much of a struggle there was, however much she laid herself open to threat and violence, he was still the motive force. Accident or not.' I repeated my lesson to encourage him, but the moment had passed. He simply spread his hands in agreement.

I sighed. There was a short silence while I reflected. 'If she were going to stay with anyone,' I said eventually, 'it would have been you, wouldn't it. She had no reason to leave you. You would have married if she hadn't been so stupid about it, maybe had a child together. A half-sibling for Naomi. Was it in her blood, then, to go from one of us to the next?'

Palastrier seemed no more interested by this line of talk than by the other. He shrugged, gave one of his rare smiles, stared out at the sea. Suddenly he spoke.

'You said Genevieve was irresponsible – do you remember? You blamed yourself, you said that while she was down here on the coast you were at home griping to Naomi about her irresponsibility. Was that because she'd gone without telling you?'

'Oh!' I dragged my thoughts back to that night. 'Partly, I suppose. But mainly because of the English girl, the cousin. Genevieve took her off in the car with her. In fact, it was because they had both disappeared that it never entered our heads that Genevieve had gone to Toulon. It wasn't the first time they had gone off, you see; we were in Sarlat the week before and they'd done exactly the same thing, vanished and made us worry . . .'

Palastrier nodded in understanding.

'As it turned out, that last time, Genevieve had dumped the girl half-way in some town, I forget where now, but when the police came to break the news we all assumed for a sickening hour or two that she had accompanied Genevieve all the way and was even then in Toulon. We sent the police off to look for her but she returned on her own, soon after they had gone . . .' I shivered. There was a breeze getting up. 'So you see,' I added, 'Genevieve excelled herself that day.'

'She certainly did.'

'The girl was a pathetic figure. She had missed the train and spent the night in the station. I took her to join Naomi at her uncle's. I left it to him to tell her what had happened . . . I was still in shock, I must have been, because I didn't give her a second thought. I wasn't even relieved to see her.'

'Understandably,' said Palastrier.

'She had a crush on Genevieve, I think. You know the way young girls are. Probably inveigled her way into the car and refused to budge.'

Palastrier gave a grim chuckle. 'Lucky Genevieve ditched her on that occasion!' he said. 'What was her name?'

'She was called Sarah.'

'*Ah bon,*' he said.

If Genevieve were going to stay. If, but she would never stay. Henri Palastrier asked her the wrong question, it seemed, and she was off.

Rings: there were rings in it everywhere. Genevieve had told me. Something about Palastrier signing the register. Something about her later being 'fooled by his ring'. Marriage, marriage; her wedding ring cropped up all the time in his discourse because he had never married, never found the right woman before Genevieve, and now he wanted to marry her.

'And she was off'? It wasn't as simple as that, surely. Nor was it easy for me to determine exactly how it was. Strange, because he was as expansive as ever on the details, when he asked her, what she did after he asked her, what happened in consequence. But the deeper currents were hidden now. There were no asides, no revealing exclamations, gestures, facial expressions. Now he became more fluent in the telling. Now he was giving nothing away.

It seemed that he gave up very easily. That was out of character, for he was a man of strong and persistent ardour. Genevieve may have been the one who had to take the risks, in the beginning, to make the enormous change in circumstances, but he supported her in every step, left her in no doubt about his trustworthiness. He had always pursued his causes with energy. He had wanted her from the beginning. Why, then, after she refused his offer of marriage, did he abandon this particular cause which was the most precious of desires? For he never asked her again.

Four years had gone by. It must have seemed the right time to him. They were contented. Naomi was settled. Their life had a good strong deep momentum, flowing along like a river current. He needed to declare himself: perhaps he felt – this he never said – that he had not done enough for her. For all his energy and support, he had taken no risks for her as she had for him. Perhaps he needed to risk. Had he said it straight out? Possibly. 'Genevieve, I want you to be my wife,' he declared – and she was gone.

And yet not quite like that. She had taken up, shortly before this, with some 'rather odd people', as Palastrier described them. He referred to them as the *camarades*. They were actors who had formed a travelling theatre company. They hated the bourgeoisie.

'Well, it was that era, my friend! Think of it! Only a few years after '68!' Palastrier exclaimed when he saw my quizzical look. He remembered Genevieve sitting in the kitchen trying to make Naomi eat her breakfast when he had announced that they could not go to Paris because there was 'rebellion in the streets'. Looking up from where she sat in her (silk) robe with the (silver) butterknife in her hand, and saying: 'Oh, couldn't we go anyway? For the spectacle?' For the spectacle! That had tickled him no end . . . It was one evening during this period that he proposed to her. She would not have him.

He said that. 'She wouldn't have me.' No reason did he give. As if it were final. Then she left for London. I need to go away, you do understand, she had said. They will put on their play in London and I will be their interpreter, they need one . . . !

He did not object. Perhaps he thought he was giving her time to think. He said merely that it would be fun for her to visit London again, and Madelon would look after Naomi. He said this, bringing his hands together with a soft clap, so be it. She knew that he despised the *camarades* and that he would never say so. Nor was he comfortable when she brought them to the villa or when he saw her photograph on their playbills, but he would consider it so inelegant to draw attention to the age difference, the social chasms now. They had long overcome these problems. He was a mature man, long accustomed to the fact that she was the daughter of a judge, that she had studied in Paris and London, that she was of that generation. She had married too young. Let him not cage her too closely at this crucial time . . .

So he said only that it baffled him rather, that she should want to go off now, to serve as an interpreter (a mascot is what he thought) to the *camarades* especially when there was so much he needed to talk about. But she must do as she pleased. He could wait a couple of weeks. I can see her listening demurely as his consideration, his reasonableness, his manners allowed her to leave for England without one single demand on his part for an explanation of any kind.

'It was nothing to do with the *camarades*, though, was it!' I broke in. 'They had no bearing on it!'

'No,' he replied, 'it was nothing to do with them.'

I was furious with her. 'So why did she refuse you like that?' I went on. 'Why did she flee? You've explained it to yourself, but what did she actually say, Henri?'

'She said . . .' He sighed. 'She said: "You have your ring and this is mine."' He held up his hand to show me the opal

embedded beneath his knuckle, and laughed. 'My grandmother gave me this. This is my ring, and she had hers. It is
logical, at least. Truthful.'

'But what did she mean!'

'That she did not want to replace hers with one from me,
presumably. Perhaps she felt that her ring protected her from
thoughts of marriage on my part. My ring too, arguably.' He
tugged, wincing. 'I'd have a struggle getting it off!'

He took my silence for doubt. 'I don't know, Jean-René.
These are only suppositions!' There was an edge to his voice.
I backed off, but reluctantly, like a child from hot bread.

I wondered. Had he really contented himself with mere
suppositions? Certainly the emotion was sincere; as he spoke
his head lifted like a hobbled ox from the remembered pain
of that episode. Genevieve said nothing, he said. She gave
no reason. He asked her, and she refused him, and went to
London.

It was six weeks before she returned. It transpired that
she had been staying in Nicholas Whelan's apartment. The
Whelans had arrived and Juliette had been furious to find
her there. Nicholas had not informed her that he had given
Genevieve a key to the place. Palastrier was furious too,
then: What is this, three days before Christmas you come
back, and not a word on the phone! Didn't you think of
Naomi? But it did no good; she departed again soon after,
leaving Naomi once more in the care of Madelon. It became
a pattern. Now she no longer said where she had been.
Finally she revealed that she had rented herself a small
apartment in Toulon, in the city centre. *What?* A flat of her
own? *Why?* She needed more freedom, she said frankly at
last; she thought it would be better if she had her own little
base, at least for the time being. What about Naomi? Naomi
can stay where she is, can't she? Nothing has changed,
Henri, I just need a little holiday from – life, Henri, I'll be
back.

'What on earth was going on!' I could hardly believe my
ears. 'Why in Heaven couldn't she stay with you afterwards?
Had things really changed so much, after one single pro-

posal, that you couldn't have been together as you were before?'

Palastrier was silent, his chin on his chest.

'You would have had her back, wouldn't you?'

My question was acknowledged only by a lift of his bushy brows.

'Which was it, Henri? Didn't she want you any more? Or didn't you want her?'

He rose to his feet. 'I'm too old for this, Jean-René,' he said mildly. 'Even as a young man I disliked being questioned. Now I cannot tolerate it.'

She would spend the week in that apartment – well, ostensibly. Palastrier, to his own disgust, took to noting the soaring mileage on her car. God knows what she did with herself. But she would come at the weekend to the villa and they would sit and watch Naomi play with the garden hose, roar with laughter as the hose leaped in her hand to squirt water and make her scream. They sat together side by side and then she would drive away on Sunday evening to her flat. She would stand with the door open, looking out at the sea, ironing her clothes like a single woman . . . Very well, I admit it, I never saw the place. I had no idea whether it had a sea view or not; whether it had an iron, come to that. Delete that from the record. But I knew that it was too small for Naomi to share with her mother. I knew also that Palastrier loved Naomi . . .

'Oh, no, Jean-René!' He forestalled me, adamant, raising one stubby admonitory forefinger, brown eyes glowing. 'Do not even think, do not even dream of charging me with that. I can see it in your face. That I kept the child as bait? The suggestion, the intimation demeans you as much as it does me. No no no, I will not have it. I loved her for herself! I wanted the best for her! She was a daughter to me!' The deep voice shook.

'She was Genevieve's daughter,' I said slowly. A spasm of disgust passed over his face, but I continued regardless. 'I for one would regard you with sympathy if —'

'Oh-ho!' His eyes popped with rage. 'The generous Jean-

René. Such fearless accusations, and then such tender sympathy!' I had gone much, much too far. 'So am I alone culpable, or will you be truly just and acknowledge the others? Who fathers Naomi now? Who now watches Naomi growing up in his house? Before you charge me, consider him!'

I gaped like a landed fish.

'Yes, the estimable Whelan.' And then, at my gaping, 'Oh, you innocent boy! Who do you think bought your blasted house? He would have died for her!'

'But it is she who is dead!' I cried distractedly. 'How can you accuse him—'

'Does it stop you loving, death?' he roared. 'Does it stop you looking at the daughter and thinking of the mother, trying to recall the mother, trying to feel, again, and again, how it used to be?' He slammed down his glass and began to pace the balcony. '*You* know! You haunt that girl: don't tell me Genevieve does not haunt you in turn when you're with her! Yes, I was guilty then, I confess it, but so are you guilty now! Don't tell me, Jean-René, that after you treat that girl in cafés you don't go home to lie in bed at night and *sweat* for Genevieve!'

'You, me, Nicholas . . . you make her sound like a brood mare.' I addressed the sea, cooling my forehead with my misted glass. 'Who will be next? What about her husband? Yes – you've said nothing of him.'

He sat quietly beside me, breathing hard. Not as young as he was.

'You must know. You know everything. Does his ghost linger lusting? Come on, Henri, let's not leave anybody out!'

By the end of the year she had almost ceased visiting Henri. She was never in her apartment. Nobody knew where she was. When she did come to the villa, or to her sister's house, she was invariably drunk. Palastrier contacted Nicholas

Whelan. Nicholas consulted with Juliette and with Madame her mother. Together, in Genevieve's absence, they began to discuss, in the most gossamer-fine realms of hypothesis, the fostering of Naomi by the Whelans. Genevieve returned and changed their plans, repossessed her daughter, bought her millstone. She never came back to Henri.

'What was she thinking of, what was she *thinking* of!' I burst out, my ears still ringing from his fury, but it was too heartbreaking, too frustrating, I could not help myself.

'Ahh,' he sighed, on a great cloud of cigar. 'What *was* she thinking of? Jean-René, you're a wily sort of chap, full of imagination. What do you think?' He was gentle now. He was chiding me.

The sun sank, the sea darkened. We had reached the end of the second September, the end of the middle phase. Such a relief to acknowledge it at last, our obsession and our pain. I leaned back and considered it, the time of Palastrier and Genevieve. I had no more questions – or rather, only an idle one.

'Xavier,' I said suddenly. 'Xavier of the teak doors. How did Genevieve stop him single-handed in the road, that time he tried to get away?'

Even in the dusk I saw the light go out of his eyes. His voice was leaden when he replied.

'She shot him in the arm,' he said.

NINETEEN

One night out of the endless nights which followed her death
I woke drunk in the darkness of my ruin. I cried out her
name from where I lay, I called and called for her but heard
only the kitchen clock and the silence. My forgetful hand
searched for the mattress and her sleeping body, for the
warmth of the woodstove we spent our winter nights beside;
I rose, and my blind hand cast about for the light switch, the
gas-lamp, the matchbox, expecting at every turn to send pans
clattering to the ground. It found none of these things,
encountering instead strange surfaces and dusty packaged
forms before coming to rest on a species of stump or totem,
a headless visitor as blind as my hand. After time and much
palpation this object resolved itself into the rough-planed
newel-post at the top of the ladder leading down from the
loft.

I swayed as the house rearranged itself around me. The
death-watch beetle ticked in the rafters above my head. A
great cry burst from my throat: *'GENEVIEVE! AIDE-MOI!
J'AI FROID!'*

I had thought that there could never again be a bereavement like that.

In the beginning she drove alone down to the coast, just

as it was getting dark. She could hear the sea but she could no longer see it. She parked and stood by her steaming automobile as other automobiles swished past, thumb stuck out, lipsticked, twenty years old.

He had a big fast car. His shirt was white and crisp against his tanned skin. They spoke little; they just sat, side by side, as he drove through the descending night.

He took her to his apartment. He poured two glasses of whisky, chatting to her about his life, his work. They drank and talked for half an hour or so. She smiled. He started to relax, running his fingers through his short black hair. The question was forming on his lips when she opened her handbag. She forced him to undress at gun-point.

It is ludicrous, isn't it. It could easily make you laugh. When Palastrier told me the mirth rose in his eyes and in mine. It rose but it died, leaving our eyes unnaturally bright.

She said, 'Until next week,' and he found himself nodding. He had enjoyed himself. He had never done it like that before. He waited in his apartment but she did not come. He had no address or telephone number; he did not even know her name. Finally he realized what he must do. He drove out along the coast road and there she was on the other side. He turned at high speed, tyres screeching. She leaped into the car, kneeled on the seat and pressed the gun against his ribs.

The third time she was covered in dust and her dress was dirty, as if she had fallen over. He was so excited that he could not wait until they reached his home so he took a side-road and they made love in the woods. Made love? She got him to drag her through the undergrowth first, according to Palastrier.

And so it went. The game became rougher. By now he was extremely uneasy but he could not bring himself to stop: besides, he wasn't entirely sure what she would do if he broke it off. Finally he made the attempt. One night soon after he refused to see her again he was driving back to the city, very late, when he saw her out on the road. He accelerated past her but she put a hole in his back tyre. I can imagine the car swinging on to the verge, Belar hauling himself out, sweating, shaking as she approached with her hair tousled and a big grin on her face . . . That time they did it in the car, and the gun was at his head.

A few weeks after this incident, incurring enormous wrath from her family – who didn't know him from Adam – she moved to Toulon and married him.

Perhaps they thought that they could contain the game better if they were married; contain it and cool it down. Perhaps they thought that if they were married they could play the game whenever they liked, who knows. History is silent on the matter of their thoughts at this point. In the event the game turned sourer, scarier, more constricted. He was frequently away from home but that only made it worse when he returned. She began to hate the city, their home, their life together. She became pregnant.

After Naomi was born they continued to play but only very seldom and very violently. Even seldom was too often – it was not long before an acquaintance glimpsed a couple, she could have sworn it was Genevieve and Paul, having what looked like a dreadful fight by the roadside. The gun was mercifully out of sight but questions began to be asked among his friends and colleagues. Desperately he tried to take the gun away from her but she was clever, she took it with her in her handbag, she locked it away in recesses he never found, she wore the key on her neck and slept like a cat. He refused to play any more – not that he didn't want to: on the contrary, Palastrier suspected that he wanted to be the one with the gun. It was one day when he was away, and they had been married – incredibly – for about five years, that she met Henri Palastrier.

'I offered her an escape,' Palastrier said. 'She must have seen at once that she could not . . . behave like that with me. Had it been merely to spite him I think she would have returned to him in a few months or a year at the most. Yes, I do genuinely feel that she wanted to stop the game. But the compulsion was beyond her power to quell totally; she went to him on several occasions when she was living with me. Once it was when she was collecting Naomi from a visit; she turned the gun on him then and he was incensed, he said that if she ever did that again he would pursue her, harry her and hunt her down because Naomi's innocence was paramount, he had always ensured that they spared the child any inkling . . .' Palastrier closed his eyes and swallowed. 'He need not have told me that she ever did it while she was with me, but he told me. In fact, the entire tale was recounted out of spite. The spite was Belar's, not hers.'

Ah, but he was a scorpion, that man. Yes, he was. Killing what it did not benefit him one jot to kill. He'd given it straight to Palastrier, all of it, after Palastrier had been living with Genevieve for four years. When she went to London after turning down his proposal he went to Belar, imagining that he might have to deal with a pig-headed man, the sort of man who would try to block divorce proceedings. For as I suspected he had not given up, my friend of strong and persistent ardour: still hoping to persuade Genevieve, he wondered quite naturally whether her husband's attitude might be the cause of her mysterious reaction. He went innocently to Belar, and Belar thrashed his tail and poisoned everything. The hapless Xavier played no part in Henri's discovery of Genevieve; news of that episode came to him indirectly long after she had gone, a nauseating coda he could have done without. No, it was I who had Xavier to thank in this respect. I asked my idle question, and the blow fell. 'Why did you tell like that! With no warning!' I had cried, and Palastrier said: 'You broke me.'

To be fair I was broken in turn by him. I lurched to my feet on that September evening and fled immediately. Seeing my distress Henri laid a hand on my arm but I brushed it aside. He apologized. He pleaded. 'Leave it, Jean-René,' he said. 'It is over, it is a tragedy, forget what I said.' I could not leave it, of course, though I deserted him that evening. A few weeks later I was back. It was during the 'final phase', our last meeting, last November, that I heard the full history of Genevieve and Paul Belar.

To hear that story recited calmly in Henri's deep gentle tones, with the sea wind rattling the shutters! It made it more obscene.

I cannot provide any account of the feelings I experienced between those two meetings. Suffice to say I once again travelled in a split-second from heat to glacial cold, from hearth to attic, from slumber to the most fearful wakefulness. From delusion – yes! because I had been proved utterly deluded – to reality. The history, when I was ready for it, was confirmation only. She had a voracious cancer and I had to see the X-ray. Back to Henri; let's have it from the start, chapter one, the testament and proof that all the time we were together and I had thought she was mine she was not; that she had been false all along; that ever since the beginning she'd had this *thing* going, God help me, with another man, the first man, her husband! Palastrier and I, cuckolders cuckolded! I need not have castigated myself for letting Nicholas Whelan take my rightful place. I knew how it had happened now. How could I or any of us have possibly superseded that history? None of us came first with her, none except Belar. I had prided myself on maturity when I settled down with her. Maturity? Infatuation it was which led me back here, jack-knifed me on my knees before her, made me love her to my very guts and she died – I know, from the theatrical cops – with a sneer on her face and one finger stuck obscenely in the air. 'Why didn't you tell me before!' I roared at Henri. 'How could you keep those facts to yourself? You knew, and you let this – killer roam off to make havoc?'

'Are you suggesting,' he had replied, 'that I should have come to you while she was alive – and I only learned of your existence a few months before she died – and informed you, behind her back, of her doings with her husband?'

'Yes! In the interests of truth —'

'Truth! It was true whether you knew about it or not, young man. She was far away from us both, Belar and myself. She had gone home to be near her family. In all likelihood it was an attempt to extirpate her compulsion once and for all. Who was I to come and tell you – you alone, without her consent – and reawaken the past!' He wagged his finger at me. 'This is Genevieve we are discussing, Jean-René!'

'But I was living a lie!'

'Were you?'

'How can you question that, when the truth poisoned it for you? You hated her!'

'No,' he said doggedly. 'No.'

'And then for three years you kept me on a hook! You could have got it over with that day you turned up in my field.'

'Ah, Jean-René,' he sighed. 'I am so sorry that you see our friendship in these terms.'

Well, I hectored him some more, in case there was any doubt about my boorishness. Then I sat for him to speak quietly and spoke quietly myself. Then I left before he could plead any more on her behalf. That was in November and I have not see him since; I got what I wanted from him, and there is no need to return. It is Juliette's voice which now echoes in my head: 'You were never her keeper!' That is the only truth.

All spring it has rained. I listen to the dialogue of guttering and drain-pipes. The gutters are more loquacious than the pipes; this accounts for the slow patches of damp on the walls and ceiling. I watch them spread. I open the door of the bedroom, peer through the shuttered gloom at the bed, perceive that the fungus has reached the mattress. Then I punctuate the drivel with a slam of the door. A black full stop.

I climb into my van, I drive around the district collecting material for my articles, I speak on the telephone. My work keeps me busy enough. One evening I stalled in the lane two hundred yards from my house and sat in a trance until Mme Pasquier's headlights glared in my rear-view mirror, and only then did I realize that night had come and it was dark.

I climb into my van and drive to my newspaper offices. I am respected by my editor. I have worked for him for seven years now and snow and flood pieces are a thing of the past. My amusing stories increase his sales; keep 'em coming, he says, and I have never disappointed him. He thinks I'm a strange man, but it's nothing he can put his finger on. There was a time – I was then at my most bereaved – when my appearance left something to be desired, but now I wear clean clothes, I keep my hair and nails tidy, my teeth – bared often in an ingratiating newsman's smile – impeccable. I know he wonders why the rapport has vanished between us. He knows I know he wonders. Perhaps one day I shall explain.

'It's the smell of the tomb,' I shall say. 'That is what repels you. I live in a tomb now.'

I meet Naomi out on the wet roads – Naomi at the wheel, her lawless uncle Nicholas beside her. Two grins, two raised palms blurred by the wipers and then they're gone. I meet Naomi again at the end of the day in a small bar on the main street. Just as it used to be – except that she no longer ties her hair up in plastic elasticated bobbles or tackles the froth on her hot chocolate with a long careful slurp so as not to make a moustache. These days she has a *pastis* with me, the beautiful hair in a chignon or a long single plait. On the last occasion she was wearing pink lipstick, a pink T-shirt under a huge indigo cardigan, pink socks pulled up over the tops of her smart leather boots, blue jeans. Earrings made of small pieces of indigo glass.

'Jean-René, when did you come here?' she asked.

I puffed out a small sigh and leaned back in my seat. We had held this particular conversation before.

'Nineteen seventy-five,' I replied patiently. 'September nineteen seventy-five.'

She has never heard the history of her mother, of course. Belar succeeded in sparing her any inkling. She makes do with the occasional morphine-repression and the now jaded intimations of her aunt. Heaven knows, I have no rights here; I cannot even call myself a stepfather. Our relationship is founded on my obsession with a woman I now hate. It is more than absurd, it degrades Naomi. She knows this; she has always known it. This is why she's trying to end it.

'And when did Genevieve die?' Yes, she calls her Genevieve now.

'August seventy-seven. Oh, Naomi . . . !'

She was as implacable as a dentist. 'And what year is it now, Jean-René?'

'For God's sake. Why do you do this?'

'You know why. What year is it now?'

'Nineteen eighty-two.' I rubbed my eyes. 'March.'

'Nearly April.'

'Nearly April,' I agreed. 'We generally know what month it is at the press offices, Naomi, even if we're not always so sure of the date.' Last year, due to a gross confusion in baling and distribution, the Fourteenth of July culture supplement had gone out precipitately on the twelfth.

I returned her unblinking stare and grinned. Her reluctant smile turned to laughter. 'Oh, God,' she said, as her implacability collapsed around her, 'you'll never listen, will you! You're . . . beyond redemption!'

The words surprised her as much as they did me. 'Is that how you see me?' I asked. 'You think I'm damned?' I signalled for the same again, ignoring her headshake and covered glass. 'Have another, don't be such a little prig. And answer me. Am I too far gone to come back? Is that what bothers you about me? I've never really been sure!'

'If you're going to play nasty tricks —'

'I'm playing no trick. I didn't begin this ridiculous catechism. You shouldn't start what you can't finish, Naomi. You're an adult now and these are the rules for adults!'

She tapped her nails against her filled glass. 'I think,' she said carefully, 'that you should move out of – that – house,' tapping in time to her words, 'before it falls down – on – your – head!'

'Hmm. Two years you've been saying that. Has it never occurred to you that I might like it there? Or don't you care? Perhaps you think I have no right to be there. I assure you it's mine as much as it was hers, after all the work I did. My money went into it too!'

She flinched. Her eyes shone. I felt cruel.

'Ah, Jean-René!' she cried suddenly. 'Haven't you noticed things changing all around you? Everything is changing, but you live as if it's still the same. Why don't you understand? You're not . . . changing! You stay the same!'

Palastrier accorded her the best of motives in coming back to St-Cyprien. I must excuse him for being deceived. It certainly looked like a genuine home-coming I interrupted. She had spent years away, studies in Paris and London, marriage and mistresshood on the Côte d'Azur. Who could have doubted that this chapter was closed by her return? She had come back, she had accepted the spoonful of forgiveness which was all Madame her mother would give her. She had set herself up on the other side of the hill from her family house, hung her little pictures on the walls, settled down to lead a quiet life under the protection of her sister's husband. (How archaic that sounds.) But she never had to go to him complaining of drips and drains; all he had to do was supply the money, because I came down the lane in my van, the hired boy, and shocked her a bit with my appearance, and walked into her house.

Naomi knew what I wanted before I did. The first time Genevieve invited me to dinner Naomi contrived to tip my plate into my lap. But her mother and I took the conventional steps. We soon picked up where we had left off in the summer. I would stay nights, weekends, days at a time in 'the ruin', as we called it. I helped her. Finally I took everything out of my van and put it in the house, and Naomi pissed in my tennis shoes. 'I didn't think little girls behaved like that!' I remarked: I was almost delighted, I was dizzy in the chaos, the house was full of well-wishers, neighbours and Whelans, cooking-pots steaming, there were candles everywhere . . .

Nicholas Whelan was right, of course; the renovation

would be more extensive than we had thought. We were determined to try. We washed in a plastic tub in the kitchen and dined off a door. We slept with our feet wrapped in coats. Naomi had a carpet on her bed. Our savings went down like sand in an hourglass, and just in time we started to bring in enough to keep going. Genevieve cadged from her family, took home typing, and sold eggs from a stall. 'How can I hold up my head,' cried Naomi, 'when people say the daughter of the old judge sells eggs in the road!' At the parents' meeting Genevieve told the principal that she kept chickens, with a wide smile: 'Not a large enterprise, you understand, I am a simple roadside vendor. My father used to say that all labour is honourable.' Naomi was apoplectic but the principal offered her a proper part-time secretarial job. I swayed on my feet at night from fatigue and Naomi was a thorn in my side but it only made the happiness keener. I went out barefoot at cock-crow to find Genevieve already outside, my woman alone in the dawn saying, 'My God, my God,' in wonder, 'How could I ever have left!'

Naomi came round. I can't remember what did it. She hated me so much that she tried to build her own house down by the river during her summer holidays. I remember one day giving her a little fruit pie, I remember taking splinters from her hands – pretending to, rather: she wanted to copy her cousin Sarah. Whatever it was I did (and it may have been nothing) by the end of the summer life had become normal. We were a family. We had nearly a year's worth of memories – like when I brought a colleague home for a little glass and found her standing in the tub in the kitchen, panicked and soapy, clutching to herself not a towel but the new fly-curtain we hadn't hung up yet. The long thin strips of plastic were a wholly inadequate shield. 'There was nothing else to hand, nothing to hide my shame!' she said to us when she had dressed. 'You came blundering in, the pair of you . . . I suppose I could have worn it like a grass skirt.' It became an affectionate by-word in the office, quick! the fly-curtain to hide her shame . . . But she liked being naked generally; when the nudist colony was set up over the hill,

Les Glycines it was called, it's gone now, she would threaten
to join whenever things got too much for her. 'You will find
me gone,' she said. 'You will know when you look in the
cupboards and find *all my clothes* . . .' She went to the school
with paint in her hair, this woman who used never to spend
less than three hundred francs on a haircut, who used to give
parties for scores of the Toulon big wheels, who knew all the
cocktails (cachet for Naomi, when she told her schoolfriends).
Who used to tear down the coastal roads in her white sports
car . . .

Two years, not even two years. Would I have found her
out in the end? There were so many other reasons for that
little veil, that little wall I detected as the months slipped by.
I excused her for that as I did for the episodes of drunken-
ness; it was easy to find excuses. 'She has much to contend
with,' I said to myself. 'We live in a small community and it
matters that we aren't married. It can't be pleasant for her,
the daughter of such venerable parents, to be known as the
runaway, the black sheep, the adulteress. To be the one who
likes her glass a bit too much, who has a scurrilous sense of
humour, who drives her daughter crazy (and me too sometimes) with her complete lack of correctness. Whose raffish
reputation precedes her everywhere . . . No wonder if sometimes she laughs at us all.'

Until last November I treasured her up, every last bit of
her. Her bouncy bottom in her too-thin cotton trousers, the
peppery smell of her armpits, the mole on her small left
breast. The way she used to press her nose against my chest
and take great deep enraptured snuffs of air: 'Ahh, ahh, if
we could bottle it . . .' Rainy evenings when she came back
with Naomi after a meeting at the school; how she opened
the door and took her shoes off and called out something to
me, I forget what, something comical even though she was
tired, out of sorts, worried about Naomi falling behind in
composition, worried about money. I used to lie in bed and
picture her just as she was at the moment when she took her
shoes off. A woman smiling, speaking, with wet hair falling
over her face. I used to lie there and picture her, and panic

when the picture began to blur with time. After she died a card came from the optician notifying her of a test for reading-glasses and I said to myself: 'My God, she was only thirty-four.' How splendid she would have been at forty-four, at fifty-four, sitting at my typewriter in her moth-eaten polo-neck and her reading-glasses. There would have been absurdities about those glasses if she had lived to get them. Naomi would have come to visit us in this house – or maybe we would have moved to another more manageable place near by . . . I kept the optician's card for a while, and then I threw it away. It was not part of her. It was addressed to a stranger who had nothing to do with our lives, a woman called Mme Belar.

Dwell no more on this, Jean-René, because the gun was her instrument of love as well as death; because it bound her to him; because it made you into a boy hired by the month to keep the rain out of the roof and divert her in bed. Palastrier may console himself if he likes by saying that he was her escape, but you cannot be proud of safe-housing a killer and a suicide. She was not of unsound mind when she shot herself. Her mind was as sound as a bell. She did it because she could not live without Belar.

Your speculations have lost their importance, not-so-young man. Let them trickle into the turf.

These are my facts. They cannot match Palastrier's, but they are all I have.

She spent the evening of the penultimate day on the telephone. I assumed at the time that he had called her, but I remember now that the telephone did not ring. She absented herself from the supper table and only after a while did we become conscious of her striding back and forth next door as the last light left the room, turning so that her bare heels squeaked on the polished wood and winding the long cord around her. Twisting it around her strong forearm as if to restrain herself or bind herself to something. She began to speak louder, faster. In the kitchen we found that we were setting pans down lightly and replacing utensils in the cupboard without making a noise, without speaking. Not that we wanted to hear, indeed we could hardly help but hear, however loudly we spoke, but rather that it was impossible to make any sound when her voice was usurping all other sound, husky, penetrating, deliberate, the words carefully chosen.

I closed the door. No: first I went to her. I stood behind her and placed my hands on her shoulders. Her hand was on her own shoulder, she was hugging herself, and as my hand touched hers it flapped me away, flutter flutter. I returned and closed the door behind me so that the girls could not hear her. Except that they still could.

'Who is it?' Sarah asked.

'Oh, no one important,' I replied. 'Just some private business. Why don't we go and see to the hens?'

Naomi opened the gate to the chicken-run and swung it back and forth. 'She should fix it with him,' she said, as the hinges creaked. 'You know how he's been sending her letters about it, on and off, for six months now and she hasn't replied to one. He's fed up with waiting for her to do something about it.'

'She told me she would do it when you go back to school – she'll have more time then.'

'Ha. Then she'll be working too, you know that!'

'She could do it in the office.'

Naomi laughed, and creaked the gate. 'Tante Juliette says that he and Maman are one of life's mysteries. Did you know?'

Bolting the coop I turned wearily to meet her dark gaze. 'And what does Tante Juliette mean by that?'

'Don't be exasperated with me! It's not me who's acting ridiculously! Look, Jean-René. Have you ever had one good talk with Maman about my father?'

'Why on earth should I want to do that!'

'Oh, I'll leave you to your temper and go and find Sarah.' She let the gate swing shut. 'Tell Maman she's crazy,' she said, raising her voice as she retreated, 'she's crazy if she thought someone like him would never want to marry again!'

But my words to Genevieve that night were banal. 'Darling, what is it?' (She was crying.) 'Don't let him upset you. I know it can't be nice to bring everything back, but the sooner you get it over with the better, surely. Have you got the papers up here? If you like, I'll help you.' 'No, darling.' (Her equally banal reply.) 'I mean . . . maybe tomorrow. Not tonight. I really need' (a tense and rueful smile) 'to be alone tonight. Look at the girls, down by the river.' (Turning to the window to distract me.) 'Isn't Sarah tall now? She always was taller than Naomi . . .' So I left her but there was no more time; there was no evening to the next day because she was gone by the evening, and it was the last day of her life.

Late afternoon the next day. The four of us at the bridge café just outside St-Cyprien. Time runs so fast, even in memory.

'I'll have an Orangina.'

'She has expensive tastes, your daughter.'

'I'll get the drinks, I have money!'

'Sarah, you are our guest.'

'You hardly let me spend anything when I come, it's embarrassing.'

'You should buy some postcards for your schoolfriends. Send them pictures of Beynac and put "Here I am in France, jolly ho."'

'If I am a guest you should be more polite.'

'I never said you were a guest! That's what Maman said. I thought you were the hired help actually, come to pick fruit and sweep up after us. It took me ages to figure out why you did no work.'

'Two Orangina and two *pastis*.'

'Well done, Jean-René, *vieux gars*.'

'Old boy old boy!'

'*Allons*, let's sit at the end of the bar and look at the river in a civilized manner . . .'

Perched high up over a river wide and shallow in the

summer. The girls cooling their cheeks against the little bottles, Genevieve lifting the heavy jug to fill her glass and mine with a cold grey cloud. Her eyes sweeping the bar, the balcony, the river; her eyes blue but almost green. She used to change at five on afternoons like that; she would change after playing tennis or driving around town in her car, or standing scarf-headed in the kitchen preparing dinner for ten or twenty. Two women liquidizing gazpacho or vichyssoise, surrounded by the unctuous squalor of culinary processes requiring many ingredients; one of them aged and lean and imposing and the other with her lasting honey tan and her eyes a paler blue than now, licking her finger – a face not blurred as it is now by wine, the eyes clear, slanted. A face with the stamp of a strange and sweet-sour hunger. She would change, gorgeous in her suede skirt which cost fifteen hundred francs and her bare calves, depilated in the most expensive fashion, tautened by high heels; her little pot of a stomach making a vee of her belly, her little breasts smothered in silk – she was like a posh velouté ice-cream, she could not sit with her legs together; on evenings like this she sat in Palastrier's villa as he poured his first drink and cupped it in his fist, and the light gleamed on the bottles and the glass sculptures and the cubed tumblers. She turned her face away from the marine walls, the reflections, the creak of leather, to gaze at the last of the high summer evening. She sat and looked at that pale incandescent blue and she thought of Belar.

I watched her glance at her own face in the mirror above the bar. How much older now, than when she came to Palastrier? She was twenty-six then, thirty when she first began to leave him. Thirty-two when she met me . . . thirty-four now? Can that be possible? I watched her stare, let her chin drop an inch, rake her blunt tongue over her white, slightly gapped top teeth. Eight, nine years.

And her skin thicker now, her eyes puffier, with a green, unavenged look in them sometimes. She was starting to freckle.

She was the same.

'Oh, Maman, are you sick, where are you going?'

She covered her eyes with dark glasses, let the hair fall forward over her face; she gathered her baggage, bag, cigarettes, lighter, and she slid off the bar-stool, saying, 'No, darling, I am not sick. No, but I must go home now.' And to me, before I could open my mouth: 'I am all right!' – which was typical, that she assumed I was going to be solicitous, that I was not going to reproach her for leaving like this and spoiling the outing. Sarah said: 'Genevieve—' She was frightened. She said it as she might say 'Mummy—'

Genevieve ruffled her hair. 'Don't worry, my sweet,' she said in English, and gave her a kiss on the cheek. Then she kissed Naomi who blushed, sombre and angry, and then she left.

She ran off over the road and through the dry grass, a woman in disarray, taking a short cut home, panting: it was years since she had done any sports, and all that smoking.

It was as if there was a thread between her and Sarah which was being pulled tighter and tighter as she ran. I watched Sarah try to pull her back, but she could not manage it. Genevieve was stronger. She was older and she had always been stronger. Fifteen minutes later Sarah herself was pulled away. She rose to her feet and faced our puzzlement, our displeasure. She said, 'You know, I think one of us—' and it was Naomi who retorted: 'Who cares about her!' tossing her head with another blush of anger. I also protested, 'Sarah, really, you don't have to, she probably wants—' but she was off before I finished my sentence.

A tall girl. Naomi's cousin. Genevieve's confidante and companion.

She is still tall, thin, fair, now that she is eighteen. She has grown up in much the same way as Naomi. When she came to see me she had just passed her driving test. She took her certificate out of her jacket pocket and showed me. Sarah Finney: had I ever known that she was called Finney? I must have. 'Look,' she said, with a tired smile. 'This proves I'm not mad. You can't be mad and drive on the roads. It's not allowed.' You ask Naomi, she said. She'll know the regulations. Wish Naomi luck for me, she said.

She is so English. When I heard her voice out in the lane calling Gene*vive*, in the English way, I thought: There was only one person who called her that. And this person, I have since discovered, is the only one who knew for sure that Genevieve still had the gun. Sarah had found out about it when she was a little girl, back when Genevieve left Palastrier. Sarah had known for years and had told no one. Sarah, furthermore, had not been dumped in some half-way town as she had us believe at the time; she had accompanied Genevieve on that final journey, accompanied her to her destination.

To know all that and yet to be unaware of the truth! Hers was a dreadful tale, distorted by delusion and more than a little tainted, in my opinion, with blackmail. When it came to the history she was as ignorant as Naomi. I left it that way once I had hit upon the root of her delusion, judging that she had torments enough without my adding to them. She departed as she had come, swearing that she had loved Genevieve and that Genevieve had loved her. She implored me not to deny this with regard to myself. 'It's just that we were the same, me and Genevieve!' she said. 'That's why we had to do it alone! We were in it together!'

May weather has come to the south-west and I have put the house on the market. I can no longer call it 'mine', not when I think how many other people have helped in its reconstruction: Nicholas, Genevieve, Naomi – Sarah herself, carting and carrying crossly all those years ago. Even Palastrier assessed the walls with his experienced eye. I shall leave it, and the memories which were made under its stubborn roof, to stand or fall without me.

But I shall take with me my friendship with Henri Palastrier, who managed to hold his own memories uncontaminated above the knowledge which snatched Genevieve from him. This achievement is the mark of the man. He took her for the New Year to the grandest hotel he could find, where the double doors were flung open as they entered the marbled foyer and the chandelier hung heavy and brilliant above their heads. He ushered her in her fur coat to the desk, his ringed hand gentle in the small of her back; he steered her thrillingly into her new status, for Palastrier's ring was a heavy opal, a gift from his grandmother, and how could he ever take that lump off for a wedding band! That is how she explained it to me. She said she was fooled by his ring; she said that his proposal wrecked everything, but it was not so.

Palastrier knew that and more. I am sure of this now. It is something Sarah said which had prompted me to reflect anew upon my final meeting with him. She was deluded, certainly, and she was gone before I could question her, but Henri's words . . . Henri's words found an echo in hers. 'We had to do it alone!' Sarah said.

I had leaped up his steps through the darkness of that November evening, pushed open his front door without announcing myself. The big salon was divided in the winter by a heavy tapestry curtain; I remember hearing his grumble from the other side. 'Who is it?' he called, as I closed the door. When I replied he said, 'Come through,' as if he had been expecting me.

They had not arranged themselves for a visitor. I walked like a duellist into a scene of intimacy. Palastrier, clad in a bathrobe and slippers, was sitting on a big black upright wooden chair. Madelon, similarly gowned, was bending over him with one knee on the corner of the seat of his chair, massaging his neck. Unhurriedly she straightened up. Palastrier lifted his head with an effort and opened his eyes.

'Draw the curtain again behind you, Jean-René,' he said. 'Hellish draughts in this place in winter.'

Madelon left the room, tightening the belt of her robe comfortably around her, murmuring about refreshments. She did not meet my eyes. She had a quiet polite smile on her face.

I remember him sitting, knees apart, looking up at me. He had aged as if a year had elapsed since our September meeting instead of a few weeks. His eyes had their usual look of sombre surprise, of gentleness, but something had gone. Friendship, I had thought at the time. Now I think it was health.

'Well!' he said, and gave one of his rare smiles. I had learned by then that his smiles were to express sadness only.

Madelon returned at that moment with a tray of coffee and cognac – one cup, one glass. To him she said, 'Don't sit up too late,' and to me, 'His heart.'

When she had gone he rose to his feet and fetched a box of cigars, the big glass dish of an ashtray, the big cigarette lighter set in a lump of quartz. 'I'll tell her,' he announced, cheeks working like a bellows, 'that you smoked them all.'

The ploy of an old man, I thought. To escape the frets of a wife. 'She won't believe you,' I said.

'She won't.' Amusement glinted briefly in his eyes.

There was a long pause. When at last he spoke it was to recount the history, from the beginning, just as Paul Belar had told it to him. His voice was deep and gentle and this made it more obscene. When he had done I jumped to my feet, roared, accused him of many things including duplicity. He said that he was sorry I viewed our friendship in these terms.

Presently I sat down again. There was a silence while I recovered myself. I dislodged cubes of ash into the big glass dish and listened to the coastal wind.

'You found this out after you had proposed to her, didn't you?' I said then. 'No conversation – no explanation. She just ran away. Of course you wondered, so in her absence you went to Belar. You never told her that you had been to see him, but she knew.'

I could no longer meet his eyes. I turned my attention instead to the tapestry curtain, passing my hand over flocks of game-birds and herds of running deer.

'She knew because she could see it in your face,' I went on. 'That you had been to see her husband, and that you no longer wanted her to stay.'

Palastrier rubbed a hand over his brow.

'Because what he told you poisoned everything. Because

afterwards you didn't love her any more. Why do you deny it, Henri? You couldn't, knowing what you knew—'

'No! No! You are mistaken!' He admonished me loudly, raising his cigar. 'No. I loved her just as much after I found out. You must understand that! I wanted her to stay. But, as you said, she realized that I knew. And more importantly she realized what I must have done in order to know.'

He leaned towards me and spread his large hands. 'I had gone behind her back, Jean-René. I had let her down. Do you think she was proud of what she did with him – had to do? Could not stop doing?'

He paused, commanding me to look at him. I lifted my head. Such depth of pain in his eyes.

'No,' I whispered.

'No,' he repeated. 'It is a sad little truth I discovered, is it not? She felt shamed before me, and although I could bear it, she could not.'

Abruptly he stood up. 'I have told you, young man, what she wanted you never to know. Belar betrayed her to me and I have betrayed her in turn. I could hardly turn you away, not now! But take account of this, my friend, before you go: my betrayal will have been for nothing unless you understand that Genevieve loved us both, you and me, with all her heart. She gave us everything she possibly could. I'm a good judge of people . . .'

His eyes filled. I never thought I would see him undone.

'Jean-René,' said Henri Palastrier, 'she was a fantastic girl!'

SARAH

TWENTY

'There is a market,' Genevieve said.

We were sitting around the table on a Sunday morning, eating breakfast.

Jean-René raised his head from the newspaper. 'A market?'

'I don't want to go,' Naomi immediately announced. 'There are things I have to do here. I'm very busy today.'

'Oh, really?' Her mother jeered. 'What things do you have to attend to? Business matters? Do you have a vast fortune tucked away – investments to make? Shares to sell on the telephone when I'm not here?' She laboured the conceit.

'You know you're the one who's spending my savings like water, you gross drunkard.'

'I certainly am not.'

'Not what? Drunk, or gross?'

'You little brute. What things do you have to do, anyway?'

'Oh, Maman, Maman, things! Nothing!' She paused. 'Sarah has things to do as well.'

'Oh, this is too much. You're extraordinary.'

'She doesn't want to go.'

Genevieve addressed herself to me, eyes narrowed, brows slightly raised. 'Domestic peace may depend on this.'

'Well, I'd quite like to go . . .' I said.

'*Oh, la vache*. Trailing after Maman wherever she goes.'

'Where is the market?'

'Oh, God, Jean-René, do you know I think I've forgotten!'

'It looks like there will be no conflict of interests, then.'

Genevieve gaped. 'You know where it is, don't you! You know where it is, from which hour, what there is to buy. But due to your massive conceit you're just going to sit there, smiling and smiling —'

'Don't repeat yourself. It makes people think you have an inadequate vocabulary. Tante Juliette —'

'Darling, you are transparent in your efforts to irritate me. As for you, *Homo superior*, you can drive us all to it. And I will buy the things we need. Saucepans, utensils. It's lucky somebody here is willing to remember our financial situation, take steps like these to avoid getting ripped off at the *quincaillerie* in town where the *salauds* the foreigners go, oh, excuse me, Sarah —'

'I'm a foreigner too, I take offence at that!' protested Jean-René.

'You're not a foreigner the way Sarah is.'

'You're always telling me I am.'

'Take no notice, Jean-René,' I said. 'She's . . . tell me the word for "hung over", Genevieve.'

She was drinking a lot but I didn't think it was a bad thing. It was only wine after all. What harm did wine ever do to a person? She said she never drank spirits; they couldn't afford them, she said, so they drank wine as an economy. Naomi, who had to take some of the bottles back to the village shop, said that it cost her dear.

'I'm so embarrassed,' she said. 'They hear me coming for miles. All I ever do is buy more wine. You could at least take the stuff at four francs, it would look better – or at least not quite so bad.'

Genevieve said that she preferred 'the stuff' at three francs, and that Naomi should not be such a thin-skinned soul as to be hurt by what other people said.

'I'm not hurt!' cried Naomi. 'I'm certainly not hurt by any of the real gossip that goes flying around at school, *merde*, you should hear some of it! They say that you take drugs in the office!'

'You see? I can't use a nasal spray in this cursed community.'

'And that Jean-René is a *gitan* and a criminal.'

'Oh, well, that's true, of course. Better cut your hair, darling, and get that licence for your bus, or we'll have the police round.'

Jean-René guffawed, groaned, stretched, rubbed his eyes, drank huge mugs of coffee, lit a cigarette at the table, groaned again when it was whipped from his fingers by Genevieve ('Some of us eat in the morning!'), retreated grumbling behind the newspaper. But he drove us good-naturedly to the market all the same, grinning at Naomi in the mirror, yelling remarks at us above the noise of the engine.

The town we drove to was one of the largest in the region. The roofs of the lofty civic buildings reminded me of Paris. The streets were wide, but there were no parking-spaces left. The main street, occupied by the market, was a broad sycamore-lined avenue patched with light and shade.

We sat in a café packed with slot-machines. People came to drink apéritifs, departed on motorbikes. From where we sat we could see the banners slung across the street, from municipal building to municipal building, announcing a coming bicycle race. The music from the loudspeakers on the lampposts deafened us. I said that every building looked like the town hall, and Jean-René agreed.

Genevieve was wearing a blouse so old it was transparent.

'You should really throw that thing away,' said Jean-René. 'I can see your bra from here.'

'Then it's as well I'm wearing one.' Genevieve peered

down at her bosom. 'What's the matter? Are you afraid we might meet one of your local government spies?' She leaned over and kissed him noisily. 'You could always ignore me, sweetheart. If I look such a tramp they won't expect you to be with me.'

'I'm more afraid that one day soon we'll meet your sister and brother-in-law. She'd only start on at me again . . .'

Genevieve put down her drink and stared. 'About what?'

Jean-René looked uncomfortable.

'Go on!' Genevieve commanded, her lips pale. 'What has she been saying? And don't stall on me in that stupid way, cleaning your glasses, your glasses are perfectly clean, you're always cleaning your glasses.'

He heaved a sigh. 'She just happened to mention to me,' he began, 'that she was a bit . . . concerned about you. Perhaps she meant that, what with your job and everything, you had too much to do – you weren't getting enough time for yourself . . .' He trailed off as he watched her face darken. I suddenly thought: He's too young for this, he can't handle it.

He cleared his throat. 'It was nothing. She was only being kind.'

'I hope you told her where she could go with her kindness!'

'Actually no, I didn't.'

'You didn't? You didn't tell her to mind her own business?'

'No . . .'

'So? What? You agreed with her?'

'No, I just—'

'Oh, I understand. You just said you did. You just slithered out of it, saying, "Yes, Juliette, absolutely, she's a slut, I've been trying to get her to smarten herself up." And look at you, incidentally! It's – it's incredible!'

'She's just concerned,' Jean-René said simply. 'Look, I might as well tell you before she does. She gave me some old clothes of hers and Katrine's.'

'She did what?'

'They're in the attic.'

'You accepted them? You took their old clothes?' Genevieve's voice faded to a whisper. 'For Naomi to wear? For *me* to wear?'

Jean-René said nothing.

'You think we would wear them? My sister's cast-offs?' She slammed on her dark glasses and leaned back in her chair, turning her face out into the street. Her lips twitched and she pressed them together.

'Maman, Jean-René, *arrêtez*, have pity on us, everyone's looking . . .' Naomi pleaded in a choked voice.

'Ah, Heavens, you and your thin skin,' Genevieve said in disgust.

The piped music began to vibrate in my ears. Suddenly there seemed to be more of a crowd. I was almost as embarrassed as Naomi. I stood up.

'I think I'll go for a quick walk,' I said. 'Naomi, are you coming with me?'

Naomi rose to her feet like a duchess, her face wooden, pushing her chair away with one foot so that it blocked the passageway. She walked past me out of the café.

'I don't mind how much they do it indoors,' she said, as I caught up with her. 'It's when she gets going in the street like that . . . that I really cannot tolerate!' She spat the words, walking on with her hands in her pockets. Then she stopped and looked at me, shading her eyes from the sun. When she spoke again her voice was calm and clear.

'I try to understand,' she said. 'But all I feel is . . . contempt.'

'She thinks she's being humiliated,' I protested. 'Being offered Tante Juliette's clothes, I mean, would you wear them?'

'Ha!' Her earrings jangled with annoyance. 'Guess whose this is, this dress! It's Katrine's, you know, hemmed up – she gave it to me. And *she'* – meaning Genevieve – 'takes things from them all the time, when it suits her, she always has! She never gets round to buying us so much as a – a sock!'

'Oh, that's not true, surely!' I said, laughing at the sock. 'What about that terrific ski-jacket I saw in your cupboard? I bet that wasn't Katrine's.'

'No, but even so . . . even so she's absurd in public,' Naomi snorted. 'Oh, never mind. Poor Jean-René, he always goes clod-hopping into it. He always comes off worst.'

We wandered back towards the crowded centre. Naomi spotted Jean-René browsing amongst second-hand books and trotted away in his direction. I drifted on up the street, looking for Genevieve. I bought some salted peanuts in a paper bag, for the sake of buying something, since I was at a market. I stuffed them in absent-mindedly, realizing as my mouth watered that I was very hungry. It was nearly three in the afternoon. I hoped we would be going soon.

A pair of hands was placed over my eyes. I giggled, trying to turn round. 'Geddoff,' I said. 'I know it's you. Stop playing!'

Genevieve's enormous basket held an enormous pan. 'Very cheap,' she said.

'You've made a peanut go down the wrong way. What's it going to be for?'

'Oh, making jam. Boiling dishcloths.'

'Boiling dishcloths!'

'I do that! Well, I will, now that I've got this.'

'Where are the others?'

'I can't see them anywhere. Can you?'

'You were a bitch in the café.'

She looked at me. A smile crinkled the corners of her eyes. 'Let's go and look at the church.'

'Shouldn't we find the others first?'

'Oh, let them stew!' she said harshly. She began to stride away from the market stalls, and I ran after her.

'No,' I said. 'No, you can't just walk off like this, just because you're angry!'

'Because I'm angry? You're amazing. Angry doesn't come

into it. I couldn't believe my ears. I could have hit him. I will almost certainly slap Juliette if I see her in the next few days.'

'I'm glad you didn't hit him. He doesn't deserve it. And Naomi was mortified enough as it is.'

'Mortified! I'm mortified too . . .' She seemed to be running out of steam.

'She says you can argue as much as you like at home as long as you don't in the street.'

'That's very magnanimous.'

'Yes, I think it is, in fact! I think she is certainly behaving more like an adult than you today!'

'Yes, she's very grown-up now, isn't she, my girl,' she said dreamily, suddenly tender. 'So. To the church?'

I heaved a huge sigh. 'I think—'

'Look, they're bound to go there sooner or later. What's the matter? Don't you want to come with me? We hardly seem to have talked at all yet. Come, for the sake of my English at least.'

'I want something more to eat.'

'OK, so we buy food. Now let's go!'

'You seem to have grown up, you know.' Genevieve tore at her sandwich, spilling crumbs on to my sleeve. 'Excuse me, I'm a barbarian when I'm hungry.'

I shrugged. 'I'm a liberated woman now.'

The grass grew green in the shade of the walls of the church. The churchyard was much bigger than the little crammed one in the village. The graves were more elaborate, too – monuments, some of them, great roofed structures decorated with flowers made of plastic or tissue paper and decked out with photos of the deceased.

I pointed at them. 'I hate that greenhouse type, it's macabre.'

'That's because you're a wealthy Protestant. No sense of family, and tight-fisted with it. I bet you think they're in bad taste. Admit it.'

'Well, yes, I do rather.'

'"Well, yes, I do rather"!' She laughed, her mouth full.

'Ha! Don't tell me you'll have loo-paper flowers on your grave! You're the fancy-pants with the family vault, not me!' I lay back so that my body was in the shade and stretched my arms above my head in the cool grass. Her back was towards me. I could see the straining bra-strap, the beginnings of a tear under one arm of her blouse. I reached out and slapped her gently. 'Getting fat,' I said. 'Old slob.'

She gave a muffled laugh. 'Young bitch,' she replied. 'Wicked brat. Expel – expulsee!'

I crowed. 'No such word!'

'Proud of yourself for that?'

'For burning that bloody skirt, yeah! Otherwise . . . Oh, I'm just thinking of the new place. I haven't met the Head yet, she was away. I've got to go and see her before term begins. She's called Miss Dupree, can you believe it. Actually,' I yawned, 'the whole thing makes me tired, I'd rather forget about it . . .'

She was engrossed in splitting blades of grass in half with her thumbnail, staining her fingers. I lifted one foot and waggled it. 'Are your feet still green, Genevieve, from the dancing? Mine are.'

'What? Oh – no. I scrubbed it all off last night with a, with a *pierre ponce*.'

'A whaat?'

'A stone, a small bathroom stone—'

'A pumice stone!'

'Thank you. My new word for today.' She split the last blade, muttering 'pah-mis, pah-mis' under her breath. She laughed. 'Pummel me with your pumice.'

'Pimple me with your, your *pierre ponce*. Or pimp me. Pimp me with Peter your ponce.'

'Sarah!'

'Don't be cross, it's a pun!'

'Remember when you came to stay with Juliette and we went down to Toulon?'

'A pumice pun.' I giggled and shut my eyes, but she jogged my arm.

'Sarah. Do you remember that?'

'Mmm.'

'Why such lassitude all of a sudden?'

'I know what you're going to suggest.'

'How can you, when I don't know myself?'

'I know you. You want to go down there, today, without telling anyone. You want to take off. I've been watching you ever since I arrived.'

Her face appeared above mine. I could see the beads of sweat on her upper lip, the bird's egg freckles. I put up my hand and tucked a lock of hair behind her ear.

'Qu'est-ce que tu as?' I asked. 'Aren't you happy?'

Her eyes filled with tears. 'You should never ask that of a woman my age,' she said. 'So few of us are happy. So many chances missed by this time! She sniffed. 'So much lost!'

'Oh, hang on while I fetch my violin!'

'You don't understand! You're thirteen, too young to know anything!'

'I thought I was grown up.'

'You're a cruel girl. You have no soul.' The tears were still streaming down her face. She wiped them with the back of her hand. Finally she said: 'He's been writing to me.'

'Who? Oh, him!' I sat up.

'He's sent me the papers.'

'What papers?'

'Divorce papers.'

'He wants to get divorced?'

'Nothing escapes you, does it, Sarah?'

'Good Lord,' I said. 'After all this time.'

We sat for a while longer, pondering. The day began to cool. We left the church and searched everywhere for Jean-René and Naomi, but the van was no longer where we had left it. They had given up on us.

We stood on the side of the road out of town, Genevieve with her huge pot, her blouse gone completely now under the arm. I was carrying our shoes. She taught me how to hitch-hike French-style, with my arm bent and my thumb groovily at an angle. *Le stop*, she said it was called. I said, Typical how you make a pose out of everything.

A lorry stopped for us and we got in. She was very excited. She said: 'Take us as far as you can along this road.'

'No!' I said. 'Genevieve, we're going home!'

'Don't you want to go on a trip, like we did before? It was your idea that time!'

'It was never my idea!'

We quarrelled. We went for miles and miles. She wanted to see the sea, she kept saying. The driver reached his turning and set us down. We waited for a long time, but nobody stopped.

'I'll go by myself,' she said bitterly, after a long silence.

'Come on, Genevieve. Let's cross the road.' For the first time during this long, stupid day I was uneasy. 'I'd like to take a trip with you, but not there again, not now! Not like this, without telling anyone —'

'Oh, don't try to tell me you don't want to. I know you do, just as you know about me.' She turned to face me. 'You're just tired, aren't you. Just tired. You don't think I should correspond and discuss and acquiesce, do you? With him of all people? You don't think that is the way to deal with him, do you?'

I couldn't bear this cooing tone. 'You wouldn't have to,' I retorted. 'From the sound of it, all you've got to do is sign the papers.'

'Yes.' She was harsh. 'Sign the papers. Sit at home and wear my sister's clothes and say thank you, everybody, for arranging things for me! If I'd done that the last time Juliette would have got Naomi. My God, Sarah, you have changed.'

'How can you say that!' I cried angrily. 'Why do you think I was chucked out of Lucifer's, for Heaven's sake!'

'I don't know. Tell me.'

I could have strangled her for that. 'Because I wasn't going to sit down under it, of course! I thought you understood that! So how can you think I'd want the same to happen to you!' I was sweating and tired. I pushed the hair off my face. She stood looking at me, infuriatingly calm.

'Haven't you done it enough?' I went on. 'My God, you've shown *him* you won't be pushed around. I don't get it; why don't you just take charge of things? This is your chance to get rid of him for good.' I took her by the hand. 'Come on. Over we go.'

She whipped her hand free. 'Ha ha ha,' she said. 'Poor little Sarah. Mummy come back and everything will be OK.'

'Oh, shut up, you're not my mother.' I crossed the road. 'Thank God!' I called from the other side.

Finally she came to join me. We waited, the evening sun behind us as we faced the traffic, the air heavy with petrol fumes, the tarmac warm under our feet.

We could have gone anywhere, to Bordeaux or Paris or even to Spain.

'Couldn't you have returned sooner, Sarah?' Jean-René had been angry, but it was with her, not me. With me he was mild and tired; it was worse. I protested that I could hardly pick her up and carry her, but we both knew that I was guilty.

'Should have left her,' was all Naomi said. 'She'd have come back pretty quick then' – as if her mother were a wayward cat or dog.

All reproaches were pointless because she made the call in the end. I was sitting in the kitchen as she spoke on the telephone in the next room. I had asked for form's sake who she was speaking to, and Jean-René had said, 'Not important,' before taking Naomi out to deal with the chickens. I sat there and played with a cork, rolled it, picked at it. It was an unsatisfactory toy. I listened to Genevieve, who was saying please now, and the word was racked with entreaty. That was all she was saying, just please, please, please.

Then there was a sudden coherence. 'No. I will come to you tomorrow. I wish to see you so that we can discuss this. No, I will send you no document until we have talked . . . !

'Yes, there is something more to discuss! Much more to discuss! Face to face . . . !

'My God, do you think that you can finish it all with a letter . . .?

'You have taken so much! You ruined me so utterly that only now do I feel . . . How can you deny me one last meeting? Would it cost you so much . . .?

'Ah . . . you would not do that! You would not dare! Not again . . . !

'Ah!' she exclaimed, 'you are poison!' and lit the third cigarette of the conversation. I heard her draw in her breath, and then there was a long, murmured stream of inaudible words. She was almost whining. Then a short silence. Then she said: 'Yes . . . Yes . . . Yes.' And then: 'Tomorrow.'

She put down the receiver and went slowly upstairs to the tower room. I put the cork in my mouth and bit on it.

She didn't reappear until the following afternoon. Jean-René was at home, typing an article about a new local canoeing club for the Summer Sports section. He didn't look up when she came in. I opened my mouth and closed it again. Naomi started humming, flipping her wooden sandals against her hard heels. It was an irritating noise.

She had spent the night in the tower. Naomi and I realized this without Jean-René having to say anything.

She sat down heavily. When offered food, she lifted her chin and closed her eyes. We took this to mean no.

She drank a glass of wine.

It was obvious from Jean-René's closed expression that he knew why Genevieve should speak so urgently on the telephone, in that voice, tearing the words out from inside her. Naomi hadn't exchanged a word with her mother since before that telephone call, but she didn't need to ask. It had been going for ages, this tussle with Belar. They were both sick of it.

And since I had listened right up to the end, there was something else I knew, that I thought the others didn't know.

So there was that – and there was the old thing, of course.

We went out as we had planned to, the four of us, for a long walk in the late afternoon. I remember I was due to leave in a day or so. We were going to take the road down through the village, follow the path up the hill, and cross the dry headland so that we could look down on the plain, on Juliette's side, where the slow loop of the river fed the fields and the castle hung like a rocket at the valley gates. Descend to the bridge, sit for a while in the café at the bridgehead (Genevieve's itineraries generally included refreshments), and take the short way home along the road.

I seemed to be chasing her all the way, walking first a little ahead of her and then lagging behind, trying to remain level with her on the wide path. But she ambled on with her hands thrust in her pockets as if she hadn't seen me there until I said 'Genevieve!' in exasperation.

'Yes, my darling?'

'Speak to me!'

'About what, sweetheart?'

I growled, at my wits' end, as we swished through the dry grass. Naomi and Jean-René were up ahead, covering the ground faster than us, chatting. Genevieve shaded her eyes to stare at them.

'Sarah.'

'What.'

'I . . . nothing.'

'What!'

'Nothing!'

'Genevieve, tell me! Tell me what's going on!' But my raised voice caused Jean-René's head to turn, and he and Naomi paused at the top of the hill and waited for us.

Sometimes it could be green and slow, as slow as when I first saw it close up, by the road beneath the troglodyte village when I had given François and Lucien a more thorough slip than I'd intended, when the sunbeams shafted the dusty air to be lost in the glass-green and I was tempted in. And when it rained it turned as brown as an old coat; Naomi and I had watched it in the past, squatting in a cold spell where the rock came down like a cathedral wall. We had watched the water's skin pucker beneath the rain of a summer squall, watched the rain clear and leave it dark and shining again, with a riverine smell. We had thrown sticks down and shrieked to hear the echo.

But on that day it was clear and shallow, gloriously wide, purling past the bridge legs in a glittering rush, heralding an estuary although it was a hundred miles from the sea. It reflected the sky, the light blue sky of the evening. The café was perched up on the end of the bridge against the sky.

She grasped my hand and squeezed it tightly. 'You're on my side, I know,' she said, speaking slowly and with certainty as she gazed up at the bridge. 'On my side.'

There seemed to be flags everywhere, flying in the breeze.

TWENTY-ONE

When I was a kid I thought she should have a sword. I thought she was like a prince or a knight, but she wasn't. She was a guerrilla, like me, taking to the hills or fighting undercover. We used to be outlaws together – we had to be outlaws. And if we fought each other it was only out of love, Jean-René. We were two of a kind. She might have laughed at me and called me a Spartan in front of you but we both knew the truth. The true colours. We were perfect, we did the sword dance with each other, step-step-pirouette, feint, parry, *touché*, as well-drilled as show-gladiators. Except of course we didn't have any swords.

I wonder if she's still out there waiting to kill me. I think I'm safe here in the tower with you because she doesn't come into houses any more. You'll protect me, anyway, won't you? She wants to kill me because she knows I'm going to tell.

I ran like fury. I'd never run so fast in all my life. Great whoops of breath, chest like a cage, heart labouring – arms flailing so that my bracelets went chink chink. Silence except for the chinking of my bracelets and my gasping breath.

She was in the car, engine running. 'You!' she said,

laughing, as if she knew I wouldn't have given up on her. I got in beside her and we drove off.

Do you know what it's like, Jean-René, when you get down to the coast? At night you could be anywhere, England or France; it's all marked out with lights but if you don't know what they mean, if you aren't a sailor, you can't tell one place from another. We had driven for miles; she was tired, I know. She was burning. I looked at her white, burning face as we drove; like a little kid I said: 'Why don't we just keep on driving? We could go to Italy, or we could turn round and go to Spain, or we could get on a boat to Africa – what do you think, Genevieve?' I was trying to joke, trying to break her out of it, but she didn't take her eyes off the road. She just smiled and said, 'Not this time. You know where we have to go this time . . .' By the time we reached the city it was completely dark.

We sat for hours outside his flat. The white building with the zigzag steps. For the most part we were quiet. Once I said I'd like to stretch my legs but she grabbed my wrist and her hand was like iron. From time to time she spoke. She told me that this wasn't the flat they had lived in when they were together. In fact, after they separated he had been posted abroad for a long time, and then he'd had several long tours of duty. When Naomi went to visit him that summer when she and I were eleven, he had only just moved into the flat. Naomi had been his first guest, she said, and she laughed. Even now he was often away.

There he was at last, climbing up the steps, unlocking the front door. A light came on inside. A shadow-man, taking off a shadow-hat. Then a click beside me as she sprang her seat-belt. She put her hand over mine.

'Don't come in after me, please, Sarah,' she said.

I don't know how long I sat there. More than an hour. I didn't know if she could see the car from the flat. I tried to distract myself by opening the glove-pocket of the car and reading all the little scraps of paper I could find by the light of the street-lights, but I couldn't take anything in. A shop-ping list, *eau de vie*, she wanted it for the walnuts, maybe? I didn't know she ever did walnuts in *eau de vie* . . . Once or twice I saw a shadow flitting across the window of the flat, but too quickly for me to tell who it was. It must have been late, very late at night, when I left the car.

I pushed open the door and went into a kind of reception room, tiled floor, a few bits of horrible big brown furniture. His hat and jacket were flung on a chair. The French hats are smarter than the English ones. The stripes on the jacket told me he was a commander. He'd been promoted, then. Last year, when she had told me about him, she'd said he was only lieutenant-commander. Though maybe they had different stripes in the French navy. The blue of the jacket was different as well, not so dark. The light in the hall was extremely bright and this made everything starker and uglier. There was no sound.

I opened one of the doors leading off, groped around, turned on the light. A living room, more horrible furniture, emptiness, dust. I wanted to call her, but each time I opened my mouth I found I had too much saliva. I had to keep swallowing . . . I went back into the hall and saw her standing in one of the other doorways.

She was leaning against the door-jamb. She had blood on her shirt. It looked for a minute as if she'd done it to herself, but it wasn't pain which was doubling her up like that. It was laughter – the kind of silent laughter you have when you've got no breath left. 'Oh, Lordy,' she said, when she could speak. 'Pass me that jacket, quickly now, we haven't got much time.'

I think I just stood there, because she had to ask me again, this time louder and sharper, and when I still didn't move or speak she pushed past me and got it herself, grabbing it so roughly that she pulled the chair over with a clatter. At that point I pissed myself. 'Genevieve!' I said, pissing and grizzling simultaneously, 'Genevieve!', like that till she called from the other room for me to shut up. Finally I went into the bedroom.

He was lying on the bed. I didn't look at him – only enough to see that his head was turned away, towards the window. Then I looked away before I saw anything else, but I had a feeling, from my quick glimpse, that he'd been shot in the back of the head. Genevieve was ransacking the wardrobe, clashing the hangers on the rail. 'I decided against that jacket,' she said. 'I think the dress uniform would be better.' She looked at me over her shoulder. '*K-tioung*,' she said, and pointed two fingers, laughing. 'You love that sound as well, don't you. *K-tioung*, *k-tioung*. You couldn't stop, you shot that bloody branch off in the end, do you remember? I might as well have brought you in with me, since you couldn't keep your nose out of it. I could have let you do it – you're a better shot than me . . . Ach, don't vomit as well! Messy kid!' She pulled out the dress uniform and threw it on the bed. She said, 'Come on, we've got to be quick. I can't find the sword. Look for the sword in the cupboard while I get started.'

I wiped my mouth. 'Why can't he wear the ordinary uniform?' My voice was tiny, it came out of someone beside me who didn't know what was going on. My jeans were all warm and wet and my shoes squelchy. But she was already feverishly busy with the clothes and it took a while for her to answer. When she did, it was to say that people always dressed up grandly before they killed themselves, it was a well-known fact. I started crying quite loudly then and she had to stop what she was doing and shake me until I shut up . . . I'm sorry, I can't help laughing, Jean-René, it's only nerves. It makes me so scared, my guts are sinking and sinking just saying this.

The cupboard was black. I took some medals down off a shelf and passed them to her but she threw them on the floor. She realized I was dawdling because I didn't want to help her. She had pulled him up the bed until he was sitting against the pillows. She made me keep him upright while she put the posh jacket on. I didn't want to touch his body so I held him by the hair on top of his head, turning away so that I couldn't see him, which was really stupid because his hair was very short and soft, and it slid through my fingers so that he fell sideways and hit his head with a great crack on the windowsill, and if I hadn't already I'd have pissed myself then . . .

'But at last she'd got him, got him how she wanted him, and we left the flat.'

When I stopped, there was silence.

We were sitting at opposite ends of the tower room. The window was broken and it was cold in there, but I was sweating. The place was inch-deep in dust, and I felt the grime sticky on my hands and face.

'I'm thirsty,' I said.

Jean-René remained silent and motionless. His face was completely blank. Eventually he moved his head against the wall. When he replied, it was to say, 'You've talked a lot.'

The silence returned. It began to rain again. We sat there for an age, listening to the rain. Although I hadn't reached the end of my tale, Jean-René didn't ask me to continue. At one point he gave a brief, toneless laugh, but it wasn't a joke he wanted to share.

When I caught sight of him coming towards me through the field I didn't recognize him. His face was pale in the faint light. He must have heard me pleading to her. I said to him, 'Quick, she's coming, run!' and then I remembered who he was. He didn't speak; he just looked at me and ran with me to the house.

Once inside he began to ask me a lot of questions which I couldn't answer. He kept asking, 'Did you see her?' and I got quite scared of him because he wouldn't stop. I was getting confused now. I wondered if he was in league with her and this was a trap. It was the way he had said, 'Did you see her?' which threw me, because I was sure he had said it hopefully.

I woke with my foot on a cushion. I had a huge blister on my heel. It was midday. I got up to wash myself and saw in the mirror that the beads on my plaits had left impressions on my face. I put my clothes on again and sat on the couch in the blankets, in silence, for about four hours. I watched Jean-René come in and go out, offer me food, sit down to work, get up again, make coffee. Occasionally he reassured me that he wouldn't leave the house and that he wouldn't let anyone come near, even if they didn't look like Genevieve.

'Jean-René,' I said finally, 'come here.'

He came. 'Only if you talk,' he said. 'You've got to talk.' He wasn't being callous. I knew he wanted the answer to everything, but I still wasn't a hundred per cent sure of him.

'She's so clever,' I said next. 'She always was, but now she knows everything. She knows what I'm thinking, what you're thinking.' The enormity of that idea compelled me to cover my head with the blanket. Jean-René sat beside me and stroked my head through the blanket. He didn't go to the phone; I had feared he might try and ring her up, since I wouldn't let him out of the house. Not that I could keep him here myself. After all, I had no gun.

I slept and found myself in a dream. I was standing on a huge green plain; I thought at first it was a battleground, but it was the playing field at Lucifer's. It was frosty, the sun was going down, and I was alone. I heard her coming up behind me and knew that I could never outrun her because there was a bandage on my knee. But when I turned round it was Flora standing there.

'Oh, Sassy,' she said. 'I thought I'd never find you.'

Then I woke up. I called for Jean-René. I was ready to start now.

'We left the flat and drove to the sea-front,' I said when I had gathered the energy to continue. 'When we got there I refused to get out of the car. I didn't want to leave her or her to leave me. I could see that she was mad.'

I thought of that sleepless dawn, the smell of the inside of the car, the way her lips stretched as she bawled at me to go.

'I even tried to grab the gun, you know. She had the

safety on. But she was stronger than me and I was scared. I tried to tell her that it wasn't too late, that everyone would realize it had been an accident, that she had to come home. But it was no use, Jean-René, because she wasn't listening.

'She gave me all her money. She pushed me out of the car and drove off. I walked all the way to the station. The sun was just coming up. I stood staring at the timetable. You have to change at Toulouse, and at Brive, I think; I don't remember. But I must have done it because I arrived at Siorac in the end. I washed my pants and trousers in the river on the way home. I remember thinking, Tante Juliette will be frantic. I'd already forgotten the whole thing by then.'

Her hands on my shoulders, fingers poking into my neck and chest, pushing me out of the car. The slapping struggle. The names, the dreadful names she called me. The final thing she did.

'She had to put the gun to my head to make me go,' I said, and after a second or two: 'Oh, yes, she did that.'

'Sarah,' Jean-René said gently. 'Leave it now. Nothing you could have done—'

'But I could!' I cried. 'I could! I should have noticed she'd taken the gun from the flat! I was too slow! I only realized when we were nearly down at the front. I had an image of it lying on the bed, and then I remembered that as we went out of the room the sheet was bare and white. I told her the moment I realized; I said, "Shit, Genevieve, you've still got the gun, we've got to put it back." I pulled her arm, I was so desperate, and we nearly hit a parked car. She was driving terribly now anyway, her legs were shaking so much that she couldn't control the pedals . . . And I was so used to her having it around, I expect she was, too . . .'

Jean-René took off his glasses. I realized that the light had been catching them and hiding the expression in his eyes.

'My God,' he said. 'My God. You knew it was hers.'

'Yes,' I replied. 'She'd had it for years.'

He held one hand to his cheek.

'She kept it in a plastic bag,' I said. 'Under your bed.'

His newly naked eyes were wet.

'Palastrier told me,' he said at last, 'how she hid it every-where. She was so cunning, so cunning, with Belar. And in this house, with me, she just tossed it into a plastic bag.'

'Yes, along with all her old make-up and things. Christ, Jean-René, it was nothing to do with you. Why should you know!'

He gave me a dazed stare. 'I wonder where she put it when she was with Henri,' he murmured.

'She probably knew you'd never look,' I said.

'She's not here, is she. She won't come and kill me now.'

'No, she won't.'

'In the woods I remembered it all, what happened in Toulon. Imagine forgetting something like that . . . !'

'Sarah, you should sleep.'

'I've done it now. I've given her away.'

What silence. The second morning, when I awoke, there was no sound at all. One cock-crow, but it was faint. It must have been from the farm. And it smelled the same there. Just the same.

Jean-René was sitting by my makeshift bed on the sofa. For the first time I noticed how much older he looked. He couldn't have been more than thirty-five or so. It wasn't the greying hair so much as the greying face. And the thinness; he had thin wrists, fingers white where he clasped his knees. Dark hairs curled over his watchstrap; a horrid, greasy, fabric watchstrap, hard to tell the original colour. Hard also to remember how broadly smiling he had been, how lithe. I had the impression he had been sitting there for a long time, but there was a steaming cup of coffee in his hand.

I reached out and touched his shoulder. 'I don't think you're happy here,' I said.

He handed me the cup.

'It must have been terrible, hearing all that,' I went on. 'She didn't want me to tell you either. But I had to get it out, even though I was dead scared she'd finish me off. At least you'll understand now, how it was an accident.'

He bowed his head.

I shook him gently. 'It was a mistake, don't you see? She didn't mean it, that's why she went finally mad. That's why she was so angry out there in the woods, because she screwed it up, she was mad . . .'

He left the room, returned to say: 'Naomi has been telling me to sell up,' left again. That was all he said. I was stunned.

By the time I got up the van had gone. I hadn't heard it. I wandered through the house. There was nothing left of Genevieve here. Even her pictures were gone. What had they done with all her things? I opened the bedroom door and shut it again quickly.

I remembered dashing down the passages aged twelve, I remembered playing jacks with Naomi in the empty upstairs rooms when they were full of sunlight and air, hearing the radio on down in the kitchen and Genevieve was calling, laughing, saying, 'Where are you girls!' She was happy here. She adored Jean-René. Couldn't he see that? It wasn't age that had greyed him; it was loathing for her, layers of it, coating him like scum. Surely he didn't think, just because she was slow about the divorce, that she had still loved Belar?

Why did she go back there, I thought I had convinced her, I thought it was all over, I never *dreamed* . . .

They were full of rot now, these upstairs rooms. Damp streamed from the walls. I found a box full of chipped wine-glasses in one of them and in a cold manner I smashed them one by one into the fireplace.

I had to leave the house after that, so I went to the village only to find that the shop had closed down. I came back, slept, woke to the smell of cooking. By this time I had no idea how long I'd been there. I turned on to my back and shut my eyes the better to speak.

'OK!' I called. 'I get it. You think I'm guilty, just like Naomi does. You think if I'd told you we could have stopped it. Jean-René, are you there?'

He appeared at the door.

'Do something!' I said. 'Punish me. Get Naomi here, tell her I let her mother go off and kill her father and shoot herself. Because that's what you think. God, have you understood nothing? God,' I exclaimed, 'can't you see how it all went wrong, it was just supposed to be a game?'

There had been a great tumult in England when I left with Genevieve. I had been running from a huge row. Something was about to happen. What was it?

I wanted to walk to the station but Jean-René insisted on taking me; he said I'd never make it with that blister on my foot. He kept asking if I'd be OK on my own in the train. I said of course I would. Genevieve had gone now and I knew she wouldn't be back.

Look, I said, proof that I'm not sick in the head, and got out my driving test documents to show him. I told him that in England, if you're at all funny, you're not allowed behind the wheel.

The rain came pouring down. All the colour had been drained from the fields and the farms. The cattle stood under the trees and shook themselves like dogs. The windscreen clouded as we swung round the corners; I was afraid we'd meet a truck coming down from the quarry, but Jean-René said that it was too wet for them to work today.

'I didn't know you had met Henri Palastrier,' I said after a pause.

'Life goes on, Sarah.'

'You told me once that he'd behaved like a, like a saint, I think you said.'

Jean-René laughed and wiped the windscreen for the fiftieth time. 'That was a long time ago. He and I, we were no match for you two. You know, Sarah, Genevieve was probably always beyond help, but you . . . I still can't understand what part you had in all this. To be frank I cannot conceive how you kept quiet all this time!'

'I've explained till I'm blue in the face!'

'I think you should perhaps consult someone.'

'A psychiatrist, you mean! A shrink for me, and for her ghost if you could manage it! Great!'

'It's not healthy to have such secrets. How long have you kept all these secrets, Sarah?'

'She told me about Belar when I was twelve, but I had always known that she and I were together, somehow, ever since I first met her in London.'

'But you were a child! How could you understand!'

He was being so thick. 'Of course I understood, Jean-René, it was about me as well! This is the whole point! It was us!' I sighed. 'When we were in London I hid her gun so that Juliette wouldn't find it. She gave me a diamond – it was fake, actually, but I didn't care.'

Jean-René gave a little twist of a smile. 'The winter of diamonds and freedom,' he said, as if he were quoting. 'She told you about that as well, I suppose.'

'Oh, yes, she went on and on about that. I can't remember what she said now – or why it mattered so much, come to that. I just get this picture of Nicholas's flat. She said it had reminded her of the hotel, you see.'

'I could never quite decide what she meant by freedom,' he said after a moment.

L'hiver des diamants et de la liberté. 'Maybe she just liked the words.'

Jean-René gave a pale smile.

I laughed. 'God, she had a colossal row with my dad! She made a real fool of herself. She called him a soldier putting his boot in, and he said, "I'm a sss . . ."'

'What?'

'I'm a sss . . .'

'Sarah? What's the matter?'

'Chirri birri birri I'm a sailor!' I hit the notes like a bell. I told Jean-René to put his foot down. I couldn't miss this train. 'I've got to get home,' I said, and told him why.

He made me promise to call him. He said that he wouldn't mention my visit to Nicholas or Naomi. We embraced. I repeated everything again so that he would not forget, and he nodded dumbly. He looked so shaken suddenly, standing there on the platform.

The trains go at tremendous speeds in France. Soon I was at the French port, soon I was at the English port. Soon I was climbing out of a taxi at my own front door.

My mother came out. She said, 'Darling, thank God, where have you been.' From her face I could tell that I was just in time.

TWENTY-TWO

When we were children they rose above us as high as a cliff-face.

We waved at them from the dock with the other mothers and their pushchairs. We had to do it for hours, they moved off so slowly. 'Jonathan, you're not looking,' said my mother one time. 'Where should I look?' he said, to be annoying, and my mother put her hands on his head and turned it in the right direction.

I remember he ducked away from the hands: 'I want to go home now,' he said, and my mother said, 'Yes, we've seen enough,' swept Flora into her arms and strode off at such a tearing pace that Jonathan and I had to run to catch up with her.

This time they seemed smaller, of course. This time there were so many people that there was no question of striding off. We had to fight our way through the crowds.

How much time would have been enough, to get used to the idea? Two days, three? A week? A difficult question, unanswerable; pointless since at the end there are still only three days and then two and then one and the previous days of waiting, so vital before, are worthless now that they are actually suiting up, spinning their radars, stoking up the noise. Steaming out.

There is a long haul ahead of them. There will be beard-growing competitions to pass the time, and the captains will judge them out in the middle of a flat glittering emptiness. Tiny figures on a metal deck in the sun.

He will judge them, Captain Finney my father. He will confer a prize on the most hirsute competitor.

My mother has hired a man to help me with the problem of Genevieve. The first time I went to see him he suggested we 'did some exploring'. I told him that was fine by me. We explored my sightings a bit, on the bus and so on, but then I got tired so we had to stop.

Clive came to see me, his arm in a sling. We sat on the sofa with our cups of tea. Slurp, comment, shloop, remark. We had a game of cards with Flora and watched the racing on TV. It was the first time I'd watched it; I enjoyed it, it was entertaining. Clive said that these days he went to watch it at the Fruit and Veg, in the office during the lunch hour. These days, he said, as if I'd been away for weeks. In fact I felt as if I had, too.

I asked him why he had got into the fight. He said that one of the men had called Vivienne a slag.

'Oh, you're joking.' I was merciless. 'Honourable Clive. Do you think that's what Vivienne wanted?'

'Hey, hey,' he said, hurt. 'And do you think I'm proud of it?'

'I'll be back working soon, when I've mended,' he said when he left. 'I wish you'd come back. The boss would have you if you asked him. He's got his uncle there, but it's only temporary.'

I said I would think about it.

All I'm supposed to do is tell the hired man about Genevieve. It should be easy but now that I've awakened the memory of the end, it blots out the rest. I think he's trying to establish that I conjured her up to rescue me from the present. 'When did you first see her?' he asks. 'Where?' He wears away at the apparitions and turns them into fits and faints and fugues. It's all fine by me.

'Why did she come?' he asked.

'To rescue me,' I replied patiently. 'You've already found that out.'

'But why her? Why not someone else?'

'Because she knows how it is,' I said. 'We're the same. We know how each other feels.'

'And how do you feel?'

'Dead.'

'But you're not dead. Genevieve is.'

'We failed,' I said after a moment. 'We tried to fight, but we lost.'

'Fight against what?'

He sat there in a listening posture, chin on fist. It was a strain, watching him listen so intently. 'I'm sorry,' I said. 'I'm trying to be helpful, but I just can't think straight.'

'You don't have to be helpful, Sarah. I'm here to help you, not the other way round.'

This, I thought, is the first hint of how annoying he's going to be in the future.

I decided to go back to work. Everyone else in my family was doing what they were supposed to be doing; studying, teaching, judging beards on the deck of a destroyer. I felt left out, sitting at home eating packet savoury rice for lunch. I was just searching out my overalls when Jean-René telephoned.

His voice came eagerly down the line, making me realize that I'd hardly given him a thought. 'It's so nice to hear your voice!' he said. 'Are you OK? Sarah, I've been thinking – I didn't realize, about your —'

'Oh, I've been doing plenty of thinking too, Jean-René,' I blurted. 'I spend all my time thinking at the moment.' I was suddenly very angry. 'I took your advice – or my mother did on my behalf. I'm having my head examined.'

'Sarah, I'm very sorry I said that. I think of you. Naomi also—'

'Much good may it do you,' I said rudely, banging the phone down as if he was a breather. I regretted it, but not enough to call again and apologize and thank him for looking after me. I couldn't have him harping on as well as the shrink. Even during that weird couple of days he had struck me as the kind of person who would be difficult to stop, once he got going.

The lawn is damp and green at my grandparents' house. The tall sons in their Sabbath tweeds laugh loudly, suddenly, the daughters-in-law clear the plates. The family rises to its feet. Grey-haired now, the uncles stroll out on the grass before returning to the places where duty leads them. Public buildings pillared and pilastered await them, ministries and acronymic headquarters where the grass is mown, the hedges clipped, the gravelled walks impeccable. Where the monuments cast a sharp black shadow. They're behaving . . . I can't describe how they're behaving towards my mother, these paternal uncles, but I keep thinking they're going to stumble to their knees in front of her. She's never got on with them, not really, and it shows, but she puts up with this behaviour. She knows they're doing it because my father has gone to war.

'There never seemed to be any sense in it,' I said. 'After these lunches we'd all go back to our grey schools and camps and ships. Wasn't she lonely without me and Jonathan? She never said so. Of course, she had Flora . . .

'Anyway, I wouldn't wear it,' I concluded. 'Literally. I burnt my school skirt and caused a fire. A small one; the rain put it out.'

'Why wouldn't you wear it?'

'It was degrading. It was a skirt for kneeling down in. Supplicating in.'

'Are clothes really that important? I would have thought the person inside was more important than the clothes they wear.'

'You know nothing. Look at you in your comfy cords and woolly. God, do I have to teach you everything before we even start?'

The ruder I get, the less I care. He's not doing his job properly, in any case, because we keep getting off the subject of Genevieve.

According to Vivienne there is a robotic announcer who delivers news of the war. She says that everyone is very concerned about the efficacy of the Argentinian missiles, and about the type of alloy used in building the British warships. Some say it's cheap and flammable; others deny this. The arguments rage back and forth across radio and TV speakers, interspersed with news of local groups for families with men at sea, but we keep our machines turned off for the most part. My mother has all the necessary information. Generally she talks to her mother.

Jonathan is at boarding-school now but Flora is at home. There are two of us and a mother, just as there were when we lived in the house on the heath, in that house and all the other, indistinguishable ones, before Flora was born and before I met Genevieve. Mother and two children walking to the shops in search of shoes, finding out where the library is and how reliable the buses are; the mother walking ahead so that we saw her tall strong back. Tying my tie and Jonathan's tie, the elastics on the socks, the painting overalls. The blue tunic and then the blue skirt, then another tunic; and the jumper and then the cardigan, and then the special beret for the convent. I put on these different clothes and studied 'capacity' in primary school maths, pouring milk-bottles of water into calibrated litre jugs and I was careful, I didn't spill a drop. Jonathan and I started the days of the week with Sunday or with Monday according to the local custom. We put the Amen after Deliver Us From Evil or we went on for

The Power And The Glory. Quick-witted about break-times and football teams, we always kept one step ahead. I tell myself I'm eighteen now; I try to prove this by looking after and entertaining Flora, but Flora doesn't need me because she knows she's really older than me. She knows that even though I sit in the pub with my friends I'm really about eight.

According to Vivienne it's better to listen to the robotic man because you know where you are with him. Since I last chatted to her I've found out that we have a special man who has sworn to my mother that he will tell us all the minute they know anything about anything. So far he has kept quiet.

'You don't know how it felt!' I said crossly. 'Having him leave, time after time!'

'It felt horrible,' volunteered the psychiatrist, and I put my hands together and laughed, rocking back in my chair.

'Yes, horrible, and?' I said. 'And the other thing it felt? What is that?'

There was a pause.

'Oh go on, guess.'

'Good?' he suggested.

'Yes!' I said. 'It felt . . . right!'

He nodded sagely.

'It was what he was *for*!' I said, as it crossed my mind that he was too young to nod so sagely.

'What you were told he was for, you mean.'

'No! No, it is, actually, what he's for! You haven't met him, you don't know what he's like! Wait till you see him! Then you'll know!'

'Write to him,' my mother said. 'You can put it in my envelope.'

BFPO Ships. Dear Katharine, dear Robert. Darling. The children are ill, the children are well, the children are bloody-minded. The children have taken apart the toaster and the radio and I am attempting, with fraying patience, to put them together again. The children are now too old, Robert, for me to chronicle their daily deeds. I am a woman of forty-two and I am too old to be writing letters like this, Robert, do you hear me, this is ridiculous, it's *grotesque* . . .

She won't say that. She gives no sign that she even thinks that. What on earth can she find to say instead?

'Nothing has happened,' I replied. 'Nothing I can possibly tell him about, anyway.'

'Then make something up!' she cried. 'By all accounts you've got a vivid imagination!'

Shaken, I said that I would.

'Genevieve wouldn't sit down under it, you see. She gave me the courage.' I yawned. I am getting so weary of these sessions.

'Under what?'

I pressed my temples. 'The thing. The whole bit. The desertion, for example; she never accepted that it was right.'

'But you said that she herself deserted her daughter. She left her with her boyfriend for two years —'

'No, no. She proved she didn't mean it. I challenged her and immediately she saw she was wrong and got Naomi back.'

'Just a minute, Sarah, I'm confused.' No, you're not, I thought. 'It wasn't Naomi's father who was keeping her, though, was it?'

'How could he? He was never there!' I laughed bitterly. 'That's the point. He wouldn't give up his life. That's why she had to leave, so she wouldn't be sucked into the whole . . . life, like we were!' I was already exasperated; a bad sign.

'But she didn't leave him,' he went on. 'Not truly. She had to keep going back.'

'Yes, I know, I've explained about that. She had to show him.'

'It sounds to me as if she couldn't let him go. When he finally decided to break off their relationship completely, she couldn't tolerate it.'

I swore under my breath. 'You've got it backwards again.'

'Sarah, I'm going to put it to you as I see it, and you can tell me where I'm going wrong. OK?'

'I think I can manage that.'

'The marriage broke down, as far as we know because he was absent for long periods.'

'Definitely because.'

'OK. Definitely because of his long absences. Fair enough. But then, when his estranged wife returns, more than once, to threaten him with a gun, he says nothing about it to anybody. He lets her do it. Now don't you find anything odd about that, Sarah?'

'He knew he was guilty! He deserved it!'

'There's a box of tissues on the windowsill behind you. And what about her? What about Genevieve? Does her behaviour strike you as normal?'

I snuffled.

'You might find it helpful to compare their relationship with that of your parents. Your parents I understand have a stable marriage —'

'Yeah, right, because my mother gave up!' I'm losing my voice.

'Really? She doesn't strike me as the type to do that. I don't doubt for a minute she worked hard at her marriage, but that's different. Take all the time you want, Sarah, but I must understand if we are to work this out.'

An age of blurred whiteness elapsed. I sat blinking.

'She only did it to scare him,' I said in the end.

'So she wanted to scare him. Why did she have to do that? And why so many times?'

'Because he had to know that she had . . . she had power.'

'Is that what power is? The ability to scare people?'

'Yes, when that's all they deserve!' The rooms in this place are soundproofed. I can shout all I like. 'He deserved it! He could go anywhere, do anything, and she was – left! She couldn't do anything about it! Don't you see!'

'It's all right, Sarah.'

'I thought she'd finished with the gun! I know she didn't mean to shoot him! It was always just to teach him a lesson!'

'OK, Sarah.'

'I didn't want it to happen!'

I can scream the place down if I want.

I haven't got the answer but I need to know. I need to know whether the fact that I came back in time will make up for it. I went down to the docks and watched him go. I need to know if this action will be enough, so I pray.

When I was young I did the right thing, don't forget that. We went from place to place and I followed and followed, walking fast, pulling my socks up, running. I pulled Jonathan's socks up for him and took him by the hand. I held on to the half-crown for the bus fare so tight that it made an impression on my hand. Remember that. I took the thorn out of Flora's foot and rescued her gas-balloon from the pine tree. I need to know if these actions are enough. Can you hear me?

I made a mistake. Long ago. I run like a dog through the house, chasing shadows. My mother too; please, think of her. It's not her fault. She's doing it too, turning into a dog again before my eyes, an old dog now, they all are, all the women. They're all whining so high you can't hear them, their dugs hanging down, waiting for the man in question to come back because their chins fit only on his knee and their old velvet ears flatten only beneath his palm. They are slobbering now. When the ships come back a bell will ring and some of them will drool for a dinner which will not come.

This is 1982, for crying out loud, we were all fooled, we thought: This can't be happening, right up to the third, the second, the last day, the last minute we couldn't believe it: and then only did we see that it is WAR coming to make you open your mouth and ram your knuckles against your teeth to stop yourself from breathing out because you might not breathe in again from terror and then you would SUFFOCATE.

I made a mistake. Please. My father should be occupying himself with his beans and marrows. Let me see his back bent in the garden. I walk past the sitting-room door and someone has left the telly on by accident, I say 'What's on?' because I think it's a movie but it's ITN, da-da, da-DAA and I've never seen a fire that size before in my life, it makes the ships look like toys. My father has no experience of such conflagrations. How can he possibly put it out?

TWENTY-THREE

Striated like rock, but softer than rock; like water-currents or thermals but more tangible.

Coloured with immaterial colours – a soft grey, a streak of moss-green, a glint of silver, a breath of blue – which inhere like the colours of a dream, in my mind's eye; distant as a cloud-formation on the sea-horizon and yet I can reach out and part it, pull out a skein or clump if I want. Small bright things live in it, slipping like fish beneath the surface, darting and shivering with joy and pain. I didn't use to know what the past was made of.

Looking for the houses of my youth I wander in my car by a shoreline mournful in summer when the horizon is clotted with haze, dreadful in winter when the estuaries threaten to freeze. I look down on the dredgers and lighters canted in the ooze as faithful as labradors, tethered by chains as thick as a man's thigh. I ponder on those whose job it is to husband the sea, the preoccupied men in small rooms ashudder with the engine's unholy roar, awash with unholy fumes of hot painted metal and fuel, and I know that the sea for them is a bristling chart, a radio report, a line seen rising and falling. It is a profit, a loss, a prize, a grave.

How ugly it is down here – and what a shame, because

the countryside is beautiful a few miles back. But this is a place of roundabouts and road systems; a flat place, where I can see for miles but there is nothing to see. Signposts loom and flick past, dotted lines split and merge and double and fill like the stripes on my father's arm. I pull over to ask the way from someone who says: 'Follow the main road and turn left past the video shop – it's new, you won't recognize it – and left again down Paddock Lane; oh, it's called Curlew Drive now since they built the close at the end, it's all changed now . . .' and yes, it has all changed, it changes constantly, and it is so noisy. In the evening it is noisy, with children kicking their footballs on the dwindling commons and the docks full, then empty, then full again with long-distance lorries as they come and go all through the night . . .

Sunset, tarmac, concrete, salt breeze. A familiar broken skyline. Yes, this feels right; structures have started to appear, iron and steel, with protrusions fixed or mobile. Long, flat-roofed buildings behind high iron gates and some-times barbed wire. Red brick, breeze block, functional head-quarters or substations for I don't know what, some called, confusingly, HMS, and others scattered, as are the signposts, with acronyms and insignia which are more obscure. They multiply now as I pass on through the hinterland, joined by warehouses, Portakabins, machinery, plastic pubs called the Nelson and the Dolphin; I'm about to stop at the next one when there is a clatter of halyards on masts and suddenly I am by the sea once more – just for a moment, that is, before the road bears me off inland – at which point, as I am lost again, I say God damn it, 'hinterland'? There's nothing else but; the whole place is bloody hinterland! And then I see it, the house on the heath, the white walls and the washing-line, and as I look I realize that we never lived there at all, that it was another family altogether, that it was a different girl I saw running to the beach, who I wanted so much to be that I convinced myself it was me.

So I drive on, here and there, A-road and B-road, roundabout, housing estate, anchorage, bridge, and there's just no way of telling where the hell I am until I'm into the city and heading for the docks.

It has spread so much now. Up over the hills, tiers of red houses and grey houses, clumps of high-rise; at night you'd see a forest of lights if you came down off the motorway and over the bridge. The people speak with a different accent from that of the county, they speak like Londoners because they are, or are the children of Londoners, some of them; and although the city was built on the sea and because of the sea there are few old salts, and the heritage is for the tourists. No fish slither glittering into wicker baskets here – it isn't a Mediterranean resort. They vacuum it in and freeze it on board for the most part. You can get fresh at the dock but not at dawn, they open at nine. Not that you would want to be down there at dawn because it can be bitter, it can be foul weather; there can be 'trouble with the pontoon at Gosport' announced on the local radio which also gives out storm warnings in the North Sea, causing the customer in the corner shop, the middle-aged mother in glasses and cardigan, to pause in mid-step, and there's nothing old-salty about that . . .

This used to be the High Street. The city's long axis, torn out after the War; all the roads lead crosswise over it, called after national heroes and impossible to cross on foot. Now there are more of those blue-crested vans and lorries about; there is a sudden flurry of acronymic signposts and gateways; there are people in blue uniforms, striding purposefully about in a different rhythm from the nine-to-five. Now the buildings are tall, imposing, red brick and above all beautiful, which is astonishing after all the ugliness, but I'm not looking at the street any more. I've seen them at last, parked two by two all along one side of the harbour, smaller and faster and more rakish in design than I ever remembered. A hot city of turrets and domes in the summer and an iron mountainscape in winter. Still here after all this time. Always here. Always, like the land and the sea.

You put your hands in the sink and stare out at the

dockyard cranes. The window-fan buzzes. You think: Must be a gale out there.

It was much the same wherever I lived.

I know what the past is made of.

'Do you remember the Father Christmas?' asked Flora.

We were sitting in my flat, drinking coffee with sugar in it. We had just been watching the documentary of the war on video.

'What Father Christmas?' I said.

'It was a party for the children. They took us out into the harbour and Father Christmas came down from a helicopter.'

'What an extraordinary thing,' I said. 'It sounds like a dream.'

'It wasn't a dream! Maybe you were too old to come.'

'After my time, you mean! Did he give you presents?'

'Of course!' Flora giggled. 'I thought he was the real thing. I still believed in Father Christmas, you see.'

The landscape of the Falklands was very like that of the Hebrides, especially when the film was accompanied by haunting oboe music. Green turf, and water everywhere.

'You didn't!' I said.

'I did, honestly!'

'That must have been fantastic.'

'Yes, it was. I remember his robes billowing out as they winched him down . . . I wonder if Daddy remembers what ship it was.'

The men cried such a lot. They cried out there and then four years later, interviewed in their armchairs in front of the cameras, they cried again.

I said: 'We'll have to ask him.'

'Yes, we will.'

There was a silence while we drank our coffee.

'So you really thought it was Father Christmas?' I said.

'Yes, honestly, I swear!'

'How wonderful!'

We laughed, and drank our coffee. Sugar for shock.

Clive joined the navy six months after the war. His sister's fiancé died in the conflagration I had momentarily mistaken for a movie. For a time I wondered if Clive had thought he wouldn't see the like of Matthew again and joined for that reason. I heard he told Suzanne he'd always fancied it even before he met Matthew, but she gave him a really hard time. She put on a lot of weight after Matthew died. According to Vivienne she started eating huge helpings of food she didn't normally go for, Bakewell tarts and so on, custard, things that Matthew had liked.

Clive's still in it, anyway. He sent me a congratulations card for my graduation, telling me he'd seen Julian at a party when he was down in Plymouth. I haven't seen Julian for ages, not since he called round at the Fruit and Veg just after the war. He said he was very happy for my family but that the whole thing was a crime.

'You and Clive, you think people like me don't know anything,' he said. 'You thought it had to be a pose, didn't you, because I wasn't involved like you. But we do have a right to think and speak, you know, all of us. We have to be allowed to make a stand.' We are a nation, he said.

There isn't much to say about us. It's all in the film, the departure and the homecoming. In any case it would be bad taste to go on about this much longer. It would be 'bad form'. My father came back and we stood there overcome by, I wish I could leave it at joy and relief, but it was also pride.

My mother is as strong as a kicking mare. I keep comparing her to animals which is regrettable, distracting since I am trying to describe the strength of a human being. The strength of my grandmothers too; they're all three of them the same. I would be tempted to say it is strong stock if I hadn't seen, over thousands of days, how it is not passed on, how you have to make it each time for yourself . . .

I saw Suzanne in the street two months after it happened. She invited me home and there were no dark clouds in their house, their house was ablaze with Matthew's absence as if the war had gone through it and left it blasted and shining. Suzanne gorging herself, alone, on puddings she can't stand, yes Julian I know it's a crime, that Matthew is finished for her and for all of them and will never come back.

Naomi is getting married. The groom is called Olivier. Beside his name on my invitation she had written *Not the same one.* She said that Jean-René was planning to drive down from Paris the day before, and why didn't I join him? I might do that; it would be more fun than going sedately with my parents. Jean-René sold the house when I was in my first year at university. A friend of his appeared out of the blue at my door, carrying a brick and a book. The book was a collection of his photographs and stories, just published. I preferred the earlier grainy ones of the north; some of the later river scenes, the Dordogne and the Auvezere, I found a bit touristy. The brick was from the bathroom wall.

I bet Naomi will look gorgeous in her wedding gear, just like Juliette did.

Naomi's mother died a long time ago, but I knew her when I was a child. She gave me food of all colours and shapes – biscuits that were a cake inside, foreign fish paste, rainbow particles of sugar. She gave me a hard clear jewel fashioned to reflect white light. And she gave me a heavy black thing to hold, which fitted my grip like the hand of a close companion, but this last thing she took back in the end. In the end she fought me to keep it and she won. When she was young she must have gone down to the quayside like us, she must have sat in her car with Naomi and watched the ship move off like a mountain, but I can't picture her waving or hooting her horn or flashing her lights. I can only see her slitting her eyes behind her shades, and her ship went off silently over the glitter because she was deaf to everything except the thump of her heart. I try not to think of that quayside any more.

She never belonged in my past. The past is made exclusively of my land and my cold sea: she had no place in it. I struggled for years to keep her there but it wasn't right, she knew it wasn't right, she came leaping out in the end. I thought it was a great game, it made me feel mighty and free, but she wasn't playing with me. Her game was different and she played it with another person, a man I never saw until he was dead. Not long ago I asked my mother: 'Did she pull a gun on you, up in the woods after Nicholas's wedding?' My mother didn't say 'What?' or 'Gun?' as you might expect. She just said: 'Why must you go on about that poor girl?' and only then did she grasp the implications of my question and her answer. So I had to tell her why I'd asked. I had been ready to do it for a long time, thanks to the sessions at Mental Health which had shrunk my head practically to the size of a pea. My mum and I, we both agreed, Genevieve didn't mean to scare her. She just couldn't help it sometimes.

She couldn't help it – I told the shrink, you can't talk about abuse, not with her. She didn't abuse me any more than I blackmailed her. She couldn't help it; she was desperate; she had been desperate ever since she left Henri Palastrier. If you want to keep a gun secret do you put it in a plastic bag under your bed? Do you train it on a man at the top of the steps, outside the door for all the world to see? Do you leave it in a bathroom cabinet in a strange flat, full of people, for anyone to find? No. She knew it wasn't right. Deep down she wanted it to be taken away from her. But I found it instead, and stowed it carefully away in a safe place, and forced her to share it with me. I made it ours.

Do you think she simply let me play out of fear? But I'd never have given her away. Surely she knew I would not have betrayed her as long as she lived!

We sat on the floor together, feasting on leftovers like a couple of vagabonds, in the drawing room which reminded her of a big hotel. She told me about the hotel years later but I didn't listen. I remember only that she cried and that I suddenly felt eight again, as if Christmas was occurring out of the clouds as silently as snow and she was teasing me for the first time and I knew I could say, I could do, anything I wanted.

*

I feel very brown and strong. When I've saved up enough money I'm going on a long trip. I quite fancy tramping along with a rucksack under a huge sky. Maybe I'll ask Jean-René for advice. He's done a lot of travelling in his time.

He phoned the other day about the wedding. I had just come back from a camping weekend. I chatted about the arrangements, dying for a bath; I was covered in wood-ash. We had lit a fire and sat up all night talking. I had sat the next morning with my feet in the warm ash, wriggling my toes, looking at the countryside.

'Sarah,' Jean-René was saying, 'on the journey, I promise I won't talk about her if you don't want, but if . . . Oh, it's so clumsy on the telephone . . .'

You get these big dry fields in England after harvest. Tall trees, small houses far away on the other side. I had sat with the shade behind me and watched a woman come out with a bucket from one of the houses. I could hardly hear her voice across the field. Genevieve used to come out like that; I made believe it was her voice I heard. A flat southern voice. A voice from another country.

'Talk all you like, Jean-René,' I said. 'Tell me about her.'